MISANTHRO

S. HENRY BERTHOUD (1804-1891) was born and raised in Cambrai, but went to Paris in the early 1830s order to join the writers of the Romantic Movement, where he did editorial work on several of Émile de Girardin's pioneering popular periodicals, including the *Musée des Familles*. He did important pioneering work in the fields of historical fiction, *roman scientifique*, fantastic fiction, fiction for children and the popularization of science, as well as the *conte cruel*. A close friend of Honoré de Balzac, his contribution to the evolution of the Romantic Movement, as a writer and editor, was highly significant and deserves to be far better known.

BRIAN STABLEFORD has been publishing fiction and non-fiction for fifty years. His fiction includes an eighteen-volume series of "tales of the biotech revolution" and a series of half a dozen metaphysical fantasies set in Paris in the 1840s, featuring Edgar Poe's Auguste Dupin. His most recent non-fiction projects are *New Atlantis: A Narrative History of British Scientific Romance* (Wildside Press 2016) and *The Plurality of Imaginary Worlds: The Evolution of French* roman scientifique (Black Coat Press 2016); in association with the latter he has translated approximately a hundred and fifty volumes of texts not previously available in English, similarly issued by Black Coat Press.

S. HENRY BERTHOUD

MISANTHROPIC TALES

Translated and with an Introduction by

BRIAN STABLEFORD

THIS IS A SNUGGLY BOOK

ISBN: 978-1-943813-53-7

Contents

Introduction

CONTES MISANTHROPIQUES by S. Henry Berthoud, here translated as *Misanthropic Tales*, was first published in Paris in 1831 by Werdet, advertised as being edited by Charles Lemesle; it was reprinted in Brussels the following year by C. J. de Mat.

Charles Lemesle, born in 1794—and thus ten years older than Berthoud—was the author of several volumes of poetry and drama issued between 1827 and 1841, as well as a curious collection of cynical aphorisms and prose vignettes, *Misophilanthropopanutopies, tablettes d'un sceptique* (1833); he might have been the grandson of the similarly-named author born in 1731, advertised in the Bibliothèque Nationale catalogue as a merchant of Le Havre, who had published accounts in verse of the conquest of England by "William the Bastard" in 1759 and 1779. The "notice" that commences Berthoud's collection was presumably written by Lemesle, and it was presumably via his mediation that the collection achieved publication.

The book was the first that Berthoud published after relocating to Paris permanently from his native Cambrai in 1830, although he had almost certainly spent some time there in the early 1820s as a student, and it was surely then that he first made the acquaintance of his friend Honoré

7

de Balzac and other members of the Parisian literary community. In the later 1820s, however, he had been working for his father, a printer by profession, who had issued a previous slim publication in volume form for him; as observed in the "Notice," he had also published items in publications issued by the Societé d'émulation de Cambrai, where "Le Fou" (translated herein as "The Madman") had appeared in 1830. Berthoud could not know when he published *Contes misanthropiques* that he would go on to publish more than a hundred other books, and contrive to make a steady living from his pen, in spite of the severe disruptions caused by the 1848 Revolution and its aftermath, while actively serving the causes of popular education and the popularization of science.

Contes misanthropiques is of some historical importance as the first collection of stories in a genre that was given numerous other titles—all equally inappropriate—by various practitioners before and after the one that eventually caught on to a greater extent than its rivals: *Contes cruels*, employed by the Comte de Villiers de L'Isle Adam in 1883. That label stuck partly because it materialized not long before such tales enjoyed something of a *fin-de-siècle* heyday, largely due to accommodation being made for them in the feuilleton slots of various periodicals, most notably the daily newspaper *Le Journal* and the *Écho de P*aris, which were filled with such material by writers including Léon Bloy, Marcel Schwob, Jean Lorrain, Catulle Mendès, Octave Mirbeau, Jules Richepin and Edmond Haraucourt. The genre had enjoyed a previous vogue, however, following the publication of Berthoud's exemplar, during the period of fashionability enjoyed by the Romantic Movement in the early 1830s, when Petrus Borel provide the best-known collection, *Champavert: Contes immoraux* (1833; tr. as *Champavert: Immoral Tales*), which he signed "Petrus Borel le lycanthrope" and prefaced with an introduction falsely lamenting the death of the eponymous supposed author. Significant contributions to the genre were also made by Berthoud's friends Balzac and Jules Janin.

The stories in question are really no more "immoral" than they are "misanthropic," but those misnamings reflected a perennial difficulty in characterizing them precisely, and "cruel" is only slightly more accurate. Lemesle's description of himself as a skeptic is perhaps even more accurate as an encapsulation of the spirit of such tales, except that the skepticism they exhibit is of a very particular kind, not only directed at human hypocrisy, which it sets out to lay bare, but more particularly at the deep-rooted hypocrisy of conventional literary representations. The most revealing of all the stories in the present collection is "Agib, ou les Souhaites" (tr. as "Agib; or, Wishes") a mock-Gallandesque tale that not only features a teller of a skeptical tales but a listener who does not like the tale he is told at all, and explains to its teller that he would have done better to fill his narrative with wonders and provide an upbeat ending—as, of course, Galland's Scheherazade had been careful to do—rather than indulging in downbeat cynicism and deflating moralizing.

What, in essence, stories in the *conte cruel* genre set out to do was to oppose the conventions of fiction that encourage embellishments of various sorts, including and especially the contrivance of "happy endings." They are stories written in the full awareness of the fact that what the great majority of readers want, most of the time, is to hear uplifting stories of heroic struggles against adversity, in which love conquers all. *Contes cruels* are produced by writers who are painfully aware that that is not the way things work in the real world, and who want to puncture the illusion fostered by conventional stories by deliberately going against their grain. Such stories are not so much "cruel" to their readers because they display horrors with a certain relish—although they sometimes do—but because they deliberately violate the ordinary reader's hope and expectation that a story will end "well." Stories are, of course, always able to do that because authors exercise godlike power over the universes of their texts, but whether they ought to do it is a different matter.

Authors who refuse to provide "happy endings" do not do it because they are "immortal" or "misanthropic," wanting to harm their characters instead of rewarding them, but quite the reverse; it is because they are extremely moral and would dearly like to love their fellow human beings that they feel compelled to express their disappointment with the vicious immorality they see around them and the dismal failure of so many of their fellows to make themselves lovable. *Contes cruels* are, quintessentially, tales of disenchantment, not so much stories as anti-stories protesting against the illusions that are so frequently and so ardently demanded of stories by readers who want to use them, at least as an escape from the dismal aspects of reality, and perhaps even as a means of illusory reassurance that things are not quite as bad as they really are.

We now know that most, if not all, of what is conventionally called "mental illness" simply consists of psychotropic side-effects of physical malaise. In the purest sense of afflictions of reason, there is perhaps only one authentic mental disease, and that is optimism, whose more extreme symptoms include faith and hope. Perhaps it is a necessary disease, at least for the young, because it is what insists that people should continue struggling against the odds, and thus sustains life in the hostile circumstances of existence—which is presumably why natural selection favors it so strongly, if it too has a material basis in our neural cytoarchitecture. A mind completely freed of the illusions of optimism could only be reckoned healthy if it were accepted that the logical consequence of mental health is despair, and perhaps suicide. Undoubtedly, the people best equipped to succeed in life—especially in the career of authorship—are those who can subscribe to the cult of optimism, or at least fake such a subscription, while supporting the disappointments inevitably consequent on reality's failure to live up to its expectations.

In the Age of Enlightenment whose advent was trumpeted in the eighteenth century, the rapid and far-ranging evolution of education, science and philosophy enabled increasing numbers of people in Europe, if not to see through the sham of optimism—including its diabolical corollary, faith—at least to become distressingly anxious about its fragility. It is little wonder that the era in question saw a great boom in literary activity, including a spectacular renaissance of palliative fairy tales and love stories, and became, in a strangely fundamental sense, the era of Scheherazade. Nor is it surprising, however, that the narrative fireworks in question cast a dark shadow, and that rebels began to emerge who were intent on undermining that quest for escape and reassurance, challenging its essential insanity.

Such heroes were, of course, swimming against the tide; they knew that it was a difficult fashion in which to seek popularity, but—not being immune to the disease of optimism themselves—they hoped at least to gain respect, to which they were fully entitled. Perhaps they also hoped to cash in on the sense of superiority that is often construed as a reward by those readers who feel themselves to be separate from the common herd, by virtue of being more fully aware of the hypocritical artifices of fiction. Pessimists are invariably proud of their pessimism, even if they learn not to flaunt it because it makes other people uncomfortable and inevitably attracts opprobrium. For them, indulgence in *contes cruels* can be as reassuring as indulgence in conventional fictions is for readers who are able, willing and eager to participate in the commonplace rewards of conventional fiction—although, obviously, the world is not as clearly divided as that, and many readers are sufficiently versatile to claim and savor both kinds of rewards, in varying proportions and in accordance with various moods.

Writers too can produce stories as well as anti-stories without necessarily laying themselves open to charges of hypocrisy, treason and money-grubbing pandering to vulgar taste. There are degrees and variegations in insanity, and even old people often require a soupçon of optimism to buoy them up when mere resignation and the inertia of the beating heart are insufficient to keep them going. Even those sufferers who succeed in minimizing the worst symptoms of the disease rarely rid themselves entirely of the virus without suffering mortal consequences.

For the young and passionate, when the fever of optimism is often at it peak of temperature and delirium, pessimism is usually an affectation; when it is not, it usually annihilates all activity, and the kind of pessimism expressed in youthful writing thus tends to be Byronic in nature—but that does not mean that it is insincere or not deeply felt. Indeed, writing is reputed to be one of the most effective treatments for the direr effects of optimism and pessimism alike; while not necessarily a mental illness in itself—although one could certainly make out a case for that contention—the activity of writing, with its attendant creativity, nevertheless mimics some of the life-sustaining side-effects of the particular insanity of optimism. Thus, the writing of *contes cruels*, especially for a young writer, can provide a kind of psychological relief that is capable of substituting for optimism even to the extent of producing symptoms akin to hope and faith. That is, in essence, the remedy that the great pessimist Arthur Schopenhauer proposed, in recommending the substitution of an Idea for the blind and insane "will to survive" that routinely and instinctively preserves life, in blatant denial of the calculus of probability and the corrosions of entropy.

One strongly suspects, therefore, that S. Henry Berthoud—who was certainly a Byronist at the time—enjoyed writing his "misanthropic" tales in his twenties, however perverse that enjoyment might seem on superficial examination, and they can also be enjoyed, in a connoisseur fashion, by discriminating readers possessed of refined taste, who are aware of the essential hypocrisy of the fictional conventions the tales defy and deny. Such readers can obtain real pleasure from them, without having to deem it a guilty pleasure; indeed, it is arguably the most virtuous of pleasures, the least tainted by illusion, delusion and fundamental insanity.

If some of the items in the collection seem a trifle primitive by comparison with the artistry that later writers acquired in the provision of "punch lines," that is because

S. Henry Berthoud was a true pioneer, roaming freely in literary territory that was largely untrodden. In fact, the most remarkable feature of the collection, viewed as a whole, is its sophistication: the broadness of its spectrum, its frequent dexterity and its occasional brilliance. The terse, economical style of the stories brings several of them close to the as-yet-undeveloped genre of prose poetry, which Joris-Karl Huysmans was eventually to describe as "the osmazome of literature," and the affectation of repeated refrains employed by several writers of prose-poetry affiliated to the *fin-de-siècle* Decadent Movement is anticipated by Berthoud in one of the "Scottish ballads" he modeled on the work of the English Romantic Sir Walter Scott.

Berthoud never produced anything like the *Contes misanthropiques* again, perhaps wisely, given that he was intent on making a living as a professional writer, and the vast majority of his works—most of which were specifically aimed at children—are doggedly conventional in supplying upbeat endings in which virtue is usually rewarded; when it is not, the failure is represented as tragedy rather than merely dismissed as the inevitable way of the world. He did, however, do it once, and that is creditworthy as well as remarkable—and he never entirely lost the skepticism that made him see the irony is what he was doing, and it frequently intruded into his works, at least as impish subtext.

This translation was made from the copy of the 1832 edition of *Contes misanthropiques* published in Brussels by C. J. de Mat that is reproduced by Google Books. Six of the stories previously appeared in the showcase sampler of Berthoud's work *Martyrs of Science and Other Victims of Devilry and Destiny* (Black Coat Press 2013), but in order to maintain the integrity of the present collection I have reinserted them here in the same positions that they occupy in the original.

Brian Stableford

Notice

for *Les Contes misanthropiques* by S. Henry Berthoud

WE have greatly praised the decided penchant of the contemporary generation for profound studies; it is one more flattery that we address to the epoch, vile courtiers who, in order to obtain its suffrage, call our youth, with so little modesty, grave and serious instead of saying presumptuous and stuck-up. Profound studies! When frivolity has never been more general, albeit a ponderous and sly frivolity, playfully erecting, to the sound of ancient monuments falling, fragile constructions that are sketched for a day. Profound studies! When, alongside the semi-knowledge that infects all the ranks of society, one never sees traces of a laborious, solid and well-digested education! You want the truth? Here it is: we are sullen and sinister boors, ignoramuses brushed by a pedantic science. These words are perhaps harsh, but the century that proclaims itself the century of independence and frankness will show poor grace in complaining if, in our turn, we undertake to be free thinkers.

For minds withered in their florescence, faded by satiety, harassed by political commotions, shaken by frantic passions, obsessed with egotistical preoccupations, menacing novelties, ambitious and cruel hopes, there are scarcely more than two kinds of reading possible: that of newspapers and tales. They alone are of a nature to satisfy our infantile curiosity, our febrile sensitivity. Don't talk to us about a thick book, an argumentation deduced at length; who can guarantee that the world will not have changed its face before we reached the last page, before we arrive at the conclusion? We are in progress, we are in a hurry, we only listen while running, and in order to be perceived, to be heard in the midst of the crowd and the tumult, a bizarre exterior is required, and it is necessary to raise one's voice.[1]

Such is, in fact, the double character of present writings. If it is true that literature is the expression of society, what does this urgency to depict the horrible, to represent humanity from the most abject and hideous point of view announce? Is it literature that is calumniating society, or society that is perverting literature?

Monsieur Berthoud, in sparing our idleness, in taking precautions against our impatience, has only, moreover, made scant sacrifice to fashionable theory. This is not Hamilton[2] escorting his reader through the labyrinth of a tale full of grace and finesse; this is not Voltaire, the bitter and mordant ironist, lavishing on human misery the scorn and derision that Goethe's Mephistopheles does not spare it. Might it be Hoffmann, of the unhealthily dreaming[3]

---

1 Author's note: "'Take my voice for the blast of the trumpet.' Chapelain, La Pucelle." Jean Chapelain's epic poem of 1656, about Jeanne d'Arc, was enormously popular, but was subsequently savaged, and the author's reputation was wrecked, by the critic Nicolas Boileau-Despréaux.

2 The Irish author Anthony Hamilton, who was brought up in France after his Catholic family took refuge there following Cromwell's revolution, and wrote in French as "Comte Antoine Hamilton"

3 Author's note: "*Aegri somnia.*" [i.e., a sick person's dreams]

imagination, straying over the dubious limit of real and ideal existence? No, any more than it is Mérimée seizing with a perfect verity the species of reality that the Germans call objective, disposing with a fortunately dissimulated skill all the parts of a dramatic action, and spreading the warm and vivifying color of his style therein.

If Monsieur Berthoud ought to be compared to anyone, it is to Sterne rather than anyone else. Moreover, his physiognomy is more agreeable than pronounced, his composition more sage than original.

With the exception of a few darts of ill-humor against marriage, a few applications of the philosophy of La Rochefoucauld and Montaigne, one cannot see that the author justifies very well his title of *Contes misanthropiques*, and so much the better. We have had more than enough of those sullen and morose writers who only see the world through a crepe and who, calmly melancholy, exploit as best they can the commonplace lugubriousness of misfortune.

Small tableaux like those of Monsieur Berthoud do not admit vulgar details. The narrower the frame, the more one has the right to demand that the painter redeems by the choice of accessories what invention lacks. We would have liked, therefore, to prune from his collection several stories whose foundation and form are too common, as well as one or two that arrive at a denouement in a forced manner. But in general, his brief narrations present a mild and tranquil interest, and end with a moral idea that gives rise to useful reflection.

One regrets that he has not taken greater advantage of historical traditions and local color, although he seems called on to reproduce them successfully. For example, the

Flemish story entitled "Le Baptême d'une cloche"[1] is one of the best in his book, but it has nothing about it that is Flemish, nothing that is special. And yet what a rich mine the author had to exploit in the customs and memories of his homeland! A resident of Cambrai,[2] a friend of Monsieur Le Glay,[3] so well-versed in Flemish antiquities, what aid might his imagination not have borrowed from the agreeable and facile erudition of that author? We know a woman who, for a long time, kept in a portfolio a series of Belgian traditions in prose and verse, but who, distracted by the duty of commerce from the muses, absorbed by difficult labors, distanced from the literary theater and discouraged by the disfavor attached to national essays, has condemned those sketches to a perpetual oblivion, while ready to applaud those who, like Monsieur Berthoud, are able to follow a career in which she has not sufficient ardor and illusions to engage.

Let us just say a few words about Monsieur Berthoud's style. He has the provincial bonhomie of writing simply and correctly. One might take him for a classicist, but for a few faults and save for certain places in which he attempts to imitate the manner of saying everything that something is and is not, of accumulating epithets and synonyms, of unfurling and folding a period like a snake that, coiling over itself, dazzles us with that continual evolution, and causes the patches with which its smooth and shiny body is variegated to stand out more: a manner that the talent of

---

1 Translated as "The Baptism of a Bell"
2 Author's note: "Several of his tales are inserted in the *Mémoires* of that town's Société d'émulation."
3 André-Joseph-Ghislain Le Glay (1785-1863), founder of the departmental archives of the Nord, father of the eventually-more-famous antiquarian Edward Le Glay.

the author of *Barnave* has rendered so seductive, without succeeding nevertheless in avoiding all its faults.[1]

It is another artifice of the modern style that seems to have touched Monsieur Berthoud slightly. That artifice has been revealed to us by a man of great intelligence, unfortunately placed under the influence of a theory that regards taste as unfashionable, a superstition, a despotism, a kind of literary feudalism unworthy of the emancipated heads of the nineteenth century: the taste that is, however, the probity of genius and the one and only safeguard of mediocrity.

That mystery of the art, of which Boileau, Racine and Fénélon had the misfortune of being ignorant, consists of substituting for abstract and general expressions words that specify sensible realities;[2] thus, the sky will no longer be serene or somber, it will be blue, red or gray; an edifice will cease to be imposing or majestic, it will be high, low or broad, and everything will only appear more clearly if it is given exact measurement. In virtue of that theory, these verses of Monsieur Chapelain, a poet that it is scarcely permissible to mock,[3] will serve as a model; they refer to

---

1 *Barnave* (1831), a historical novel featuring the controversial Revolutionary orator Antoine Barnave, was the work of Berthoud's friend Jules Janin.

2 Author's note: "See the poetics placed at the end of *Poésies de Joseph Delorme*." *Vie, poésies et pensées de Joseph Delorme* (1829) is a collection of prose and verse by Charles-Augustin Sainte-Beuve, a leading member of the French Romantic Movement

3 Author's note: "One sees in the *Correspondance de Grimm*, Part I, vol. II, p.160, that a certain M. de Caux de Cappeval had announced, in 1757, that he would correct the style of *La Pucelle*, the plan leaving nothing to revise. What he did not do, some of our fashionable poets appear to be accomplishing; their verses are only Chapelain 'revised and corrected,' and that is not an epigram." The reference is to the Encyclopedist Friedrich Melchior Grimm's *Correspondance littéraire*,

the beautiful Agnès:

> One sees outside the two ends of her short sleeves,
> Emerging uncovered two long white hands,
> Whose unequal fingers, round and slender.
> Imitate the swelling of round and fleshy arms.
> *La Pucelle*, Book V.

Is it not evident that that doctrine, pushed to its final consequences, will tend to materialize poetry, introducing thereinto Condillac's theory of sensation?[1] Is it not often more poetic to go from the effect to the cause than from the cause to the effect, and are objects not far less interesting in themselves than in the impression that they make upon us? That the sky might be azure, or a blue of varying deepness, I do not oppose, but its aspect renders my soul serenity. It is from me that I depart to appreciate its spectacle, and when I say that the sky is serene I am neither more trivial nor more false that when I describe its color.

It is necessary to be grateful to Monsieur Berthoud for not allowing himself to be caught by these paradoxes. To admit our entire thought, the author in question is more worthy of merit in our eyes by virtue of the faults that he has avoided than the qualities of which he gives proof. His book is nevertheless a work of good sense and taste, which one can read without danger to the mind or the heart, which is a great thing today, and if he does not manifest therein any great fecundity of imagination or high range of

---

philosophique et critique (1753-1773).
1 The empiricist philosopher Étienne Bonnot de Condillac (1714-1780) published his famous *Traité des sensations* in 1754.

intelligence, we will answer for him, while conserving the
difference between verse and prose:

> I agree that, in making verses
> My career is well-furnished;
> My genius already unharnessed
> As soon as I have scribbled both sides of the page.
> However, my Aristarchus demands that the muse
> No longer leaves me on the road,
> That my verve has a tomorrow,
> That such beautiful fire is less quickly used up,
> And an honest volume warmed until the end.
> But weakness is my excuse;
> Sloth, in its turn, delightful venom,
> Numbs me when I think of putting on my boots,
> Or changing my bagpipe for a clarion.
> It is necessary to cede to one's destiny,
> Good Sancho, has your innocent mount,
> Ever been able to match the speed
> Of the impetuous Rosinante?
> Or the indolent mule of Bonneau
> Follow Agnès' mare with the golden bit?[1]
> Such is my muse, I say so without mystery.
> It's also, if you wish, the solitary lamp
> That is extinguished when the sun,
> The pure and vermilion timepiece
> Comes to announce to the earth
> That it is time to wake up.
> It is the valetudinarian drinker,

---

1 Agnès Sorel and the counsellor Bonneau are historical characters
featured in *La Pucelle*.

By Broussais put on a diet,[1]
Who limits himself, sighing,
To saluting every grace
Of a unique glass where the ice
Tempers the fuming garlic.
It is the timid shepherdess
Whose dog serves as her guide,
And who, at a rapid pace,
Down there by the ravelin,
Goes to consult in secret
The pious anchorite,
Possessor of the wand
And the knowledge of Merlin;
But who, far from the village,
Never goes, wise girl,
Within the walls of the city,
To show her simple attire,
Her corset and her figure
Beautiful in timidity.

     De Reiffenberg.[2]

---

1 The reference is to the physician François-Joseph-Victor Broussais (1772-1838), a great advocate of bleeding as therapy, and thus a very dangerous man.
2 The quotation presumably comes from one of the two collections of poetry published by the Belgian historian Frédéric de Reiffenberg (1795-1850) in 1823 and 1825.

MISANTHROPIC TALES

My Uncle Bertrand's Friend

A Paradoxical Story

1825

Homine nil miserius (Pliny.)[1]

We would desire little ardently if we knew exactly
what we desire.
(La Rochefoucauld, *Maximes*.)[2]

WHAT a singular man my Uncle Bertrand is! What
he feels and what he does never seem to be in accord with what he says.

To hear him, generosity, affection and virtue do not
exist, but I do not know a better, more sensitive and more
respectable man than my Uncle Bertrand. Recount a good
deed in his presence: tears begin coming to his eyes; then
he will demonstrate to you pitilessly that it has only been
produced by a calculation of egotism. He delights in his

---

1 The quotation from Pliny, reproduced by Montaigne (where
Berthoud presumably found it) is actually *Solum certum nihil esse certi,
et homine nihil miserius aut superbius* [The one thing that is certain is
that nothing is certain, and nothing is more wretched or superb than
a human being].
2 The Duc de Rochefoucauld's *Maximes* were first published in 1665,
although more were added in later editions.

rich library; he loves to be surrounded by his friends, and his affection for me, the sole member of his family spared by death, has never recoiled before the greatest sacrifices; nevertheless, not a day passes without my uncle crying anathema upon the satiety produced by study; no one expresses himself with such virulence on the folly of unfortunates stupid enough to believe in amity, in blood ties or gratitude. In sum, the sweetest and most cherished illusions dissipate before his bitter sarcasms, before his reasoning that drives one to despair. If my Uncle Bertrand's life were not there in its entirety to belie his paradoxes, it is certain that once having heard him, one would no longer believe in anything.

One day, when I was dining with him with several other people, the conversation turned to happiness, and everyone, as you will understand, set about defining it in their own manner. After much verbiage, however, everyone fell into agreement that a young man, rich, healthy, educated, intelligent, endowed with sensibility and great physical advantages, could not fail to be happy.

My Uncle Bertrand, who had not said a word until then, formed a pitying smile and shrugged his shoulders, after which he passed his left hand over his elevated forehead two or three times; that is what my uncle always does when he is getting ready to tell a story.

A great silence then descended among us.

My Uncle Bertrand began speaking in these terms:

"There's no one among you who hasn't read in La Fontaine's fables the story of the ill-advised King Candaules.[1]

---

1 This oft-recycled story, as told by Herodotus, relates how Candaules, king of Lydia (from 735-718 B.C.) boasted of his wife's beauty to his

"What happened to that poor prince also happened to me.

"Smitten with Lucile B***, as one is smitten at twenty-five, I thought I was in love with her, as one thinks one is in love at twenty-five. My marriage was soon due to take place, and there would have been something lacking in my joy if Léopold de Merville, my childhood friend, had not been a witness to it—because, when one is twenty-five, one believes in friendship.

Lucile's marriage was celebrated six months thereafter, but with Léopold de Merville. My tender fiancée had preferred to poor Bertrand, a young man whose good looks and intelligence were enhanced by an annual income of fifty thousand francs.

"That is how it came about that Merville was married and I remained a bachelor."

In spite of the jocular tone that my Uncle Bertrand was trying to give his story, his strained voice and a pause of a few seconds revealed a painful emotion.

He resumed thereafter:

"Alas, they did not enjoy the happiness of that union for long; Merville found himself a father and a widower on the same day.

"Eighteen years after that disastrous event, I received a letter from Merville; he only had a few days to live, he told me therein, and he begged me, in the name of a friendship very unworthily outraged, to watch as a father over Lucile's son, that orphan, whose excitable character inspired the most ominous presentiments.

---

skeptical bodyguard Gyges; in order to prove what he said he arranged for Gyges to see her naked, but the offended queen then arranged for Gyges to murder the king and usurp his throne. Plato offers a different version of the story in a classic passage in the *Republic*.

"I left within the hour, and it was in pressing Léopold's icy hands that I pronounced the oath to become a friend and a father to Gustave.

"Merville's death cast his son into a somber and taciturn sorrow. As there is no grief that does not yield to distance from the place where one has suffered it, when the sight of new and curious objects preoccupies the imagination, I undertook a long voyage with Gustave into the interior of France.

"As I had anticipated, the memory of his father, at first so poignant, soon degenerated into a mild melancholy, devoid of bitterness, and not of a nature to give rise to any anxiety.

"After six months of traveling we arrived at Dieppe, where a fall from a horse forced me to stay for a while.

"During the first week Gustave did not leave my bedside. The affectionate cares and delicate attentions that he lavished upon me rendered my annoying situation almost tolerable, and, redoubled the attachment inspired in me by his good qualities, of exquisite sensibility and becoming exaltation.

"And then again, his voice, although a little more emphatic, resembled Lucile's sweet voice so strongly; he had a gaze in his big blue eyes so similar to Lucile's that he could not speak to me, and I could not see him, without the memory of Lucile softening me. In that fashion, my amity for Gustave became identified with the love I had had for his mother, and it seemed to me that in preserving him from grief, in turning him away from a reef, I was worthy of Gustave and the woman I would have liked, during the insensate dreams of my youth, to surround with happiness and love.

"I did not take long to perceive that Gustave was experiencing some great chagrin; if he read to me, I saw by the monotony of his voice that an insurmountable preoccupation was drawing my young friend's imagination far away from the thoughts of the book. Moreover, in the care that he was now giving me, duty was evident rather than the active and attentive affection that had previously inspired it. He abandoned me to my solitude for entire afternoons, and when he returned, he remained silent, as if absorbed in some overwhelming thought.

"Every time I interrogated him, he strove to evade my questions, or only replied by attributing his depression to the death of his father.

"He was hiding something from me, that was certain, and I experienced the greatest anxieties.

"It was then two months that my fall had confined me to my room, and I was finally beginning to recover. Surprised not to have seen Gustave all day, although night was beginning to fall, I dragged myself to his apartment. After having knocked several times in vain, I suddenly noticed that there was a faint groaning coming from within. I called for help; the door was broken down. Gustave lay there dying; a letter deposited on the table told me that he had poisoned himself.

"Fortunately, it was not yet too late. Prompt help recalled the unfortunate young man to life, and after a night passed in the greatest anxiety, I finally obtained the certainty that he was out of danger.

"Gustave had been gripped by a fervent passion for Clara Patternich, a young Mexican who was staying in the same hotel as us. Clara's father had surprised the two lovers in a very tender conversation and, as the affairs that had brought him to France were concluded and a vessel was about to set sail, he embarked with his daughter, whom he had promised to businessman in his homeland, and whom he had no desire to marry to a foreigner, I don't know how many leagues from America.

"Gustave, in despair, had taken an overdose of laudanum. Returned to existence, he conceived and executed a folly almost as great: that of running off to Mexico after the beautiful Clara.

"Remonstrations, prayers, tears—nothing could turn him away from such an escapade. It only remained for me to go with him, which is what I did.

"After a long and tedious crossing, we arrived in Santa Cruz. My first visit was to a merchant to whom one of my friends, his correspondent, had recommended me in the most pressing manner. That recommendation disposed him greatly in my favor, and when he had finished reading a postscript that authorized him to open me a credit of thirty thousand piastres, his protestations of devotion knew no bounds. That postscript doubtless also stopped him laughing in my face when it was necessary to tell him that I was the quinquagenarian Sancho of a young European Don Quixote in pursuit of a Mexican Dulcinea.

"'Are you certain that the young woman's father lives in Santa Cruz?' the merchant asked me when I had finished.

"'Not the slightest clue in that regard,' I replied.

"'It's just that we have at least thirty Patterniches here,' he said, 'and I know that each of them has a string of daughters capable of furnishing a Clara to all the lovers in Europe. You can't decently go from door to door knocking and crying: *Is the one that I love here?* Wait, though—it's nearly time for mass, and if the object of your search is in

Santa Cruz I'll guarantee that you'll encounter her shortly in church . . . or this evening at the tertulia—that's what we call our soirées. If not, leave for another Mexican city, for Señorita Clara isn't in Santa Cruz.'

"We went to rejoin Gustave, and the merchant took us to the church.

"I've traveled in Spain, and people there are far from observing a very edifying decorum, but a Spaniard would be scandalized in a church in Santa Cruz. There is a racket and a stir that stupefies foreigners; people talk there either about pleasures or business; they strike bargains and slip one another love-letters; rosaries in hand, they all accost one another, chat, joke and laugh with less restraint than at the end of a fête in France, when eyes are shiny and cheeks are red and burning.

"Gustave ran around the nave in all directions; he did not find Clara.

"Our guide then proposed that we go and wait for the crowd at the exit from the church: by that means we could pass all those it contained in review.

"Outside the door there were a great many carriages, and especially many horses. Their high saddles rise up four or five inches in front and behind, in order to give the rider a more solid support on the steep and mountainous roads of the region. To the right and left of the saddle and on the breast of the mount, the hide of some long-haired animal falls almost to the ground. At every moment we saw numerous riders departing rapidly, pricking the flanks of their admirable horses with gigantic spurs. They all had their heads passed through a cloak holed in the middle, whose form is reminiscent of a priest's chasuble, with more amplitude. To complete that bizarre equipment, a sword, enormous in dimension, was attached by straps to the left of the saddle, and their feet were supported by large wooden stirrups.

"'Come and rest at my house now,' said the merchant, when we found ourselves alone outside the closed church. 'We'll have dinner shortly, and you can continue your search this evening at the tertulia of one of our richest merchants.'

"If you're sober, and don't like tumult and shouting at table, may heaven preserve you from ever dining in Mexico. Silent and grave at first, all the Mexicans who were dining with us soon delivered themselves, and almost instantaneously, to the noisiest conversations; one couldn't hear oneself think. We saw worse toward the end of the meal; they started taking the liberty of making deafening toasts, and twelve or fifteen people, permanently on their feet, never stopped shouting, or rather howling, with the accompaniment of all the guests: *Copas en mano! Union y libertad!*

"The delicate and reserved Gustave suffered at the sight of that orgy, and I was able to convince myself completely that he was beginning to repent of his mad escapade. The annoyances of the journey and everything that came before his eyes had contributed marvelously to that. Only self-respect and habitude—for habitude also has a powerful influence on a man's imagination and desires—made him persist in his search. The best means of encouraging those fortunate symptoms was to pretend not to perceive them; in consequence, as Gustave's enthusiasm cooled, I redoubled my zeal to find Clara, and I did not ease up until my ward and our host were walking to the tertulia with me.

"The merchant, our guide, was European and he had decorated his house in the continental manner, so it was without preparation that Gustave found himself in the room where the tertulia was being held.

"Like my young friend, you might have expected to see a splendid elegance deployed in that gathering. Well, imagine a bare floor and a whitewashed wall devoid of plaster; add for a ceiling a circumflex dome of beams and joists, with the scales of a mantle of tiles extended above it; fill all that with the thick smoke exhaled by four hundred cigars, along with piercing cries, the chords of a mandolin and bursts of laughter that give you vertigo, and you'll have an almost exact idea of a Mexican tertulia.

"Yes, Messieurs, it's there that two hundred women in dazzling costumes are arranged along the walls, in an automatic position, so to speak; it's there that, by virtue of a disagreeable contrast, men in boots and cloaks, their hats on their heads, circulate or group together around gaming tables. At each of the corners of the apartment one sees a stone table, on which a massive candlestick stands, charged with a wretched candle that only serves to render the obscurity more visible. Behind that glimmer, for I dare not say light, appears, beneath a glass globe, a statuette of the Virgin, the patron saint of Mexico, which the devotion of the mistress of the house has covered with artificial flowers in detestable taste. In the middle of the room, hats and shawls are heaped on a large table, among the glasses and refreshments. Finally, nurses and old domestics are walking back and forth, chatting with their own masters in a very familiar manner entirely unknown in Europe.

"I rejoiced in the stupefaction and disgust expressed by Gustave's physiognomy.

"'Is she here?' I asked him.

"'Eh? How can one tell in such smoke?' he replied, in a tone half-impatient and half-melancholy. I seized his arm, and by that that amicable constraint I obliged him to accompany me from group to group. Suddenly, Gustave shivered; he had recognized the person in search of whom he had crossed the sea. She was smoking a cigar with the best grace in the world, laughing in bursts, and her slightly deformed figure announced that the girl had become a young woman. In any case, a tall fellow came to talk to her in an entirely conjugal fashion, and our guide said to us: 'That's Señora Bemposo, married four months ago when she returned from the continent. Her family doesn't live in Santa Cruz; her father is a Mexican businessman.'

"Gustave dragged me out of the house rapidly, without saying a word.

"The next day we embarked on a ship sailing for France; the day after, he was laughing at his misadventure."

"But Uncle," I exclaimed, "Gustave isn't unfortunate for having committed a folly; become wiser by virtue of the tribute he's paid, he'll now be on his guard against an imagination too vivid and too excitable."

"Yes," my uncle replied, "last year he married a very pretty, very passionate foreign singer without an écu of dowry."

"Well, what need did she have of a dowry to marry Gustave, with an income of a hundred thousand livres? He's happy now, with a woman he loves and who loves him."

"Yes," my uncle replied, for the second time, taking a piece of paper from his pocket. "This is the last letter he wrote to me; it's to press this solicitor to arrange a separation; my nephew can no longer live with the woman he loves and who loves him."

"Where, then, does happiness reside," I exclaimed, "since sensibility renders one unhappy, and fortune only serves to satisfy insensate desires whose accomplishment one curses?"

"I once knew," my Uncle Bertrand replied, for the third time, "someone who said: *In order to be happy, it's necessary to have rich savings, an evil heart and a good stomach.*"

"Fie on such happiness!" we all cried.

"In that case," my uncle countered, for the fourth time, "tell me, pray, what you mean by happiness?"

Lang-Mao-Li

A Chinese anecdote

Stroke a tiger and it will devour your hand.
(Yu-Xiao-Li.)

IN the province of Fo-Kien, so celebrated for the beautiful rock crystal that is found in its mountains, there was a comfortable little house, over the construction of which taste seemed to have presided rather than opulence. It was surrounded by trees that embellished it with the variety of their foliage and their delicious fruits. The ly-chee was bowed down by the weight of its scarlet apples, alongside the chi-tse, whose flavorsome berries mingled their perfume with that of the seeds of the mui-chu. Not far away, on the banks of a limpid stream, an old domestic was collecting melons and a kind of almonds called longyen, the smooth yellow rind of which covers a white winy flesh, in immense vases of coarse porcelain. Further away, appetizing pyramids could be seen that he had just formed with pa-tsians, tcheou-kous and fan-pole-myes, the delightful fruits known in Europe as pineapples.

The peaceful proprietor of that pleasant retreat, young Lang-Mao-Li, was composing verses under a bilimbi arbor.

His forehead supported by his left hand, his right was getting ready to trace, with his ivory brush, the ideas inspired in him by the profound calm of that enchanting abode, when a frightful roaring and plaintive cries suddenly interrupted his meditations. He got up precipitately. An enormous tiger was pursuing a young woman. Without hesitating, Lang-Mao-Li launched himself in front of the ferocious animal and plunged his dagger into its heart; but he paid dearly for his victory, because his enemy, in writhing, sank its redoubtable claws into his left arm.

An old servant of Lang-Mao-Li, named Fan-Po, after having placed an initial dressing on his master's wound, took him to the apartment where the young lady who owed her life to him was waiting for him. She advanced timidly toward her liberator and, lifting the veil that enveloped her, showed him the blushing features of a rare beauty. Her head was ornamented with a feng-hoang, the spread golden wings of which covered her broad brown forehead; the tail, of the same metal, rose up in a tuft, and the neck, terminated by a sharp beak, extended over her nose, whose remarkable smallness matched that of her eyes. Finally, her figure offered a bosom full of grace, and her tittering and uncertain gait indicated sufficiently the admirable exiguity of her feet.

Young and poetic, Lang-Mao-Li could not see those attractions without a keen sense of admiration; he was unable to say a single word, so much was he troubled. Fortunately, he had time to collect himself somewhat while the beautiful stranger told him the name of her father, Namb-Ki, a rich merchant of Fo-Kien.

"I was going to the home of one of my relatives," she added, "when a tiger pounced on the two slaves who were carrying my litter. The monster would have torn me to pieces if you hadn't saved the life, at the risk of your own, of the unfortunate Iu-Sa. May the great Fo recompense my liberator!"

Lang-Mao-Li wiped away a tear, and was more troubled than ever.

When his compassion had calmed down slightly, they deliberated as to the means of informing Iu-Sa's father of the danger she had run and the place where she had found shelter. It was decided that Fan-Po would leave at daybreak the following day.

The beautiful Iu-Sa then withdrew to the apartment that had been prepared for her, and Lang-Mao-Li spent all night dreaming about the charming young woman's little eyes, and composing verses in which he compared their brightness to that of the aster, the favorite flower of Chinese poets.

Timid and respectful, as one is the first time one is in love, Lang-Mao-Li dared not infringe the strict laws of etiquette, which forbid a Chinaman to present himself before a nubile young woman. Sighing, he deposited in the threshold of Iu-Sa's apartment a basket of the rarest flowers and most delicate fruits; then he waited with a keen impatience for the return of Fan-Po.

Fan-Po finally appeared, accompanied by a little old man whose sly gaze sparkled with cunning and guile.

Namb-Ki—for it was Iu-Sa's father—prostrated himself at Lang-Mao-Li's feet, as if he were saluting a mandarin. "May the great Fo," he cried, "envelop with the mantle of prosperity the man who combines the courage of Meang-Ni with the wisdom of Confucius and the poetic talent of the divine Ibionam!"

The young man received these eulogies blushing with pleasure and modesty, and then hastened to offer the merchant a rural repast, at which the delicious wine of Nam-Hung was served. Namb-Ki then redoubled his eulogies and his protestations of amity; he shed tears, and raised his arms to the heavens, pressing Lang-Mao-Li to his bosom. Finally, it was necessary to separate; the merchant had his litter advance and placed his daughter therein himself.

Fortunate Lang-Mao-Li! Iu-Sa raised her veil adroitly, and darted at her savior a glance full of gratitude and tenderness.

The young poet's gaze followed the litter enclosing Iu-Sa for as long as he could. She had disappeared some time ago, but he still kept his eyes fixed on the road she had taken. Sad and pensive, experiencing an emptiness that had been unknown to him until then, he tried to devote himself to his cherished occupations, but it was in vain; the memory of Iu-Sa occupied his mind entirely, and he could not trace anything on his tablets but the harmonious name of the beautiful woman.

The night, which he passed in a cruel insomnia, further augmented his excitement, and in the morning, Fan-Po was astonished to see him dressed in a large-breasted scarlet jacket fixed on the right by five golden buttons. Rich trousers in white taffeta, which fell over his pointed shoes, rendered the elegant costume complete. Lang-Mao-Li went to ask Namb-Ki for Iu-Sa's hand.

"How happy I shall be," he said to himself, in the road. "The great Fo is recompensing my courage with a divine and admirable generosity; I know how beautiful the woman I am going to marry is, and I'm not running the risk of seeing a deformed monster emerging from the nuptial litter, of whom I can only rid myself by paying her father a large forfeit!"

As he approached the house of Namb-Ki, he felt his courage draining away, for he feared that the modest ease he enjoyed might seem very little in the eyes of Iu-Sa's father. "If he doesn't grant my wish, nothing remains for me but to die!" he said to himself.

How forcefully his heart was beating when he entered the merchant's house! How red-faced and embarrassed he was when it was necessary to explain the purpose of his visit!

"What are you asking me?" cried Namb-Ki dolorously. Then, after a moment's silence, he went on: "How can I refuse my daughter to the generous man without whom I would never have seen her again? Why am I not richer? But only let the great Fo cast a favorable eye on my enterprises, and I will share my fortune with you . . . what am I saying? I shall give it to you in its entirety!"

Lang-Mao-Ki protested against such a speech and, to prove his disinterest, added that he wanted to espouse the one for whose hand he was asking without a dowry. Namb-Ki raised his arms to the heavens in admiration, and the marriage was celebrated a few days later, with an extraordinary pomp and splendor; it cost the poet more than a year's income.

It would be difficult to describe the happiness that the two spouses enjoyed during the first three months of their union. Namb-Ki visited them almost every day, and his son-in-law's table became, in a sense, his own. His good humor and frankness ended up gaining him the poet's affection, so it was not without a sharp chagrin that the latter observed the change that came over the character of the merchant in a matter of days. He was somber, taciturn and while he ate, large tears ran down his cheeks.

All that amity, of the most tender and most pressing nature, was put to use by Lang-Mao-Li to divine his father-in-law's fatal secret. Finally, he discovered it: he was about to be ruined and dishonored; he had to pay a sum of thirty thousand sequins at the end of the month, and the recent loss of a ship rendered the payment impossible.

Lang-Mao-Li did not hesitate; he sold more than half of his worldly goods and, a week later, he gave Namb-Ki the thirty thousand sequins that would prevent his ruination. The latter received them with the most enthusiastic transports of joy and gratitude, promised his son-in-law to pay them back in a few months, and wanted to give him a written acknowledgement that declared him to be indebted for that sum; the literate rejected any such proposition, and Namb-Ki did not mention it again.

Some time afterwards, an important affair obliged Lang-Mao-Li to go to Peking; Fan-Po went with him. It was necessary to tear Iu-Sa from her husband's arms. Needless to say, the poet hastened his return, and he was overjoyed when he found himself with his wife again after an absence of two months.

While Iu-Sa was telling her husband everything that had happened during his voyage—a story that he interrupted more than once with tender caresses—a pale man enveloped by vestments in disorder entered the house precipitately and prostrated himself at Lang-Mao-Li's feet.

"Scholarly literate," he said, "soldiers are pursuing me, and if you refuse me shelter, I shall fall into the hands of a powerful enemy. My crime is to have revealed in a satire the exactions of the mandarin of this province . . ."

Lang-Mao-Li did not give him time to finish, lifted him up and swore to him that he could regard his house as his own so long as he was in danger.

After having changed his clothes, Tit-Se-Lo—that was the name that the stranger gave himself—came to rejoin Lang-Mao-Li, who marveled at the good appearance of his new guest. He had a long conversation with him, and was so charmed by the erudition and intelligence of which he gave proof that when he left him he ran to the bilimbi bower to compose a set of verses against the unjust oppressor of Tit-Se-Lo. The latter appreciated the literate's satire greatly, rating it far above the one that had earned him so much persecution, and asked for permission to make a copy of it—permission that was immediately granted to him.

Iu-Sa showed Tit-Se-Lo at least as much tenderness as she testified to Lang-Mao-Li, so the latter waxed ecstatic all day regarding his wife's generosity of heart, and blessed the great Fo for having given him such a sensitive wife.

His old servant Fan-Po was not exactly of the same opinion. One day, he took it upon himself to insinuate to his master that the amity of Iu-Sa and Tit-Se-Lo was not as entirely innocent as he would like to believe. Lang-Mao-Li immediately dismissed the wretch who had dared to calumniate the model of friends and the most ideal of wives.

The literate sage In-Miopo has compared calumny to a mite that attaches itself to a garment; it is an imperceptible insect devoid of strength, but it leaves ineradicable traces and often ends up eating away the fabric entirely. That was exactly what happened to Lang-Mao-Li; he was scornful of Fan-Po's absurd suggestions, but, in spite of himself, he paid closer attention to the conduct of his friend and his wife. It did no good to take refuge under the bilimbi bower; calm and poetry had quit that delightful redoubt, to give way to anxiety and jealousy; in vain he passed his inked stick over ivory tablets; he did not trace a single word, and solitude, far from soothing is chagrin, sharpened it even more.

In order to extract himself from such a state of agitation and the ridiculous suspicions at which he blushed, he made the decision to undertake an excursion in the mountains, and went out one morning announcing that he would not be back until the evening. He had scarcely been gone for half an hour when his litter broke and it was necessary to return home. Half laughing and half cursing his misadventure, he went to find Iu Sa in her apartment to tell her the story . . .

The faithful Iu-Sa was asleep in the arms of the virtuous Tit-Se-Lo.

Lang-Mo-Li uttered a cry of rage, launched himself upon the perfidious couple, and fell, stunned by a violent blow that the robust Tit-Se-Lo brought down on his head . . .

When he came round, more than an hour later, Iu-Sa and her seducer had disappeared.

Corrupted by vengeance, the literate set forth to denounce the guilty parties to the mandarin, and bring down that magistrate's rigor upon them.

The atrocious penalty by which adultery was punished seems too mild to him; it is not enough to see Tit-Se-Lo and his accomplice, naked, their faces smeared with chalk, their ears pierced with darts, dragged through the streets with an ignominious drum on their back; he would like to make them expire himself under the blows of the pan-tse and sate himself on the spectacle of their torments and their tears.

How long the journey to the mandarin's palace seems to him! Finally, the porcelain towers on which the scarlet dragon shines appear to him in the distance; that sight reanimates his courage; he takes a few more steps, but, out of breath, exhausted by the blood that is flowing from the wound in his head, he is soon obliged to suspend his progress momentarily.

A bench is offered to his gaze; he sits down there, his forehead supported in his hands. Suddenly he is seized and gagged by armed men to whom Tit-Se-Lo is giving orders, and who drag him before the mandarin, without telling him the reason for such treatment.

How surprised Lang-Mao-Li is, and how terrified, when he sees that redoubtable magistrate, his eyes sparkling with anger, pointing with his finger at the satire composed against him on the day when Tit-Se-Lo came to seek refuge in the literate's home! It is in vain that the unfortunate tries to speak; his gag is not removed, and the mandarin casts a sheaf of five little sticks on the ground. At that signal of vengeance, two officers seize Lang-Mao-Li, lay him down full length, remove his garments, and apply to him as many strokes of the pan-tse as the mandarin has thrown down sticks.

Lang-Mao-Li's torture does not stop there; the mandarin declares all his property confiscated, and condemns him to the cangue for a month.

That sentence is carried out immediately; the head of the unfortunate literate is encased by two enormous pieces of wood that do not permit him to see his feet or to put his hands to his mouth; a seal is applied to the joints of the pieces of wood, and he is ignominiously expelled.

Bruised by blows and staggering under the weight of the cangue, Lang-Mao-Li heads for his father-in-law's house. There, at least he will receive consolation; there, at least, he will not find an ingrate. A sweet recompense for a good deed, he thinks; I helped Namb-Ki in his misfortune, and if I had not done so, the thirty thousand sequins I lent him would have been confiscated with the rest of my fortune, and would not remain to me; what is better still, I shall have a friend to commiserate with me.

Alas, the reception he received was very different from the one he expected.

As soon as Namb-Ki saw him, he ordered his slaves to drive him away, to throw out of his house a scoundrel who would cover his old age with dishonor. Then, turning to the people who were surrounding the literate and heaping insults upon him, he said: "How unfortunate I am! I gave him my daughter in marriage; I shared my fortune with him, and you see how he proves his gratitude!" And he started shedding tears with such bitterness, by which the people were so moved, that they abused Lang-Mao-Li even more harshly, and went so far as to cover him with mud.

The unfortunate fellow could not resist those further torments; he fell down unconscious.

When he came round, he found himself in a distant place, next to an old man who was giving him aid; it was his old servant Fan-Po.

Lang-Mao wanted to express his gratitude, but his sobs prevented him from doing so, and he could only offer him his hand.

"Come on, my old master," said the old man, in a slightly doctoral tone, "bear your misfortune with more courage. It's hard, I agree, to think that one has introduced to one's wife a bad lot like the mandarin's son, especially if one has taken it into one's head to give him a piece of verse that one has made against his father, but after all, it's necessary to admit that his plot was woven with a great deal of skill, and it required all my penetration to suspect it.

"Have courage, I tell you; a month is soon passed and the beating that one receives when the cangue is taken off never exceeds twenty strokes. You can come with me then to live in a hut I have in the mountains, and, by working harvesting tsi-chu varnish you can earn enough to live. It's a slightly dangerous métier, but it brings in at least ten sequins a year. If you become rich again, don't risk your life for a woman, don't expose yourself to the anger of a mandarin for your wife's lover, and don't entrust your father-in-law with thirty thousand sequins. Above all, don't recompense the sage advice of an old servant by throwing him out ignominiously."

"You're right!" Lang-Mao-Li exclaimed. "I no longer believe in amity or gratitude. But do you think that Iu-Sa, when she knows how unfortunate I am, when she recognizes the full extent of her fault, won't come to implore my forgiveness and help me to support the weight of my misfortune? Oh, I know her tender attachment to me too well! Without the infamous seductions of Tit-Se-Lo, that monster who stole her love, poor Iu-Sa would never . . ."

"Come on, it's getting dark, let's go to my hut," Fan-Po interjected, shrugging his shoulders and smiling in pity.

Lang-Mao-Li got up. The old man helped him to carry his cangue, and they both drew away, at a slow pace.

The Madman
A Ferraran Tale
1586

I can't help smiling in pity on seeing men pride
themselves on the talent, genius and reason that
hazard has given them; for all that differs so little
from the human degradation called madness that
every day, at every moment, one is mistaken for
the other.
(Paolo Frienzi, *Il Pergamo*.)[1]

TWO strangers of distinction, arrived in Ferrara a
few days before, visited the hospital—or rather the
prison—of Sant'Anna, in which unfortunates deprived of
reason are locked up. The head of the older of the travelers
was entirely bald, and his physiognomy presented a mixture of naivety and malice, bonhomie and nobility. Every
time he interrogated the vulgar guide given to them by
Father Antonio Mosti, the prior of the hospital he attached
a piercing gaze full of fire to the coarse and impassive features of that hideous jailer, and seemed to want to read his
responses before he had pronounced them in a hoarse and
sinister voice.

1 This reference is fictitious.

The nobleman accompanying him appeared to be a few years younger. His perfumed hair escaped from a toque sparkling with gems; a short, richly-embroidered cloak of scarlet velvet enveloped his shoulders with elegant drapery, but nevertheless allowed a glimpse, over a doublet trimmed with ermine, of the large and shiny links of a magnificent golden chain. His hand, covered by a silken gauntlet, was posed on the pommel of an épée suspended from a satin sash, and only the noise of his silver spurs troubled the silence of the long corridors through which he moved.

"This jailer seems as stupid to me as he is frightening, Étienne de La Boëtie,"[1] his companion said to him, in French, "and he surely won't be able to give us any information about anything we see here. I regret that, for my curiosity is keenly excited by the strangeness of these places."

At these words, a young Italian who was walking in the corridor advanced toward them and, expressing himself in French with facility, offered to guide them in their visit to the hospice. "I can inform you," he added, "of the particular kind of madness of the unfortunates who are suffering here, and to whom one might apply the line of Virgil: *abstulit atra dies, et funere mersit acerbo.*"[2]

"That offer is made with too much good grace for Seigneur de Montaigne and me not to hasten to accept it,"

---

1 Author's note: "Étienne de La Boëtie is far more celebrated for the friendship that linked him to Montaigne than twenty-nine sonnets that are only found in the first edition of Montaigne's *Essais*, printed in Bordeaux in 1580, the duodecimo edition of Jean Richter printed in 1587 in Paris and that of Abel l'Angelier in quarto in 1588."
2 "[Whom] a black inauspicious day cut off, and sunk in an untimely death."

La Boëtie replied.

"Yes," murmured the jailer, with an odious smile, "let Strozzi guide them; I'll be dispensed from replying to their intolerable questions. He'll talk as much as they want." Then he retired slowly to the extremity of the gallery, where, standing with his arms folded, he leaned against the wall. His broad shoulders and stout, thickset figure were scarcely perceptible in the shadows; only a bunch of keys that he was holding in his hand sometimes emitting a slight clinking.

Strozzi took Montaigne and his friend along a long corridor formed by narrow cells, before which he stopped in order to explain, with considerable sagacity, the genre of madness of the unfortunates imprisoned therein. His reflections, full of precision, and the agreeable form in which he presented them, charmed the two foreigners; they interrupted him several times to tell him how glad they were to have encountered a guide who combined so much amiability and instruction with the cognizance of that sad abode.

More than once, Montaigne and La Boëtie wiped away tears. "It's necessary to admit," said the first, "that I have a marvelous weakness for mercy and forbearance; I sense the misfortunes of others almost as keenly as the sufferer, and there is no anguish I have seen of which I cannot say, like Aeneas, *quorum pars magna fui.*[1] The Stoics would look at me with compassion—me, who pride myself on seeking wisdom—if they saw how the spectacle that we have before our eyes moves me to pity, because they considered

---

1 "[So many terrible things have I seen] and in so many of them I played a large part."

pity as a vicious passion, *quasi inutile vitium*;[1] they want us to help the unfortunate, but not to weaken and sympathize with them.

"It's all very well, however, for them to say that to let one's heart yield to commiseration is the effect of a softness and indulgence of the soul, and cite in support of the thesis the example of children and vulgar individuals who soften more easily than the vigorous, masculine and pitiless heart of a mature man; let them come here, and see how they support these groans, these wayward gazes, these dolorous and incoherent speeches."

"For myself," La Boëtie added, "I'm far from boasting of stoicism, and I'll blush rather than remain an indifferent spectator to the sufferings assembled in these places, the sight of which moves me to compassion."

The poet and Montaigne were doubtless about to yield to their liking for dissertation when they were suddenly interrupted by the noise of a cell whose door was screeching on its enormous hinges. A man covered in rags and curbed by misery rather than by age emerged from it cautiously and darted anxious glances around him. His beard and hair were unkempt, but his pale and wrinkled features nevertheless offered something strangely noble and imposing.

He advanced mysteriously toward the foreigners and, taking a letter from his bosom, said to them in a low and solemn voice: "If you are Christians, enable this writing to reach the Princess Leonora d'Este."

La Boëtie exchanged a smile with Montaigne and Strozzi while the former took the piece of paper in order

---

1 Author's note: "Like a superfluous weakness." [The improvisation does not appear to be a quotation].

not to offend the madness of the unfortunate who had spoken to him.

"I appear to you to be insane," the latter continued, "and you are confusing me with the debased beings into whose company I have been cast. Alas, I don't know myself how I've been able to conserve my reason in the midst of the infamous torments that are heaped upon me. Plunged from the bosom of a brilliant court into a noxious cell, torn from sweet illusions of glory, amity and love to groan for seven years alone—alone or among the insensate and persecutors, to curse the fatal gift of genius and glory attached to my name . . . oh, who could support such an existence?

"In the name of the mother of God," he cried, embracing Montaigne's knees and bathing them with tears, "put an end to this horrible torture! Let Leonora learn I what place I am groaning, and she will come to deliver me . . . but you're hesitating; you're afraid of her brother. Oh, yes, fear him, for his vengeance is frightful, implacable! Well, tell Gonzaga, the Prince of Mantua, or my childhood friend, the faithful Cardinal Cinzio,[1] that here, under a supposed name . . ."

Suddenly, the formidable voice of the jailer rang out, and the echoes repeated his heavy and precipitate tread. The unfortunate shuddered, fell silent, and ran fearfully to take refuge in his cell, the door of which the impassive guardian closed upon him, without interrupting the *canzonetta* that he was humming in a low voice.

"That madman's mania," said the young Italian to the emotional travelers, "is to believe himself to be loved by

1 Cinzio Passeri Aldobrandini (1551-1610).

a great lady; sometimes he washes with tears letters that he imagines having received from her; sometimes he is heard despairingly recalling fêtes, tourneys and triumphs; sometimes he recites verses and traces them on the walls of his prison when he is accorded a little light for mercy's sake—for his madness has nothing furious; it's a profound melancholy, a somber and continuous sadness. His verses are always consecrated to the imaginary object of his tenderness, and that letter he has given you is, I'm sure, full of amorous expressions . . ."

"That's true," said Montaigne, who had just read it; he writes to the Princess of Ferrara as if the august Leonora reciprocated most tenderly; he talks about nocturnal rendezvous that she accorded him, and has no doubt that she will come to free him as soon as she knows that he is here." With a sigh, he added: "Poor human nature! From all that I have just seen here one could obtain a very strong argument to support Pliny's bold assertion: *Homine nil miserius aut superbius.*"[1]

In the meantime, a vague and confused murmur became audible in the hospital. A few moments later, Cardinal Cinzio, whom old Montaigne had seen at court, entered precipitately, followed by the prior Antonio Mosti. His features expressed the most vivid emotion, and a burning blush covered his face. Father Mosti took the enormous bunch of keys from the hands of the jailer and opened the thick door that had just closed on the insensate about whom the travelers were still talking.

---

1 Author's note: "Nothing is more wretched, and nothing more prideful, than human being. (Pliny. *Natural History*. Book II, chapter VII.)" The correct quotation is cited in a footnote to the notice.

Cinzio threw himself, weeping, into the arms of the unfortunate prisoner, who looked at him with a dolorous and stupid joy. "Oh my friend," cried the cardinal, when his sobs permitted him to speak, "my friend, is it thus that you are to be returned to me?"

Then, turning toward the spectators of that touching scene, he said, with a surge of indignation: "Foreigners, see how the Duke of Ferrara recompenses genius! Tell your compatriots, and the entire universe, that Torquato Tasso has been moaning for seven years in this infamous place, while the world mourned his death!" He added: "Come, my noble friend, let us flee this impious land. Come—Rome reserves palms and triumphs for you!"

After their departure, Montaigne, slightly confused by his mistake, remained silent for a few moments. Then, finally, taking his leave of Strozzi, he thanked him, in an affectionate tone, for the complaisance with which he had served as their guide.

"What?" said the latter, gravely. "You're quitting me without adoring me?"

At that question, Montaigne looked at him with astonishment.

"Vulgar mortal," the young Italian continued, "has not my sublime genius, which has plunged you into admiration, and the gift of tongues that I possess, revealed to you my mysterious divinity?" Seizing Montaigne by the throat at that moment, he cried, furiously: "On your knees! On your knees, profane! Adore me or I'll strangle you!"

La Boëtie and the jailer hastened to extract Michel from the madman's hands, and while he was dragged to a cell, Montaigne, adjusting his simarre, said: "My friend, we certainly cannot hold our heads up proudly today in vanity of the accuracy of our understanding, since we have admired the intelligence of a madman and mistaken for a madman the greatest genius in Italy. In truth, Socrates was right to profess that he only knew one thing, which was that he did not know anything, Pliny to write *Solum certum nihil esse certi*,[1] and me to say after them: "What do I know?"[2]

---

1 Author's note: "Nothing is certain but uncertainty."

2 Berthoud was apparently delighted with this anecdotal narrative, and transposed it twice more as an episode in longer works. It was previously translated in 1833 in the *Boston Literary Messenger*. It is completely fictitious; Tasso was imprisoned in Sant'Anna between 1579 and 1586, but the modern consensus holds that it had absolutely nothing to do with Leonora d'Este, that Tasso really was suffering from paranoid delusions, and that his patrons treated him as kindly as was feasible; he was not held incommunicado and maintained a voluminous correspondence with various people; he did get very upset, however, when he learned that his masterpiece *Gerusalemme Liberata*, had been revised and published by other hands. Writing stories that played fast and loose with historical events became something of a habit with Berthoud, who never let historical accuracy get in the way of a story he wanted to tell his own way.

Maria Ovenson
A Scottish Story
1802

It's her! Oh, yes . . . if I could still doubt it!
(Shakespeare, *Richard III.*)[1]

AWOMAN, and a young child she was holding by the hand, were wandering at midnight in the immense street in Edinburgh that extends from the castle to Holyrood and is named the High Street. To the extent that the pale light of the street lamps, further veiled by snow that was falling abundantly, permitted it to be judged, the cut of the poor garments that the two unfortunate creatures wore, iridescent with snowflakes, indicated that they were inhabitants of the other side of the Solway Firth. The child was a little girl, thin and paltry, whose valetudinarian pallor was further augmented by the rigor of the cold; she might have been nine years old. Her mother's features, strongly defined and even a little harsh, announced an energetic character, but they expressed no more at present than the

---

1 I have back-translated the alleged quotation from the French; nothing like it occurs in the original, or even in *Richard II*, which includes a scene in which it might fit, but it was not uncommon for Shakespeare's plays to be very extensively rewritten in French versions.

complete dejection produced by mental anguish and bodily suffering: a depression that is absolute, especially in strong souls finally vanquished after a long struggle with despair.

Perceiving a stone bench at the door of a town house of prosperous appearance, she brushed away the snow covering the icy stone and sat down. Then, effortfully drawing her daughter on to her knees, which could scarcely support her, she strove to warm her up, hugging her against her bosom and pressing the blue and swollen hands of the poor child in her own stiff hands. A few moments later, one might have thought that the girl was asleep, if convulsive efforts to huddle closer to her mother had not announced that dolor alone had closed her leaden burning eyes.

The red-hot iron under which quivering flesh screams and writhes, and the saw that stirs and slowly eats away the bone stripped of its flesh by the scalpel, produce a physical pain too intense to allow the soul further mental anguish: the exasperating dolor that they cause annihilates, while it lasts, even thought itself; but one of the bizarrely atrocious symptoms of cold is to cause a mental anguish more execrable than the icy malaise that penetrates the bones and grips them so horribly; oppressed by a dolorous and unquiet stupor, one is prey to a kind of nightmare that collides in the sick imagination with all that memory has of the most heart-rending; one experiences simultaneously all the torments of sleep and wakefulness.

Such was the situation of the unfortunate woman who, by virtue of a mechanical movement, was pressing her child to her bosom; involuntarily, she remembered her misfortunes, and the past, like a phantom, appeared before her, hideous in all the horror of the present.

Who had ever drained so completely the bitter cup of despair? Her older daughter, beautiful, virtuous, seduced and abducted, and who had dared to offer her mother the ignominious price of her sin! She would have forgiven, oh yes, her repentant daughter, but she rejected with horror the gifts and numerous letters of the courtesan. Heaven, however, had not taken account of such an austere virtue; unforeseen misfortunes destroyed her peaceful and mild mediocrity.

Her husband departs in the hope of gathering a little wretched detritus of his fortune; scarcely arrived in Edinburgh, he falls ill. In winter, alone, on foot, her child in her arms, she undertakes a long and rigorous voyage in order to come to console her spouse; she reaches the end; her husband has been dead for two days . . .

Meanwhile, the snow continues falling, piling up in a white icy veil over the immobile group formed by the two unfortunates. The unhappy mother's strength abandons her; her stiffened arms refuse to sustain her dying daughter. It's necessary to die or beg. Oh, if only she were alone! But she casts her eyes upon her child, and a hand knocks on the door of the prosperous house, and a plaintive voice implores the aid of those who reside in it.

A domestic appears, but it is to send her away with a vulgar and disdainful insouciance. She is drawing away in a bleak and stupid despair when a chambermaid with an imprudent and alert face appears. "Good God, George, how hard you are!" she says. "If my mistress knew that you treat the poor like that, you'd be far from her good graces. Know that Miss Ovenson...or rather, Mistress Clarence . . ."

"Ovenson!" cried the mendicant, with horror. "Come,

my child, let's flee!" And she disappeared, dragging her daughter.

"She's crazy," said the chambermaid.

"Assuredly," replied the phlegmatic George.

"But what's become of her? She couldn't have quit the High Street, but I can no longer see her. My God! Let her become what she wants! I won't catch a chill for a madwoman."

As she finished speaking, the soubrette launched herself lightly over the soft carpet with which the stairs were covered, and George soon perceived her at the top of the spiral stairway that led to the apartment of the celebrated actress Miss Overson.

It is therefore true that a veritable love is not the exclusive privilege of pure and virtuous souls; it hastens the palpitations of the heart of the courtesan as it swells the bosom of the ingenuous virgin, and it renders its transports, its devotion and even its virtue to the degraded individual by whom it was most profaned.

At least one senses some consolation in thinking that it is often a virtuous individual who inspires that real love, capable of the greatest sacrifices, and in which one recognizes less of the egotism with which all human actions are imprinted. That love, I say, causes the person it inflames to recover something of the innocence lost: the most savage and depraved of men is domesticated by the virginal smile of the young woman he loves, and, tamed by a child-like caress, he becomes momentarily mild and good once again in her presence.

Such was the beautiful Maria Overson. Drawn into the traps of seduction by a wretch who only deceived her to throw her into the arms of the rich Lord Paterson, she became the mistress of the opulent old man. To brave the opinion of the vulgar and put on a display to the scandal of their plebeian gazes is doubtless a refinement of the pleasures of powerful men; Maria's superannuated lover wanted her to be known and admired by all England. Endowed with fortunate dispositions for the theatrical art, protected by a powerful and rich lord, she soon became a celebrated actress.

Lord Paterson did not enjoy his handiwork for long; he died a year after Maria Overson's debut, and by means of his testament deprived his heirs of an immense fortune, which he bequeathed to his mistress.

Favored by the prestige of a great reputation, young, beautiful and rich, Maria soon gathered around her a numerous group of suitors for her hand. More than one dandy took his place in the ranks; more than one baronet offered her his title; a lord even proposed to the interpreter of Shakespeare that she exchange her tragic crown for that of a duke and peer. To all those honors she preferred the brilliant existence that a celebrated actress enjoyed, especially in London, an existence that combined the independence of men with the homages and pleasures that surround women. The enthusiastic transports of an entire public, subject to the power of talent, and the adulatory cries that saluted the presence of a cherished actress, had become a real need for Maria. Perhaps, too, the satisfaction that her vanity collected in refusing such seductive offers contributed somewhat to making her persevere in her disdain.

And yet, London suddenly learned, with astonishment, that Miss Overson was renouncing the theater. That unexpected retirement was attributed to a thousand different causes; people talked about it for a week, and then no one gave it another thought.

What, then, could have caused such an abrupt change in the resolutions of the beautiful actress? It was a young author, meek and timid: the amiable Arthur Clarence. He inspired in Miss Overson one of those ardent passions called romantic, and which, in spite of the positive ideas of our century, are perhaps less rare than one is tempted to believe.

She was in love! From then on she deemed herself glad to sacrifice to the vague dreads of a jealous and idolatrous lover her most precious possession, her glory and her success. Abandoning the London theater without regret, she had come to take refuge in Edinburgh a few weeks before, where she lived happy and unknown with Arthur, who had become her husband.

Daylight was beginning to appear through the thick curtains that enveloped Maria's windows. Half-dressed in a furry robe, her beautiful arms enlaced around her lover's neck, she contemplated Arthur's smile ecstatically; by turns playful and tender, mutinous and affectionate, she suddenly fled only to return immediately to be embraced again, and to run her delicate fingers through the beautiful blond curls of his hair.

Then, drawing the curtains from the window, she started engraving with her ring, on the panes on which frost had embroidered the elegant flowers of its crystals, Arthur's monogram. He, mildly moved, watched her silently.

While she was devoting herself to that task with a child-like attention, she chanced to perceive, through the diaphanous contours of the monogram she had just etched on the opaque glass, a group assembled around an object covered with snow.

Moved by a mechanical curiosity, she opened the window, which resisted the weak efforts of her dainty hands for a long time.

Oh! It was two rigid cadavers that were being propped up against a wall.

She attached an indescribable gaze to them.

"Mother! Mother!" she cried—and Arthur received her in his arms, motionless and icy.

The Prima Donna

Return to me, he said, my songs and my burden,
And take back your hundred écus.
(La Fontaine, "The Cobbler and the Financier".)

NEVER, oh no, never had the fresh and pure voice of a young woman, never had the celestial harp of an archangel, sighed a melody more delightful and ravishing! She finished that sublime song, and for a few seconds more a great silence reigned throughout the vast all, among all the motionless groups: a silence untroubled by the rustle of a dress or a breath of respiration. Then, suddenly, there were deafening transports, clamors of enthusiasm and regret, eyes moist with tears, hands throwing garlands and wreaths. Three times she bowed, in order to draw away, and three times unanimous cries, amorous cries, called her back.

Finally, however, the theater curtain, separating the public and the cantatrice terminated the long adieux. Then a young man ran forward; he surrounded her tenderly with his tremulous arms; he pressed his lips to the charming young woman's white and semi-naked shoulders.

"Now, nothing—oh, nothing—can tear us apart," he murmured, in an emotional voice. "You belong to me, yes, to me alone! There's no more Béatrice, it's Lady Clarendon that people will call you! It's my wife, my beloved wife!"

It required all the tenderness the young woman had, it was necessary for her to love Edward as her ardent soul was capable of loving, in order for her eyes not to overflow with bitter tears, in order for her to renounce such triumphs, such an intoxicating glory.

Now, here she is, the proprietress of a vast and rich estate on the wild and picturesque banks of the Clyde. Numerous domestics await her orders; couriers are ever ready to set forth to satisfy her most frivolous and costly caprices. There are sumptuous fêtes, brilliant and varied, renewed every day; there are women jealous of her beauty, her wealth; there are young lords who solicit as a favor a glance from the beautiful countess.

But above all, there is the love of her husband, of Edward, so noble and so tender! Every morning, leaning on his arm, she climbs some high crag in order to contemplate the sun rising among ruddy clouds; or, after a long walk, after having consoled a few invalids, after having rendered happiness to some indigent family by means of rich alms, she goes down to the seashore and relaxes on the sand to the sound of waves that break with a melancholy roar. During that voluptuous repose, Edward says words of love to her so sweet, which move the soul so forcefully when one listens to them, arms enlaced, beside, close beside, a cherished being in an immense solitude . . .

They both finally possess it, that happiness about which they talked so much in the midst of cities, when importunate obligations cast them into an indifferent world and isolated them from one another. At present, they only live for themselves, together, always together; their existence is one long ecstasy of amour and felicity.

Soon, and insensibly, a vague and mysterious trouble, confused regrets of the past, dolorous impulsions toward an indefinable object, render the Countess of Clarendon pensive and tarnish the child-like freshness of her complexion. Gradually, her reverie becomes a bleak and somber sadness, and her languor degenerates into a mortal depression.

When Edward saw two sinister red patches on the pale cheeks of his beloved; when, by force of love, he could no longer obtain from her anything but a languid smile, he set himself on his knees before her; he took her thin hands and begged Béatrice to pour out into the bosom of a husband the cause of her secret dolors.

"Oh," he said to her, "become once again, become again that insouciant and playful young woman whose infantile gaiety and joyous sallies would have cured the most incurable troubles of the soul; become the Béatrice of old again. Have no fear of demanding immense sacrifices to grant me that benefit—what does all my fortune matter to me when I see you suffering, suffering without being able to bring a remedy to your illness?"

"I'm happy," she replied, in a faint voice, "as happy as I can be here. Alas, my Edward, I don't know the cause of the languor that is consuming me. Everything that surrounds me testifies to how much you love me, and how could anything but our love make me happy?"

Edward went in search of the most celebrated physicians, at great expense. "Cure her," he said, "cure her and I'll give you gold, as much gold as you want, but cure her—oh, cure her!"

The men of the art promised that Béatrice would soon be reborn to existence, but after having attempted vain and hazardous remedies, it was necessary for them to admit in low voices that she was lost beyond hope, and they went away sadly.

If you have never been cherished by a tender and adored woman, if you have never seen her perish slowly before your eyes, you cannot possibly understand Clarendon's agony.

He calculated the progress of the terrible malady despairingly; he said to himself, with inexpressible anguish: "In another month, I shall be alone on earth!" And he prepared with a cold despair the denouement of that brief future: she that day, and he the next.

Mention was made to him, by some chance, of a physician once renowned, an enthusiastic old man of an uncommon originality. Without the slightest hope, Edward summoned him to see Béatrice. Does not a drowning man willingly clutch at a wisp of straw he sees floating on the surface?

Dr. Griffiths was not easily convinced to come to Lord Clarendon's house. When he saw the poor invalid, he took up residence in the castle unceremoniously, and did not leave her thereafter for a single moment. By night, he kept watch on the disconnected words she uttered in her dreams; by day he tried in a thousand different ways to make the patient's soul spring forth, but there was no unexpected shock, no clue as to the cause of her illness. The doctor's experience, skill and knowledge remained fruitless.

One morning, he precipitated himself, semi-naked, into Edward's room, crying: "I've saved her! I've saved her!"

Edward threw his arms round his neck and almost choked him with his hug. I should think so! It was the sole glimmer of hope that had consoled him in two long years of anxiety and despair.

"That's long enough to stand here in our nightshirts and behave like lunatics," the doctor finally exclaimed, slightly embarrassed by his incongruous attire. "Quickly, a carriage, horses and let's be on our way to London. But don't impede my projects, or that will be the end of her!"

A fortnight later, the Drury Lane Theater was full of an innumerable crowd from the morning onwards; they were waiting to see the celebrated prima donna Béatrice.

She finally appeared on stage, pale and hesitant; cries and transports of joy immediately greeted her. When silence had fallen again, she began to sing, but tears filled her eyes and sobs were mingled with her voice. She collapsed, unconscious, and little Dr. Griffiths launched himself from the wings on to the stage, crying: "She's saved! She's saved!"

From that moment on, in fact, Béatrice recovered something of her former gaiety; the illness that was consuming her disappeared, and six months later, a mild pallor was the sole trace of it that remained.

The old doctor had divined Béatrice's illness; he had understood that glory is a sublime disease that cannot be cured by wealth, pleasure, or even love.

The Nose

A French Anecdote
1830

Ridicule dishonors more than dishonor.
(La Rochefoucauld, *Maximes.*)

HAVE you ever found yourself in a comfortable and good post-chaise—yes, a post-chaise pulled by four vigorous horses, guided by a generously paid postillion? Was it at the end of a warm day in September? Was it on a road that extended between a double enclosure of tall trees? Did you see, to the right and left, far, far away, in the fantastic light of a pure and ravishing moon, vacillating, fleeing, continually reborn and vanishing, woods, houses, crags and hills?

In that case you must remember sensations simultaneously soft and impetuous, vague thoughts, confused desires devoid of any real object, the need for an even greater speed than that imparted by the impulsion. Then, too, there are melancholy reveries, pleasant memories, impossible projects; and then one becomes agitated; one lifts oneself up as if to hasten the carriage, and yet, when it stops, one is sorry to have lost the heavy rumble of the wheels, the rattle of the windows, even the rude and continuous movement, including the jolts that penetrate all the limbs with I know not what torpor, and I know not what bizarre sensuality.

Yes, I would have given a great deal if, when it stopped, my carriage had not interrupted such sensations; yes, I would have liked to feel them last even longer. But we had reached a relay, and while our horses were being changed, I was obliged to get up from the cushion on which I was sprawling and open the window of my door in order to breathe in fresh dry air, perhaps more salutary but certainly much less soft than the mild warmth enclosed in the carriage.

We found ourselves outside an inn of rather meager appearance. Near the door, a man was standing, surrounded by a numerous group of peasants and little guttersnipes, all laughing and jeering, all throwing projectiles at the stranger, which, although not dangerous, were nonetheless very disagreeable. Weary of being the object of such insults, the unfortunate man cleared a path through his enemies and went to sit down not far away, on a stone bench. He covered his face with both hands, and remained in the attitude of a man in despair.

The peasants, more insistent than ever, seized him and recommenced their cries. I could not contain myself any longer; leaping down from the vehicle, I marched straight toward the unknown man, and the sight of a gentleman dismounting from the post-chaise began by imposing silence on that entire multitude. I signaled to them to go away; that gesture, marvelously seconded by the postillion's stout whip, was obeyed.

"Monsieur," I said, drawing near, when I had saluted the unknown man with all the more respect because his attire was decent and seemed to announce a decent man, "is it indiscreet to ask you the reason for the insults that were being heaped upon you? Can I not help you to put an end to them?"

He replied without raising his head: "Habitude ought to have resigned me to such things a long time ago. The subject of those people's mockery, the reason that obliged me to quit the diligence and stop on the way when my affairs ought to have required the greatest celerity in my journey—in brief, the cause of all the misfortunes of my life—you will know only too well by looking at me, Monsieur."

With those words he drew his hands apart, and the crowd immediately resumed its jeers and abuse.

For myself, I stood there, immobilized by amazement. Never, from any human face had a nose protruded to compare with the stranger's nose. Imagine this: it almost covered his cheeks, only leaving visible the two corners of his mouth, and descended—I speak in all conscience—as far as his chin.

Having recovered from my astonishment and mastered the mad desire to laugh that was suffocating me, I offered the stranger, if his destination, like mine, was Paris, a place in my carriage.

I had scarcely pronounced the last word of my sentence than he had leapt upon a portmanteau lying at his feet and was standing up, hat lowered, next to the carriage door. It was a strange thing to see him at grips with the politeness that forbade him to climb in before me and the desire to get away from the persecutions he was enduring—a desire that spurred him terribly to launch himself into the carriage immediately.

We took our places and the horses set off at a gallop. There was a silence between my traveling companion and me that lasted seven or eight minutes. The man with the monstrous nose was the first to break it.

"Monsieur," he said, "I don't know how to express my gratitude to you. I find myself all the more sensible to the interest that you have testified to me because the sentiments that I inspire ordinarily are very different." Turning his head as if to hide his enormous nose from me, he went on: "Nature has made me ridiculous, and, although I'm owed compassion, I only excite sarcasm. How can people take pity on an unfortunate who presents himself in a grotesque form, who gives rise to risible remarks?

"I won't mention the persecutions that I had to endure from the moment I began to conceive a few ideas, until my emergence from the boarding school in which my father, a merchant in Bordeaux, had put me; whatever the consequences of my deformity were, that epoch was nevertheless the most bearable of my life. It was permitted to me then to punish those who insulted me; I did not find myself perpetually oppressed, as in our polite and civilized society; my two vigorous fists reestablished equilibrium, and I forgot my ugliness in thrashing the little mockers. Alas, I soon learned, after my entry into society, that even that compensation no longer remained to me, and that it was necessary for me to bow down under a humiliating resignation.

"This is what happened. I was walking in the country one evening, when I encountered three young officers whose noisy burst of laughter, at the sight of me, rendered my face crimson with anger. However, I continued on my way, my heart beating precipitately, my fists clenched with rage, trembling with a thirst for vengeance. One of the boors wanted to outdo the others. He ran after me and addressed me with I know not what crude joke. He received for a response a terrible punch in the face. Half an hour later I was involved in a duel, and I had killed a man.

"The family of the unfortunate sublieutenant was rich and powerful; they wanted to avenge the death of an only son, the heir to a great name; it was necessary for me to leave the country and take refuge in Rome.

"There, well-enveloped in my cloak, with a broad-brimmed hat pulled down over my face, I could go out by night with impunity, and even sometimes risk doing so during the day. It was thus that I visited Rome, its monuments and its ruins. Placid and ignored, finally removed from ridicule, I experienced a wellbeing and a calm of which I had never previously had the slightest idea. It was doubtless due to that relaxation of my ill fortune that I allowed myself to be drawn into a romantic adventure, of which I shall tell you the story.

"I had noticed, in the church of Saint Peter, to which my liking for music often took me, a young woman of rare beauty. Soon, and gradually, seeing Lauretta—that was what her mother, who always accompanied her, called her—became for me a kind of veritable need.

"Every evening when she came to kneel down at mass, she found me nearby, considering her with ecstasies of amour and pleasure.

Those frequent and mute encounters rendered me madly in love with the charming creature. I slipped a note into her hand while she was leaving the church, in the midst of the crowd, and the next day I received a response; it was not too discouraging.

"That went on for a month.

"Gradually, the young woman's letters became affectionate, tender and passionate; then she granted me a rendezvous.

"Oh, Monsieur, you can't imagine my joy when I was greeted by the emotional voice of the young woman, when I felt her hand trembling in mine, when I, previously the object of sarcasm and disdain, heard myself called tender and sweet names, when a ravishing young woman lavished the most touching evidence of love upon me.

"Lauretta was poor; I offered to marry her; she consented with transports of tenderness and joy. I mentioned my ugliness to her; she swore that nothing could render me less dear to her love. It was therefore resolved that, the following morning, I would come to ask her mother for her hand.

"As I was going out, the happiest of men, of the dark room where she had received me, a lantern carried by a passer-by illuminated my face. Lauretta saw me, shivered, and the next day, when I went to her mother's house, I was told that she and her daughter had left for the country, and would not be returning before autumn. I understood the full extent of my misfortune, and resolved to quit the places that had become unbearable to me."

The poor man's story had moved me to tears, for I understood how bitter it must have been, for the unfortunate fellow, to lose in that fashion the only affection he had ever inspired. But I looked up mechanically at his strange nose, and, by virtue of an eccentricity of the human organism, and involuntary smile parted my lips—and that sight diminished my consideration considerably, if it did not cause it to vanish entirely.

My traveling companion continued the story of his adventures; his nose had always rendered him unfortunate. Time had calmed the wrath of the powerful family that was persecuting him, and he had been able to return to France and devote himself to operations of commerce, but no merchant had ever been able to deal with him with composure, and the ridicule of his face had constantly rebounded on his speculations, which nevertheless did not lack soundness, and which he planned with an uncommon talent.

In brief, he lost his entire fortune, and found himself reduced to going to request employment from a businessman to whom a friend of the family had recommended him.

He had taken the diligence to reach his destination. Five commercial travelers, who filled the vehicle with him, employed in his regard the fine and sensitive amiability that one sometimes encounters among those gentlemen, and heaped him with pleasantries so unbearable and ways of acting so outrageous that he wanted to avenge himself and challenged one of them, but the five young men responded by a redoubling of their bad behavior, and the fur-coated legislator of the little ambulant realm, the conductor, had refrained from reprimanding them because they were good fellows who sang licentious verses delightfully and their victim had a ridiculous nose and never said a word that did not occasion laughter.

It was therefore necessary to get off. That expedient, as we know, only served to deliver him to other persecutors.

When we arrived in Paris my traveling companion gave me the warmest thanks and left me, covering his face as best he could with a large handkerchief.

I met him four months ago, in the greatest stress, and devoid of employment. The wife of the businessman with whom he had been placed was pregnant; she feared, for her child, the consequences of the sight of a deformed nose like that of the new clerk; the poor fellow was, therefore, sacked without delay.

The Punishment
A French Adventure
1815

O woman, woman, woman! Weak and deceitful creature, No animal created can match her instinct. (Beaumarchais, *The Marriage of Figaro*, Act V.)

Now, the good sire, for two years, in the Holy Land, rode from vespers to matins and from matins to vespers, breaking lances, striking and receiving hard blows of edged weapons and swords, saying incessantly: "With the ransom of this miscreant my lady will buy a headdress of rubies and white pearls; with the price of this good and beautiful armor damascened in gold she will distribute largesse to her varlets, pages and ladies-in-waiting."

And he immediately sent a squire to place at the feet of his beauty all the treasures so dearly bought by him. One day, finally, he came back from the Holy Land, wrecked by spear-thrusts, pitiful and needy. That was the day of his beauty's wedding to a sire who had not departed for the Holy Land. (*Fables* of Pierre Mahu.)[1]

---

1 This citation appears to be fictitious.

OH, how frightful it is to be deceived by a woman, by a woman by whom one thought one was cherished, by a woman for whom one has sacrificed one's rank, one's fortune and even the repose of one's conscience!

The duties of his rank as major kept him away from her; he renounced that rank, obtained by dint of wounds and patience. In order to surround her with opulence, to satisfy her most frivolous caprices, he sold his patrimony and everything he possessed in the world; he reduced himself to a condition bordering on poverty. If he had only done that! He deserted a virtuous wife who loved him with the most tender affection. He left her, in spite of the despair of the unfortunate woman, the plaints of an outraged family, and remorse, the unbearable remorse of his conscience . . .

Wretch! Wretch that he is! Such a thought turns his face crimson, crushes his heart!

He has betrayed a wife for a mistress; his mistress is now betraying him; what is happening to him is the justice of heaven.

He has no right to complain.

No, but was it Maria, Maria so tenderly beloved, so recklessly adored, Maria, Maria who had to punish him for sins he had committed for love of her?

Malediction! Deceived! Deceived coldly, by calculation, for a little gold! A handful of gold preferred to him, to him, who loved her more than his fortune, more than his honor, more than his conscience! Maria selling her kisses to an old man! In such ideas, there is death, there is hell!

He requires a vengeance! It must be terrible, inexorable. Come on, let him make her weep! Let her wring her hands in despair! Let her drag herself to his knees in inexpressible anguish! Let him be able to calm her with a word, a gesture, a glance, and not say that word, or make that gesture, or look in her direction!

Vengeance! Vengeance!

He runs . . . he arrives beneath the widows of the house whose aspect once made his heart beat so delightfully; he penetrates into the obscure corridor, reaches the hidden stairway he has so often climbed; now he is before the door that only ought to open for him!

There he stops; his strength abandons him, his knees buckle beneath him; a cold sweat trickles over his forehead. All his happiness of old, now a heavy memory, atrocious and brief, weighs upon his breast and crushes him with the most horrible torments to which a man has ever been subjected.

He listens. She isn't alone. She's talking. Oh! What is she saying?

"You don't know how much I love you, beloved of my heart! You don't know! Tell me, do you know that I shall love you forever, forever?"

The same promises that she swore to him yesterday! The same inflections of her voice, the same emotion. Oh, get it over with, let it end! He is suffering too much to hear that!

Suddenly, the door opens; he appears, pale and pitiless.

Maria faints. Her aged lover remains motionless with surprise and fear.

"Tomorrow," cries the major, "tomorrow you will be free to come back, to hear her sweet words, to receive her embraces. But tonight, this last night will be for me, for me alone. For me, whom she has betrayed, for me, to whom she still belongs!"

The old man tries to resist; a terrible hand, which rage causes to tremble, grips his weak hand; the cold barrel of a pistol is placed against his forehead; he shivers and disappears.

When she recovers consciousness, she finds herself alone with the man she has outraged.

Standing there, arms folded, he was waiting for her to wake up, in a calm a hundred times more frightening than the most terrible outburst of anger.

He took out his watch, presented it to Maria, and said: "Take it."

She turned her head away and refused.

"Take it," he repeated, in a low and hollow voice. "Take it; it's the sole possession that remains to me; it's the price of the night that I'm going to spend with you. Take it; it's my last present; take it, I want you to!"

She would have liked not to obey, but she could not escape the influence of that somber voice; subjugated, she took the watch.

After that he sat in an armchair a few paces away from her and asked her a question: "What time is it?"

In a trouble and confusion of inexpressible ideas, she raised the eyes that she had kept lowered until then, to look at him, and replied: "It's eleven o'clock."

"In one hour," he replied, "you'll return to me all the diamonds, all the jewels, all the cashmeres you had from me; I'll destroy them."

With an abrupt movement, she tried to launch herself toward her bell; quicker than her, the major seized her by the arm, forced her to sit down again, and showed her the weapon concealed in his coat.

She fell back into her armchair.

Midnight chimed without either of them having said a single word.

A few moments sufficed to break and trample underfoot the richest jewels, to tear the precious fabrics into pieces. When he had finished he threw what remained out of the window.

Then he sat down again, calmly, and asked for a second time: "What time is it?"

Maria did not want to reply, but he put his hand on his pistol, and she replied in a choked voice: "Midnight!"

"In an hour, I shall break all this furniture, all these mirrors, everything there is in this apartment furnished by me."

The clock chimed; it was the first broken, followed by all the rest. The major's armchair and Maria's were the only things spared.

When he had finished, he asked the question for the third time: "What time is it?"

Her hair scattered, dying of terror and shedding bitter tears, she threw herself at the major's knees; she begged him to have pity on her; she asked for forgiveness for the past, she made the most touching promises for the future.

"What time is it?"

That devastating question was his response.

"One o'clock."

"In an hour, I shall strike you in the face with this whip."

She fell unconscious. Coldly, the major threw water in her face and brought her round.

What anguish Maria was subjected to during that long hour of expectation and despair, that hour which preceded a dolorous torture, a torture that would stigmatize her for life!

And no hope of softening him! Not even daring to try!

Two o'clock chimed.

He struck her in the face, and threw her bleeding on to the floor.

Then he took out his pistol and deposited it on the debris of a table. Those preparations were followed by the terrible question: "What time is it?"

To die! To die! That was the idea whose horror took hold of Maria, and made her get up, trembling and bewildered.

"Oh, life!" she cried. "Life! Life! Leave me life! Strike me, trample me underfoot, but conserve my life, let me live!"

He smiled, bitterly, pushed her away with his foot, and asked: "What time is it?"

This time, she did not reply. She was only thinking about death.

Three o'clock had just chimed.

The major loaded his pistol, put one of his arms around Maria's waist and showed her the weapon.

She tried to ask for mercy one last time, but her contracted lips could only articulate a confused sound.

He enjoyed her terror momentarily, and then he said; "You're not going to die."

And then, placing the pistol in his own mouth, he pulled the trigger, and the shot rang out.

The domestics came running at the sound of the detonation and broke down the door.

They found their mistress enlaced in the major's limbs, covered with blood and debris that was still palpitating.

She had been fortunate enough for the blow she had received in the face not to leave a scar, and a few days later, moving to another district and changing her name, she did not take long to find a new lover.

Maria is now the mistress of one of our richest bankers. I saw her a few days ago; she was cheerful and lively.

The Ivory Fan
A Spanish Story
1816

I despise you; in consequence I no longer love you.
(Love letter.)

WHEN the first act of *Il Barbiere di Siviglia* had concluded at the Della Cruce theater, Léopold de Monterant, a young Frenchman who had only arrived in Madrid the day before, came to sit in the stalls that formed the first compartment of the parterre—a compartment designated by the Spaniards, if I remember rightly, by the name of the "principal lunette."

The foreigner looked around, his gaze curious and full of astonishment, for the Della Cruce has an appearance quite different from French theaters. First of all, a meager and poorly distributed illumination only produced a false light, a kind of half-light, in the three rows of boxes and the two galleries, a vast and high semicircle that seemed to embrace and stifle a narrow parterre. It was necessary to fix one's eyes for some time on the same point in order to distinguish, above the parterre, the Alcalde sitting gravely in a box hung with crimson fabric. That important individual held two small gray eyes immobile, never saying a word, never moving his long, stiff body, formal, wrinkled and ponderous, except to lower a blanched face toward eight hulking alguazils. Those worthy creatures were standing directly below the Alcalde, vast hats on their heads and white sticks in their hands. In the jaundiced faces of those honest agents of the public force there was a repulsive mixture of stupidity, self-importance and malevolence. In brief, imagine physiognomies as Beaumarchais has painted them: physiognomies in the manner of Bazile and Brid'oison.

The functions of alguazils consist of precipitating themselves, at the slightest signal from the Alcalde, into the parterre, where they take hold of disturbers of the tranquility of the spectacle and take them away to throw them in prison. Now, to receive such gracious treatment, it is only necessary to applaud, or to let loose one of those whistle-blasts that relieve a poor spectator so much when one of the fine works of Mercadante, Paisiello or Rossini is pitilessly flayed before him.

Then, to the right and left, there were monks of all colors; there were men of solemn bearing with bronzed faces; there were women uniformly clad in black, their foreheads, hair, bosom and arms covered by the inevitable mantilla. Léopold could not help making a secret comparison between that heavy and graceless veil and the shrouds that envelop the heads of caryatids on Egyptian monuments.

All those women were waving their fans, sparkling with sequins, with the rapidity, the agility, the grace and—I almost said the expression—that only Spanish women know how to give them. That uniform movement among all those motionless figures, in the midst of the great and profound silence that was maintained in the hall, added further to the singularity of the spectacle offered to Léopold's gaze.

Soon weary of seeking to divine a piquant physiognomy under the sad pleats of the mantilla, which was, thanks to in the demi-obscurity of the hall, created more by his imagination than seen by his eyes, Léopold devoted himself henceforth to the pleasure of the spectacle, and concentrated his attention on the stage where Lindor, costumed as a soldier, was mystifying the guardian Bartholo.

The patrol had already arrived, and the admirable finale was being sung that terminates the second act, when a fan fallen at hazard from a box struck the young Frenchman's shoulder and tumbled on to his knees.

He raised his head; he perceived a charming face to which that slight accident had doubtless summoned a blush, for a white hand devoid of a fan was attempting to veil it. You can well imagine that Léopold, as any well-brought-up man would have done in such a circumstance, picked up the pretty ivory item, and, when the curtain came down, hastened to return it to the person who had dropped it.

That act of politeness was its own reward, for the fan belonged to a young señorita with creole eyes and an elegant figure.

On his return to the "principal lunette," Léopold raised his eyes several times toward the box where the white fan was agitating, but either by chance or affectation, he was never able to encounter the señorita's eyes looking down at him.

Mental wellbeing is like physical wellbeing; one appreciates it not when one has it but when one desires it, or, alas, when one has lost it. Isolated in the midst of a people who speak another language than one's own, thrown into a strange city, what would Léopold not have given, on emerging from the spectacle, to lean on the arm of a friend—what am I saying?—even to see walking beside him one of those people to whom one is only bound by cold and indifferent relations! At least the features would have been familiar. Oh, how happy he would have been if he had only heard a few words of his sweet native tongue resounding in his ear! What a delightful emotion he would have experienced if the edifices, the houses lit by soft moonlight, had resembled, even vaguely, the edifices and houses of his homeland!

But he was alone. Alone! He could neither take comfort in pleasant habits, nor find himself among cherished beings, nor communicate his ideas to them, nor cheer himself up with their joy. There was a desolate void, an intolerable solitude. If the most unfamiliar man, the least worthy of being a friend, had shown the slightest sign of interest in him at that moment, he would have run to him; he would have taken his hand affectionately in is own; then he would have deemed himself happy. But he was alone. Alone!

Do not believe that such emotions only belong to an exalted imagination; Léopold was numbered among those men in whom contact with society has produced an insouciant dryness, a calculating egotism—and yet Léopold was experiencing the vague symptoms of homesickness. That indecisive sadness had even caused him to recover a kind of sensibility, for sadness renders one better and more compassionate, and if virtue exists anywhere, you will find it among those whose smile is languid and whose eyes are often moist with tears.

For want of any other object, therefore, the señorita with the white fan took possession of Léopold's imagination, and he transported to that almost ideal woman, whom he had only glimpsed, the vague need for affection that he did not know where to focus. He dreamed about her all night—for one sleeps so badly in a bed that is not one's own! He was preoccupied by her all day; he imagined seeing the pretty lady's two large dark eyes through every Venetian blind; and when the Angelus had sounded, it was with a kind of emotion and desire, a need to see his unknown woman again, that he finished dressing elegantly and set off toward the Prado.

Between one and three o'clock, a silence and solitude descends on Madrid so great that if the Caliph Shahriman returned to the world and took a walk in the city at that moment, he could have believed himself still in the kingdom of the Black Islands, all of whose inhabitants had been turned into red fish and relegated to a lake. No work, no carriages, no passers-by, not one shop open; everything is asleep, buried in a profound siesta.

But when the Angelus has sounded, the aspect of Madrid suddenly changes; emerging from a thousand different places, in noisy swarms, come monks, soldiers, workmen clad in rags and enveloped in large mantles, picturesquely draped. Carriages cut through the flow of that multitude, and the immense crossroads of the *Puerta del Sol* and the long, broad pathway of the Prado become as populated as they had been deserted a little while before.

The sight of Madrid's principal promenade surprises and disconcerts people who only know Spain via novels and who, always in accordance with the gravest authorities, think they see in every Spanish woman a poor Desdemona hidden from view by a terrible Othello. Ladies walk there one by one, in twos or threes, as hazard brings them together, and rarely—very rarely—do they have a cavalier beside them who accompanies them. One might think that the mantilla and the fan, which they never abandon, serve them simultaneously for companionship, protection and countenance.

That was what Léopold thought as he plunged an anxious gaze into the groups of strollers, and even into the depths of the carriages, mostly ancient, with which that pathway of the Prado reserved for vehicles was full . . .

Suddenly, he increases his pace; he has seen her! It's her! There she is! She still has her white fan in her hand. She has recognized him, for she blushes when he bows to her.

The man who is giving her his arm, who is calling her Juana, who can he be? Her husband? No; he seems too old for that . . . and then, that resemblance . . . there's no doubt about it; she is out walking with her father.

While making such reflections, Léopold follows the young Spanish woman, and, almost at the same time as her, finds himself at the door of the lodgings into which she enters with her father.

While he tries to recognize the street in which he finds himself, two men hurl themselves upon him unexpectedly and strike him with their daggers.

"Good," says one of them, on seeing him fall. "That harebrained Frenchman won't cause me any anxiety during my absence."

It is necessary to have spent long nights by the bedside of a dying man, to have interrogated the beating of his heart, trembling to feel it motionless; it is necessary to have shivered at every sigh that his breast exhales to understand the interest that the object of so much concern and dread inspires. One might think that we have given him back that existence conserved with such difficulty; one might think that it was our doing. Yes, one experiences for the patient something of the tenderness of a mother for her son. After that, when one sees his eyes, fixed for a long time and icy, expressing gratitude; when his pale lips murmur confused words, when his thin hand gently presses the hand that presents him with a beverage, one experiences a sad and sweet joy; tears come to pause on the edge of the eyelids. Oh, how well recompensed one is!

And if one is a young woman of sixteen, a Spanish woman, the only child of an idolatrous father; if the patient, a handsome young man with blond hair, with a gracious physiognomy, has perhaps been stabbed for love of the person who is now stationed next to his bed, imagine what sensations inundate her and what thoughts agitate her!

Such was the situation of Doña Juana. She had heard Léopold's cry of distress; she had recognized the fleeing murderer and, triumphant, by dint of prayers and tears, in spite of the suspicious prudence of her father, she had forced him to take the poor wounded man into his house; she had not wanted anyone else to watch over him.

But finally, here he is, emerged from the delirium that had overwhelmed him for so long, during which he talked more than once about the ivory fan; now he is parading an astonished gaze round him . . .

He has seen Juana . . . he had smiled languidly . . . may the saintly Madonna be blessed! She shall have her novena, she shall have the nine candles promised to her.

A month went by, and Léopold, his wound healed, had quit the house of his benefactress.

One evening, the rich businessman Merendas, Juana's father, was sitting placidly at his desk, reading the letters that a clerk had just brought him. The first one he opened, the handwriting of which he had recognized, informed him of the arrival tomorrow of Luis Perez, Juana's fiancé. The second was from a correspondent in Paris; it asked him to seek to discover what had become in Madrid of Léopold de Monterant, a young man of honorable family, although not rich, who had left for Madrid to take care of important affairs and of whom no news had arrived since the day of his departure; the keenest anxieties were experienced with regard to his fate. If Señor Merendas could discover the young man's whereabouts, he was requested to do so most urgently.

When he finished reading that letter, Merendas turned his head to his daughter, standing behind him.

"Ah!" he said, with an expression of contentment. "You've come at a good time, Juana; you can know the good news immediately; your fiancé Perez is arriving to-morrow from Saragossa."

"My fiancé will never be my husband," the young woman replied, solemnly.

The worthy Merendas looked at her, open-mouthed, with a strange expression of astonishment and consternation.

"Here, look," she continued. "This is the dagger that was taken out of Léopold's wound. Do you recognize it? It belongs to Luis. Do you want me to be the wife of a murderer?"

That argument was not irresistible for Merendas; a dagger-thrust given by a rival did not seem to the old Spaniard to be a very atrocious crime. He tried to disculpate Luis, and even to present his ambush as proof of an extreme love.

But Juana shed tears; she threw herself into her father's arms; she lavished the most tender names upon him; she used threats; she delivered herself to the most frightful despair; she begged forgiveness; she got carried away even more violently; then she threw herself into her father's arms again, and wept there bitterly.

When she left her father's study, he had consented to Juana's marriage to Léopold.

In the first transport of her joy, she ran to her lover's nearby lodgings in order to tell him that joyful, unexpected news. She climbed the stairway rapidly; she found herself outside his door; then modesty regained its power, momentarily suspended by delight. Her cheeks covered with a blush, she remained standing there, not daring to open it.

Her indecision increased further when she thought she perceived that Léopold was not alone.

She listened carefully, in order to make sure.

Yes, he was talking to someone.

"Henri," he said, "how glad I am to see you again! In truth, I'm astonished by my good luck; I needed a friend to receive my confidences of happiness, and here you are! Yes, I'm going to marry the daughter of a rich businessman who counts piastres by the tonne. Juana ought to be confessing her love to him this evening, and there's no doubt that he'll approve; he never refuses anything to the most eccentric caprices of his only daughter.

"I've promised the young woman to live in Spain—may heaven preserve me from keeping my word. No, on my soul! I shall see my beautiful homeland again! I'll rebuild the ruins of the old Château de Monterant. My God! Living on the thrusts of Spanish daggers and French language lessons given to one's nurse! One pays well for that in Madrid; I've received a good price for them!"

"Is she pretty?" asked a voice.

"She has a dowry of a hundred thousand piastres," Léopold replied.

Two days later, the marriage was celebrated of Señora Juana Merendas with Señor Luis Perez.

I'm told that Luis became a widower three months after his wedding.

The Beggar
A French Adventure
1822

"A morsel of bread, my good lord, for I'm very
hungry!"
"I have nothing to give; may God help you."
"I'll make him speak the truth, for I'll set fire to his
farm."
(Venbeerg Berthavel, *A Week in Flanders*.)[1]

AT present I'm living in the finest quarter of Paris in
a comfortable and plush apartment: a bookcase full
of elegant volumes, soft carpets that the feet tread upon
soundlessly, long muslin curtains that spread their diaphanous pleats over the scarlet folds of silk curtains.

Add that I possess the greatest wealth of all, a complete,
limitless independence.

If it suits me to scan the pages of a new work noncha-
lantly, I can. If I prefer to go for a long excursion, sprawled
in a carriage driven by a domestic in brilliant livery, drawn
by two black horses whose heads stand up proudly and
whose feet strike the ground impatiently, yes, if I'd rather
do that, I can do that too.

---

1 Fictitious.

Once, I lived on the sixth floor in the Rue Saint-Jacques, in a dark little room at the very end of a steep, dirty, endless stairway. A poor law student, reduced, in order to live, to giving lessons in Latin at fifteen sous a time, or even illuminating images at five francs a hundred, I deemed myself fortunate when I could fill my smoky little fireplace with wood through the winter. If I became rich enough to eat at a restaurant on Sunday, and sit down after that in the parterre of the Odéon or a petty theater, oh, that was a day of veritable prosperity!

And yet, there isn't an hour of my life when my memories don't go back with emotion and regret to those times of my youth, which went by so quickly—and forever, alas.

That's because I was so content, ensconced in that free-and-easy life, that voluptuous insouciance, living entirely in the present, without any anxiety for the future.

And then, when night fell, I heard rapid footsteps on my staircase, the rustle of a dress—oh, how happy I was then!

It was Joséphine!

She came in out of breath, unable to say a word, her hair in disorder and her cheeks covered in a moist blush.

Her arm fell on the back of my chair; she put her head on my shoulder, and looked up at me with her large eyes, smiling.

Happier than I can say, I dare not make the slightest movement; I was too fearful of losing my sweet burden, and no longer feeling her sweet and pure breath moistening my face.

Suddenly, the young woman got up abruptly, and, a capricious and playful sprite, upset my papers, opened my drawers and scattered everything; after which she sat down again, feigning an infantile gravity, and started saying serious things to me, which didn't take long to turn into tender foolishness.

Then she had a whim to go for a walk, and it was necessary to obey her immediately. Her arm enlaced with mine, we wandered through the somber streets of the Latin Quarter, or directed our vagabond course all the way to the boulevards, so animated in the midst of the patchwork illumination in which so many lights, people and objects were confused, so many voices and different sounds murmuring, repetitive and overlapping.

Isolated in the middle of that crowd, we only lived for one another; we only needed a word, a glance, or a pressure of the arm to exchange our impressions, to sense ourselves penetrated by an ineffable ecstasy of happiness and love.

And then, there were continual alternations of fits of joy or tender emotions: the plaintive song of a veiled woman, a dispute among vulgar people, the lurching walk of a drunkard, or a caricature displayed in a shop window inundated with gaslight offered us spectacles at every step that awoke compassion in us or made us burst out laughing.

One evening, as usual, we were walking along merrily, when a lamentable voice and the sight of a stranger barring our path put an end to our jokes and brought us to an abrupt halt.

It was a beggar.

I had never encountered a similar physiognomy in all my life.

He was tall, thin, low-browed and hollow-eyed; his stiff gray hair was escaping everywhere from the holes in his hat; a long brown coat enveloped his figure, slightly stooped but full of vigor. He was, moreover, older in debauchery than years.

I enjoined him rudely to let us pass; he only responded with insolent pleas for alms.

Irritated by his obstinacy, I pushed him away with the cane with which every law student was armed in that epoch; he resisted; driven to the limit, I knocked him down, roughly.

He stood up in an anger that made Joséphine tremble and went away, making a gesture of vengeance at me.

I laughed at his threats, and, reassuring my companion, we resumed our walk. We had soon forgotten the beggar and his anger.

It was beginning to get late; we were heading back to the Rue Saint-Jacques, occupied in building I don't know what castles in Spain for the future, which were never to be realized. Suddenly, Joséphine interrupted me. "Look! Oh, look," she said. "What a pretty shawl!"

And, with the extended forefinger of her delicate hand, she showed me the most charming cashmere headscarf that any French factory had ever produced.

There was so much desire in her shining eyes, she would have been so happy to possess that pretty shawl, that I promised myself firmly that I would buy it for her the first time I was rich enough to make the purchase.

For that, I needed at least twenty francs.

I took Joséphine home, for we had seen the beggar prowling around while we were looking at the shawl.

On returning home, in order to realize more rapidly my project of acquiring the cashmere for Joséphine, I set about working through the night. Imagine my satisfaction when the time came to go to the law school. I was harassed by fatigue and I had to go to bed, but I had earned a quarter of the value of the shawl.

Throughout the rest of the week I tripled my work in that fashion, and refused to go out in spite of Joséphine's insistences. So, when Saturday came, the manufacturer of images who employed me counted out the sum I so desired of twenty francs.

I didn't sleep that night; I made such a great feast of Joséphine's surprise when we would go together the next day to buy the shawl.

I have no need to tell you that no day ever seemed so long to me as that Sunday.

To complete the frustration, Joséphine did not come until very late; her greeting seemed to me to be restrained, less tender than usual, and that caused me an indescribable trouble, although I attributed it to my refusal to walk with her on the previous days.

We set forth; my heart was sadly contracted; I found nothing to say to Joséphine, and she did not squeeze my arm once during the long journey from the Rue Saint-Jacques to the Boulevard Bonne-Nouvelle.

I made her stop outside the shop window. The shawl was no longer displayed there.

"Someone must have bought it," I said, sadly.

Joséphine shivered.

That shiver did me good. *Oh*, I thought, *how much affection she will lavish on me when I make her a gift of an adornment desired to that extent, which I've bought by means of so many nights of hard work!*

I therefore went into the shop; Joséphine went pale, withdrew her arm from mine and remained on the threshold.

"Come on," I said, laughing. "Who knows? There will doubtless be another shawl like it, and seeing your pretty face, they'll make you a gift of it."

Her emotion increased.

"Come on, come on," I added, no longer master of my joy, while I forced her to follow me. "Come on, and if we don't find anyone gallant enough for that, I'll have to buy it for you."

There was a fat clerk in the shop with a resonant voice; he watched our struggles with a mocking expression that displeased me greatly, so I spoke to him with the dry tone of a law student who is not disposed to allow anyone to laugh at him.

"I'd like a shawl similar to the one that was displayed in that window a few days ago."

The fat clerk started laughing.

Joséphine darted a suppliant glance at him. That glance caused a thousand thoughts and a thousand suspicions to seethe within me. I felt my face turning crimson.

"No," said the clerk, continuing to snigger. "As Mademoiselle knows very well, it was the last. Ernest must have told her so when he made her a gift of it."

I looked at Joséphine; he was telling the truth.

To slap the clerk, promise him a rendezvous for the next day, to forbid Joséphine ignominiously ever to appear to my sight again: all that was as prompt as lightning, without knowing what I was doing, as if it were an anguished dream.

As I went out, a horrible burst of laughter struck my ears, and I saw the atrocious face of the beggar disappearing into the shadows.

The next day I had to fight a duel with the clerk, who was better at handling a yardstick than a sword, and whose fear was visible. I was ready to conclude a combat that was too unequal by giving my adversary a slight prick when the hoarse voice of the beggar cried out a few paces away from me. The unexpected noise caused me to shiver; the clerk took advantage of that abrupt movement to pierce my breast; I collapsed, dying.

While I was carried away, I thought I saw near the river the mocking and wan specter of the beggar; I wanted to shout at him to go away, but an impure hand was extended over my mouth, blood choked me, and I lost consciousness . . .

The fat clerk who had wounded me, whose attentive care made no small contribution to my cure, carried me down from my sixth floor and served as a support during my walk, which was not long.

The poor fellow, in despair at nearly having killed a man because of a bad joke, had not been far from my bedside while I had been in peril; during my long convalescence he had spent all the time he could spare with me. Touched by that proof of interest, I had almost conceived a friendship for him.

Then again, he had promised to help me avenge myself on the accursed pauper, the cause of all my troubles: Joséphine's infidelity, my duel, and my wound. The beggar had handed the poor girl letters from the clerk Ernest, who had been in love with her for a long time; he had told the young man how much she desired the cashmere scarf; he had introduced it furtively into Joséphine's room and had hastened to come and relate at the shop Ernest's success and my fate.

After concluding my walk, as I was about to go home, we perceived a large crowd assembled at the end of the street; in the middle of the crowd, two wretches gorged on drink were rolling in the mud, uttering obscene cries. I recognized the beggar's voice and, in spite of my weakness, ran to the place from which it was coming.

At the sight of me, a mocking smile contracted the scoundrel's lips; he raised himself up on his elbow, and, showing me the woman who was lying beside him, he asked me: "Am I avenged?"

My companion dragged me away very rapidly, in a pitiful state. The creature who was sharing the beggar's infamous orgy, alas, was Joséphine.

Three Scottish Ballads

Gregor
1520

> True love is like the woodcutter's ghost; many
> highlanders talk about it, but none has seen it.
> (MacMorlan.)[1]

WHAT Scotsman has not climbed the crag of
Inverness, which rises on the banks of the Clyde,[2]
and of which a narrow grotto crowns the summit? Not
long ago, the shadow of that rock scarcely covered the ring
of grass that snakes around its enormous flanks; now, it
extends over the waves of the river and almost touches the
opposite bank: that is the signal that ought to bring to
the spot the charming Anna, Gregor's lover—poor Gregor,
whose mother died a week ago, alas.

Here she comes. Her pretty mouth lets a murmur of
discontent to escape; a sudden incarnadine colors her

---

1 There is a character named MacMorlan in Walter Scott's *Guy
Mannering* (1815); Berthoud appears to have derived everything he
knew about Scotland from reading Scott's novels, but appears to have
misunderstood the dimensions of a claymore, in reality an extremely
bulky sword wielded in both hands.
2 As every Scotsman knows, Inverness is on the Moray Firth, a very
long way from the Clyde.

cheeks, for her dark eyes have scanned the river and the plain in vain; she has not seen Gregor.

She sits down on some rocky debris, and her plaid, which falls from her shoulders, forms a variegated drapery around her elegant figure, to the vivid colors of which the ruddy rays of the setting sun give an even brighter gleam. She passes her delicate fingers through the black curls of her hair, retained by a virginal snood, and then she darts another glance at the river and the plain—but she does not perceive Gregor, poor Gregor, whose mother died a week ago, alas.

Her pretty foot stamps on the ground; chagrin fills her eyes with tears; she sits down again; she gets up again. She is going to go away.

"Oh no," she says. "My departure would afflict Gregor too much—Gregor from whom all the young women in the clan would buy a smile at the price of their finest plaid; Gregor, the laird's favorite; Gregor, who never wanted to take a wife so long as his old mother required his care, his old mother who died a week ago, alas."

Suddenly, a slight sound reaches Anna's ears; it is that of oars; it's Gregor, whose boat is gliding over the waves; already she can make out his melancholy gaze; already, he has saluted her with his hand. Now he's leaping ashore; he climbs the rock.

"Oh, pity me," he said, taking Anna's hand. "Pity Gregor, poor Gregor, whose mother died a week ago, alas."

Large tears were running down his cheeks, and he tried in vain to hold them back. Twice, he tried to say something more, but his sobs prevented him from doing so.

"Console yourself, Gregor, console yourself," said Anna. "Do you not still have a friend, a friend very faithful?"

The highlander raised his eyes and fixed them on the young woman.

"Take this plack," she added. "Cut it with your claymore; give me half, keep the other, and may heaven punish Gregor if he isn't faithful to his oaths! Let it punish Anna if ever she ceases to love Gregor, poor Gregor, whose mother died a week ago, alas."

The highlander strikes the coin with a stroke of his claymore, whose two halves sprang apart. His eyes sparkling, he presents one to the young woman; but a convulsive movement suddenly agitates all of Gregor's limbs.

Anna takes from Gregor's trembling hand the half-plack, the sacred pledge of an indissoluble union; she detaches the black ribbon that floats over her white shoulders in order to suspend the symbolic fragment therefrom; the knot is already half-formed when she feels Gregor's hand on her arm—poor Gregor, whose mother died a week ago, alas.

"Anna," he murmured, initially in a low voice, and then in a solemn tone, "before saying to me: 'I'm yours,' wait until I've revealed a secret that might drive you away from me forever, a frightful secret that my mother revealed to me on her deathbed.

"My mother always told me, as you know: 'Your father has departed for a distant land.' When I saw the sad pallor of death on my mother's face, I implored her to tell me for what distant land my father had departed. Oh, what dolor suddenly contracted her features! 'Your father,' she said, 'is rich; he's rich and powerful; I'm not his wife . . . never . . .' She didn't finish; her hand remained immobile and icy in Gregor's hand—poor Gregor, whose mother died a week ago, alas."

Standing up, her eyes lowered, Anna listened in silence to that sad tale; the highlander, folding his arms over his chest, waited for her response for a few seconds, but Anna, motionless, did not raise her eyes.

"Oh, I see!" he cried, despairingly. "Anna only loved the laird's favorite, and despises the wretched bastard!"

Anna did not reply, but the half-plack fell from her hands and came to rest at Gregor's feet.

The highlander draws away slowly. Twice he stops, twice he turns round, for he thinks he hears her calling to him . . . but no; she is still standing still, her eyes lowered.

"Oh, it's too much!" he says, and, seizing his claymore, he plunges it into his heart, and collapses, darting one last glance at Anna.

Gregor, poor Gregor, whose mother died a week ago, alas!

"Gregor! Gregor! Oh, don't keep that terrible silence; it chills me with terror! I want to be your wife! Reply to me, reply to your Anna . . . !"

It is too late. It is in vain that she rips up her plaid to bandage the large wound from which gouts of blood are escaping. Gregor, poor Gregor, is reunited forever with his mother, who died a week ago, alas.

Half an hour later, the laird, accompanied by his wife the duchess and a few servants, arrived on the bank of the Clyde.

"By Saint Cuthbert!" cried the noble lady, "what a frightful spectacle! The bloody corpse of a highlander and that of a young woman! Let's go to help them."

Old Jobson, the laird's confidant, retained his master by the arm; he was pale and trembling. "It's Anna's corpse," he murmured, in a low voice. "It's that of Gregor, poor Gregor, whose mother died a week ago, alas."

The laird goes as pale as his old servant; he raises his hand dolorously to his face; a tear falls on his wrinkled cheek, and he leans on Jobson's shoulder. Then, after a long silence, he says: "Peace, peace to those who cause misfortune! Peace to the unfortunate Anna! Peace to Gregor, poor Gregor and his mother, who died a week ago, alas."

Mary
1538

If I believed in happiness, I would refrain from
seeking it in a brilliant and agitated life; it is in the
peaceful calm of obscurity that I would hope to
find it.
(Owen.)[1]

MARY, the most beautiful daughter of Scotland, was
about to perish in the waves of the Solway; Halbert
saved her life at the peril of his own, and when he deposited Mary on her father's bosom, the old man pressed his
hand, saying: "She will call you husband!"

Halbert was grave and serious. The old men loved to
talk with him about work in the fields and events of old;
no one sang sentimental ballads better than him in the
evening, and mothers always welcomed him with a favorable smile, for they said to themselves: *Fortunate will be
whichever of our daughters will call him husband!*

And yet Halbert was not the most skillful hunter in
the region; he did not spend his days and nights pursuing

---

1 Presumably John Owen (1563-1622), whose Latin epigrams were
once popular; the citation does not appear to be genuine, but is not
atypical of his thinking.

wild fallow deer; to all those noisy pleasures he preferred chatting with his venerable grandmother, who talked to him about his mother, who was dead, and young Mary, who was to call him husband.

Already, all the preparations had been made for the wedding; a hundred tables were set up; the bagpipes resounded everywhere; the usquaebach was already flowing, slaking the thirst of the crowd of relatives and friends, who had come in a flood to congratulate the fortunate Halbert and the woman who was to call him husband.

"Mary! Mary!" they called to her in vain; her aged father, tearing out his white hair, wanted to die, and cursed the guilty daughter who would cover his old age with shame by fleeing with a jack that she did not call husband.

It was Lovcar who had made her forget the holiest duties, Lovcar, the famous hunter of the clan; the red deer or the fallow deer always fell when he directed his arbalest at them; it was always the head or the heart in which the bolt was embedded. He had no flock, but he made adventurous excursions into the lowlands, and it was said in whispers— for Lovcar was wild, and his bolt, everyone knew, always hit the target—that he had seduced more than one young woman who had never called him husband.

Can a highlander love for long that which he scorns? Halbert wept over the culpable Mary, but time and reason consoled him, and the beautiful and mild Anna soon came to live in his placid abode, and made him shiver with happiness when she raised her blue eyes to look at him and called him husband.

Fifteen years went by. The fortunate Halbert returned to his cherished mountains after a short voyage; he was singing his favorite ballad, because his children were waiting for him impatiently, and he was eager to bounce his lastborn on his knees and press his lips to the fresh cheeks of the woman who called him husband.

It's pleasant, he thought, *to have suffered, and to be able to recount one's sufferings sitting peacefully by the hearth; but is the man not fortunate who never quit that hearth, and who says to himself: Blessed by Saint Cuthbert, who has preserved me from so much harm, and who has never separated me from the woman who calls me husband?*

Suddenly, he perceived a lady mounted on a palfrey who was fleeing, pale and distressed. Her clothes were bloody. "Save me!" she said, weeping. "Save me! The inhabitants of the lowlands are pursuing me; they've murdered my son and the man I called husband."

Halbert shivered at the voice of the stranger. He covered her with his plaid and took her to his home, where she received the most tender cares of the woman who called Halbert husband.

On seeing the happy family surrounding with their arms that good father, who was smiling, the stranger turned away, and a bitter tear ran down her cheek. Alas, she had never savored that peaceful happiness, for it was a wild and terrible man that she had called husband.

A week went by. She had the pastor who had given her shelter approach her deathbed. Raising an extinct gaze to look at him, and pressing the highlander's trembling hand in her icy hand, she said: "Halbert, don't you recognize Mary, Mary who caused her father to die of grief, and who was to call you husband?"

The Mariner
1533

> Do not leave a ewe to chase an eagle that you will
> never attain; for when you return to your ewe,
> forgetting the wool and milk she gives you, you
> will say, scornfully: "She cannot fly."
> (Scottish proverb.)

THE YOUNG hunter who ventures imprudently into a Scottish bog can no longer distinguish, when night falls, the perfidious light of a will-o'-the-wisp from the light shining in a hospitable house; he looks at them by turns, anxiously, and bitterly regrets not having gone home when the moon appeared in the sky, as he had been advised by his mother to do. At least, when the first rays of the sun redden the vapors of the bog, he will shake his plaid, and hasten to regain the roof where he is awaited anxiously by the young woman with the blue eyes to whom he promised the roe deer his arrow has pierced, and, swearing to be more prudent in the future, he will embrace his mother tenderly.

But the man who, disdaining an obscure and tranquil fate, attaches a holly branch to his cap, which is formed from the skin of eagles, mounts a spirited courser and never has any livestock except for cattle that he guides with his spear and has stolen from some inhabitant of the lowlands, from an unfortunate man who weeps on seeing his stables deserted and his cottage devastated, where his mother can no longer sit down; and the adventurous highlander who, trusting the perfidious tales of a traveler, goes to seek treasures beyond the seas—those men, I say, would dearly love, like the young hunter, to have only one night to wait to see their birthplace again! How many times the one, letting his bridle drift over the neck of his horse, and the other, sitting on the ropes at the stern of a vessel, plunged in a profound reverie, will cry: "Mother!"

Alas, alas, they will never find happiness again, even in the bosom of Scotland; they will no longer savor any charm in striking the agile roe deer! How could they resign themselves to spending in the highlands a life as uniform as a loch, which never reflects anything but a gray sky and the high crags that protect its waters from the breath of the wind? The young eaglet, once escaped from its nest, can no longer find pleasure there, although it must procure, at the risk of its life, the nourishment that its mother lavished upon it.

Sitting sadly beside her fire, old Anna was thinking about her son. Lindall loved Jenny, but he only had a tiny flock. "If I marry Jenny," he said to his mother, "could I see her suffering? When she tries to hide the tears that poverty draws from her, will I not be the unhappiest of highlanders who wear the plaid and the dirk? Oh, it's necessary that I enrich myself!"

And one evening, Lindall did not come back to his mother's house.

And for six years, Anna did not know what had become of him. She would have died poor and alone if Jenny had not nourished her on the produce of her labor, talked to her about her son and embraced her, saying: "He'll come back, he'll come back; he'll still call me his Jenny; he'll still call you his mother."

Suddenly, there was a knock on the door. Anna's spinning-wheel ceased its monotonous whirr, and a stranger, whose garments were crimson and covered with gold, asked for the hospitality that the Scots never refuse.

"Be welcome," she said, "but you'll only get poor nourishment here, for I'm poor and my son abandoned his mother a long time ago."

The stranger took Anna's hand and the old Scotswoman, raising her eyes to look at him, cried: "My son!"

It was Lindall, Jenny's lover, who had not come back to his mother's house one evening, in order to run after fortune.

Is there a happiness greater than that of a mother rediscovering a son she thought dead? Anna's sobs prevented her from speaking for a long time, but when she had given them free rein she said: "How happy Jenny will be! Jenny who has nourished me with her labor and who said to me: 'He'll come back, he'll come back; he'll still call me his Jenny; he'll still call you his mother!'

Jenny was behind her; she came forward, blushing, and threw herself into Lindall's arms. Lindall kissed one of her vermilion cheeks, and started relating the evils and the perils to which he had been exposed since leaving his mother.

Then he emptied on to the table a large purse full of gold coins, which the vacillating light of the lamp caused to glitter.

"Oh!" cried the worthy Anna. "Now you're rich, and no flock to match yours will roam these highlands!"

Lindall smiled and replied: "This isn't much. It's for you, Mother. Three ships belong to me, all three laden with merchandise and gold. With the value of one of my three ships I could buy all the houses of the clan and the castle of the laird himself, so keep that small amount of gold; it's for you, Mother."

How happy Jenny was! And yet, Lindall—the man for whom Jenny had supported so many difficulties and abandoned her mother—was slow to talk about love and marriage.

Alas, one day, two days, three days, went by, and Lindall did not mention marriage. His gaze was cold and distracted, and he often sang a mariner's song or whistled a martial tune, while his mother was talking to him.

One morning he said: "I'm going away."

Jenny stood there, as motionless and pale as a bog phantom.

"I'm going away," he repeated. "My children and my wife are waiting for me. Goodbye, Mother."

He had disappeared a long time ago, and his mother was still gazing at the hill he had climbed. She turned round and called to Jenny. Jenny, as motionless and pale as a bog phantom, no longer replied to the woman she had so often called mother.

Two years later, a stranger, whose garments were crimson and covered in gold, appeared in the highlands. He asked for Anna.

"She died a long time ago," an old woman replied. "But for me, no one would have closed her eyes, no one would have prayed beside her body, and the laird carried the head of the coffin himself.[1] She's over there, as she requested, beside Jenny, the young woman for whom her son, Lindall, had abandoned his mother."

---

1 Author's note: "In Scotland, when the deceased has no close relative, it is the laird who carries the head of the coffin. See Sir Walter Scott, *The Antiquary*."

The Unfortunate

A French Story

1829

Your eye, like Satan, has measured the abyss,
And your soul plunging therein, far from light and God,
Has said an eternal farewell to hope . . .
Woe betide the man who, from the depths of life's exile,
Hears the concert of a world he desires!
Of the ideal nectar, as soon as he has tasted it,
Nature makes repugnant the reality.
(Lamartine, "L'Homme:
Meditation on Lord Byron.")[1]

IT was fourteen years ago that I left the college of Grenoble, and yet I still cannot help feeling a sweet emotion at the memory of the notable day on which I was awarded there, in rhetoric, a second prize for Latin translation, a second prize for Greek translation, two first places and three seconds in the examinations.

More a hard-working student than one endowed with brilliant dispositions, that was the first and only success that I obtained in my life; you can easily imagine what a

---

1 Alphonse de Lamartine's poem "L'Homme" [The Man], addressed to Lord Byron, appeared in his *Méditations poétiques* (1820).

profound impression it produced in me, what a pleasant memory remains to me of it, and with what puerile joy I take pleasure in remembering it here.

Having returned to the college dormitory, surrendering myself to the most cheerful thoughts, I gladly started making my preparations for the following day's journey. The joy of my worthy mother on seeing her son again, the possessor of two crowns; the wellbeing of feeling liberated from scholastic servitude; the pleasure of a long journey, of seeing other objects than the sad town of Grenoble and the convent walls of our college—such were the only ideas that occupied me then. Bent over the small trunk that enclosed my modest wardrobe, I was singing loudly when an arm surrounded me with an amicable embrace; it was Charles de Belleville; he had come to say goodbye.

The most tender amity bound us together. During the eight years that we had spent together in college, we had never been apart, and never had the slightest argument or the slightest chill troubled that narrow union.

Our characters were, however, very different.

Nature had endowed Charles with an ardent and romantic soul, an exquisite sensibility, a rich imagination and a rare facility for study. He was an excellent musician, drew with talent, spoke several languages and always maintained an incontestable superiority over his comrades. Nevertheless, there was not one to be found among them who did not cherish him, for he showed himself to be constantly good, modest and highly skilled at ball games.

Personally, I was what is known as a toiler, and far from possessing any of Charles' brilliant qualities; he exercised over me an extreme ascendancy, difficult to understand if one does not know how forcefully attached men of weak character become to energetic souls whose superiority subjugates them.

I possessed for Charles, therefore, a disinterested and almost fanatical attachment. In order to give you an idea of it, I felt happier when he squeezed my hands, when, with tears in his eyes, he talked to me about my successes, yes, I felt happier then than at the solemn moment when my name was called out and the rector placed a crown on my head, congratulating me with a citation from Virgil.

After a long conversation, an affectionate conversation; after having sworn a hundred times that nothing would ever diminish the tender amity that we experienced for one another; after having promised to write to one another as often as possible, it was finally necessary for us to separate.

In quitting me, Charles left with his father in a post-chaise. The following morning I climbed up on to the imperial of the diligence, and returned to my mother, who lived in Bourgogne.

The widow of a brave captain who had died in Germany, my mother had nothing to live on but a modest pension scarcely sufficient for her own needs. I made every effort only to be a burden to her for the shortest possible time; I soon succeeded in that, thanks to my former rector, the worthy man who had complimented me in Latin on the day of the prize-giving; I was appointed as the teacher of the seventh form in a small town thirty leagues from the one where my mother lived.

My salary was not considerable, but was sufficient for my maintenance, and permitted me, every year, to go and spend the vacation with my mother. That pleasure, combined with my taste for study and my scant ambition, rendered my modest existence quite supportable.

One chagrin, however—a very bitter chagrin—troubled my tranquility for a long time: Charles' letters, at first very frequent and very long, soon became rare and short; eighteen months after leaving the college of Grenoble, they even ceased completely. I wrote several times, but received no response; it was necessary for me to renounce that correspondence, my heart heavy with regret. Since then, I had only had news of the ingrate once, and indirectly; one of our former schoolfellows told me that Charles' father, when he died, had left him a considerable fortune, and that the young heir was devoting himself recklessly to the pleasures that an annual income of a hundred thousand livres, a handsome face, intelligence and talent can procure in Paris.

Nine years went by. I had become the third form teacher in my small school, and the same position had just become vacant in the town where my mother lived. It was vacation time; I resolved to solicit that place, and left for Paris.

Having arrived two days before, and taken futile steps, I was about to return, very disappointed, to inform my mother of the sad news, when I learned that Charles was in Paris and that he had an uncle who was a minister; a single word from him could enable me to obtain the position I had solicited. I hesitated for a long time as to whether I ought to have recourse to the ingrate who had testified so much indifference toward me, but my mother's life was at stake, for, ill and weighed down by the chagrin of years, she required care that only her son could give her. It was necessary for me to overcome my reluctance and have recourse to Charles' protection. The following day, I went to the house where he resided, in the Chaussée-d'Antin.

I was introduced into an elegant study; his head supported on his two hands, Charles appeared to be deep in thought. Scarcely had the domestic pronounced my name than he was in my arms; his emotion appeared so vivid that it was a few moments before he was able to speak.

"Edmond, Edmond!" he finally exclaimed. "I'm an ingrate! You alone in the world have ever loved me, and I was able to repay you so outrageously!"

That welcome dissipated the scant rancor that I had been able to retain for him, and we soon rediscovered the confidence and affection for one another that we had experienced at the college of Grenoble. It was decided that we would spend the day together, that Charles' door would be closed to everyone, and that I would be introduced to the minister the following day.

I found Charles much changed.

His face was pale, his forehead balding, his eyes hollow, his gaze melancholy; throughout his physiognomy there was an indefinable expression of bitterness and disdain.

The sad confidences he made me explained the causes of that baleful change only too well.

Charles found himself under the weight of the bitter despair that, when it takes possession of an energetic soul, imprints it permanently with bitterness and irony.

He had, however, only experienced the chagrins that are the deadly privilege of well-ordered men, uncomprehended by the fortunate indifference of the vulgar: thirsty for love and friendship, he had been miserably treated.

But the disenchantment that slowly and insensibly produces egotism in a mature man, in whom experience and human contact have gradually worn away the loving faculties, sudden and terrible in him, had exasperated a new soul and abruptly stripped away his dearest illusions.

To extract himself from that moral void, the ardent thirst for love, an intolerable malady that desiccates and consumes, Charles had delivered himself to everything that the sciences and philosophy contain of the most positive and the most desolate.

Needless to say, those fatal studies, far from soothing him, had ended up destroying the few illusions that still remained to him.

Unhappier than before, he sought in fêtes, in worldly pleasures, the means of numbing himself and escaping from himself; for lack of affection, he sought the success that only flatters vanity; he fashioned his lips and gaze to express sentiments that he did not experience. Soon he became a skillful seducer; the vivacity of his intelligence, his ardent imagination, and perhaps even the perpetual irony, the vague and indistinct bitterness that he mingled with the most tender words, contributed to facilitating his successes. Everywhere, he was ardently sought out; everywhere, he was envied . . . oh, if only people had been able to read his thoughts!

Unhappier than ever, he was scarcely able to obtain from the moral intoxication of society the vulgar forgetfulness that the artisan finds in the physical intoxication of drunkenness. To succeed, it was necessary to pretend to believe in the love that he would have given anything in the world to obtain, which he knew to be impossible, and whose impossibility drove him to despair. He resembled one of those invalids who drink and drink in order to slake an inextinguishable thirst, but who only redouble the fiery fever that is desiccating and consuming them.

Charles study could have given an idea of the mental disorder of that unfortunate, sated by science, disgusted with sensuality, disabused of the most cherished beliefs, despoiled of the most cherished illusions.

A concerto by Hummel was open on a piano laden with flowers and weapons; further away, an unfinished painting rested on an easel; instruments of physics were to be found in the midst of apparatus of chemistry, and human bones, to which the anatomist's art had given the whiteness of ivory, lay on an herbal of enormous dimensions.

My gaze was particularly struck by the immense desk at which Charles was sitting when I arrived: there, open and piled up pell-mell on top of one another, were found Milton, Destutt de Tracy, Montaigne, Byron, Rabelais, Locke, Racine, Gall, Lamartine, Helvetius, Broussais, Hugo and Voltaire. It was evident that Charles had, by interrogating those authors in turn, sought to distract himself, and that, despairing of vain efforts, he had pushed the books away, in order to make other, equally fruitless attempts. An unfortunate Faust, the abuse of sciences and pleasures was for him a horrible Mephistopheles.

When I talked to him about my modest wishes, when I talked to him about the joy I would have if I were finally permitted no longer to be separated from my mother, he wept; he squeezed my hands and said to me with a convulsive emotion: "Oh, if you knew what I would give the world to believe again in what you believe, to savor like you an obscure and tranquil pleasure in leafing through a book, in taking a solitary stroll! Yes, if mild and cheerful thoughts could be rendered to me; if I were able to believe once again in amity, in love, in virtue; if I could sleep peacefully every night, I would give all the immense riches that people envy me in exchange. I abjure the deadly knowledge that is insistent in persecuting me, like the phantom that an imprudent magician has evoked and cannot expel. To extract myself from myself, I'm going to make long voyages, but alas, I'm undertaking them without any hope of cure; there's only one remedy for what I endure, and that's death!"

I left him, my breast taut with pity, sorrow and anxiety.

The next day, I had an audience with the minister; I obtained the favor I requested, and after having taken my leave of the unfortunate Charles, I climbed into a carriage in order to return to my mother.

Another four years went by, and many fortunate changes took place in my lot. My mother's health was restored, thanks to the presence and care of her beloved son; I had married a young woman, fresh, good, naïve and above all, an excellent housekeeper; finally, a son, a charming child, had come to augment my family and my domestic enjoyments. Add to that the fact that I had been promoted from the third form to the chair in rhetoric, and, given the character you know me to have, you will see that I had not a single desire still to form.

I came back one evening from a little stroll with my mother, my wife and my little boy, when a letter was handed to me that had arrived during my absence. I recognized Charles' handwriting; he had just arrived in my small town.

I ran in all haste to the hotel that it indicated to me. I could not retain a cry of surprise and dolor at the sight of the unfortunate; he was scarcely recognizable.

"You see, Edmond," he said to me, with a smile that I cannot describe, "you can see that I only have a few days to live. I wanted to die in the arms of the only friend I had in the world; I wanted to confide a secret that I can only reveal to you."

I urged Charles to come and lodge in my home, where my care and those of my family would be much more salutary for him than the services of strangers bought with money. He consented, and was immediately transported to my house.

The next day, he confided his sad secrets to me.

I've reported that he had left Paris at the same time as me; I added that he had the intention of traveling in various lands.

Scarcely had he set forth than ill health obliged him to stop in Aix-la-Chapelle. He had letters of recommendation to a rich banker, Monsieur Reisladst; the latter, an estimable man, did not take long to appreciate Charles de Belleville, and the invalid became the baker's intimate friend.

Madame Reisladst was English. She had her sister with her, Lady Maria Nelson, who had been married a year before to a Duke, the oldest, the surliest and most egotistical in the three kingdoms.

Charles became smitten with Maria, and was loved in return.

Disappointed so many times, it was in vain that he saw the young woman lavish upon him the most touching proofs of a delicate, modest, passionate and boundless affection, a kind of affection of which the romantic young man had dreamed so many times, and which, in his despair, he had called a chimera; Maria's love was for him a dream that he expected to see vanish at any moment. It only required for that, he thought, an absence of short duration, or a frivolous caprice.

Judge what anguish must have resulted from such a doubt for poor Charles, whose imagination was further excited from day to day.

One evening, contemplating Maria's angelic features, on seeing her beautiful blue eyes fixed upon him for a long time, he finally abjured the horrible doubt that was stabbing him and, in a delirious transport, seized the young woman's hand and pressed it to his lips.

Lord Nelson was present; the next day he departed with his wife for an estate he possessed in Ireland.

A month after that cruel departure, Charles received a letter from Lady Nelson; no woman had ever expressed such tenderness.

I dared not, she wrote, *when I was with you, Charles, confess how much I loved you, but now that we are separated forever, and that separation renders you distraught—oh, how much I sense it!—I want to tell you that I love you; I want to repeat to you that I love you, as no man was ever loved!*

I could never receive your letters; milord's jealous surveillance raises an insurmountable obstacle to that; all the people surrounding me are spies. If you knew the anguish that I am experiencing, the dangers to which I am exposing myself in writing this letter and getting it to you! But it ought to make you less sorrowful; may I count on something from you?

Charles had thus received, at long intervals, letters expressing a celestial tenderness. He never thought it possible for him to reply.

Some time after that, a young German came to Paris whom Charles had often met in the home of the banker in Aix-la-Chapelle; he had arrived from Ireland. He had seen Maria, for whom Madame Reisladt had given him letters.

The German told Charles coldly that he had only made two visits to the Duke's home; he added that the manor house was a very tedious abode, and that poor Lady Nelson's society was uniquely composed of the aged lord and a young man, his nephew, undoubtedly a very good pianist, for he had found him on each occasion making music with Lady Nelson, whom he knew had too much taste to be able to please herself in that fashion with a poor musician.

It required no more for vague and cruel suspicions to afflict Charles henceforth; they soon became a frightful certainty for the insensate, for he did not receive any more letters from Maria.

Despair completed the ruination of his debilitated health; the germs of the malady of consumption that was destroying him slowly suddenly developed rapidly, and, sensing that he was dying, he had wanted to see me once more and confide his bitter dolors to me.

"If Maria writes again," he told me, in conclusion, "you'll receive her letters . . . but she won't write again," he added, "she won't write again." He shed a few tears, turned his head away, and then expired.

On the day of his death, a letter from Lady Nelson was forwarded to me from Paris.

Three more letters arrived, at long intervals.

The last was sealed in black; it stated that the old lord had died three months before; it indicated the address to which Charles' letter should be sent.

It was me who replied.

Since then, no more letters from Lady Nelson have ever arrived.

The Roses

A French Story

1825

She was of this world, where the finest things
Have the worst destiny,
And, a rose, she lived as roses live,
For the space of a morning,
(Malherbe, "Ode on the Death of a Young Woman")[1]

It is in human nature to love to deceive oneself,
and to believe that one will be happier or wiser
than the unfortunates who have failed, and thus
not to recoil before a peril to which another has
just succumbed.
(Love letter.)

"DON'T play with those roses, Maria, don't enlace them as you're doing in your beautiful hair, don't knot them in your belt; leave the flowers to me, oh, I beg you, leave them to me. If you knew what sad memories they recall to my mind! If you knew where I picked them, Maria!

---

1 The lines are from François de Malherbe's "Consolation à M. Du Périer sur la mort de sa fille" (1598).

"It was from a young woman's grave. She had the pretty name of Laure. She was beautiful, gentle, cheerful and insouciant, just like you; I loved her as I love you, because, you see, Maria, she went to sleep on my knee many a time. Later, I shared the games of the mischievous little six-year-old, and then, when she had become a beautiful adolescent, timid by nature, it was with me alone that she forgot her fifteen years and became a joyful child again, that she delivered herself with a delightful abandon to a thousand frivolous caprices.

"Almost every evening, we took long walks in the country together; leaning on my sexagenarian arm, sometimes grave and sometimes impish, she indulged in ingenious repartee, made those ravishing speeches, spoken with so much charm, that only a virginal mouth can pronounce. Laura delighted in her easy and insouciant life of a young woman, the life that still embellishes a thousand happy reflections of the past; everything she said expressed a placid happiness, devoid of desire and devoid of projects; one might have thought that the future would never arrive for her, nor appear to her more austere and sinister.

"So, when sudden and terrible misfortune burst upon poor Laure, it struck her with a mortal blow.

"But why tell you that painful story, which will make you sad all day? I'd rather see you cheerful, as you are now.

"Oh, you can squeeze my hands, desiccated and browned with age, in your pretty hands, as much as you like; it's in vain that you're putting your imploring arm on my shoulder, in vain that you're lavishing me with those delightful caresses that make me obey your slightest caprices; this time, I assure you, your uncle won't give in . . . yes, yes, even if you promise to sing him some of those old songs that he loves so much, even if you offered him a game of piquet this evening!

"Good! Now she's putting on a sulky face . . . come on, Maria, come back, leave the window where you've taken refuge; come back to me, my child, I tell you, and since you insist, listen . . .

"One day, Laure's mother made me a confidence: a rich young man, elegantly turned out, whose intelligence and good qualities she had heard praised, had come to ask for Laure in marriage.

"He lived in a country house near ours, and soon he no longer quit Laure during the day.

"The young woman didn't take long to fall madly in love with her fiancé. Everyone encouraged that naïve love, and every time we saw her blush when he arrived or go pale when he left, her happy mother exchanged mysterious gazes and intelligent smiles with me.

"The fiancé left for a voyage of short duration. At first, we received his letters almost every day; after that he stopped writing, and a week, a month went by. Then he wrote again, but to say that he had renounced Laure's hand.

"I can't describe Laure's bleak despair, or her mother's anguish, or my indignation, Maria. Oh, if I hadn't been so old, the coward wouldn't have done so much harm with impunity, but he knew full well that Laure's mother was a widow and had no one in the world but her daughter.

"A few months later it was necessary to take Laure to Paris; the physicians of the province had declared the malady of consumption that was devouring the unfortunate girl beyond all human remedy. Alas, the doctors in Paris confirmed the terrible sentence.

"They were only too right; a week after our arrival, Laure was laid to rest in Père Lachaise cemetery.

"I'm the only one who sometimes goes to put wreaths on her grave or pick a few of the flowers that have been planted there. I'm the only one because her mother . . . her mother . . . she lost her reason.

"You're weeping, Maria? When I tell you that the author of so much evil is happy, brilliant, sought after, that he's welcome in this very house, that it's Jules de Beaumanoir?

"She's gone pale . . . ! She's tottering . . . ! Maria! Maria . .! Oh, now she's coming round, thank God!

"Well, naughty child, was I so wrong not to want to tell you that lugubrious adventure?"

The day after that confidence, I departed for a voyage that was to last several months; imagine my surprise when I received, a short time after my departure, a letter from my sister-in-law, which told me that Maria was marrying . . . guess who? Jules de Beaumanoir!

A note from Maria was attached to that letter.

Dear Uncle, it said, *I have an idea of your surprise, but before criticizing me, listen to me. Jules has been very culpable, but it was because of me. He saw me, and after that, he ceased to love poor Laure. Is it for me, Uncle, to judge him? Is it for me to punish Jules for loving me more than the repose of his conscience? He has made that confession to me, Uncle: remorse, very cruel remorse, pursued him, troubled him even during his sleep. Oh, I want to devote my whole life to him; for the price of such a love, I want, by force of solicitude and tenderness, to render him calm and happiness.*

What could I do, me, a poor absent old man, except groan?

Maria became the wife of Monsieur Jules de Beaumanoir.

To hear her, Maria is the happiest of wives; however, nothing of her former gaiety remains; she has become pale and melancholy, and I've often surprised her shedding bitter tears.

Never have I, her old friend, been able to obtain the confidence from her of the troubles she is experiencing.

Although I rarely leave my entresol, I've often heard it said that Monsieur de Beaumanoir is one of the most amiable and sought-after men in Paris.

Polycarpa Salavarieta[1]
A Colombian Story

Sacred love of the fatherland,
Render us audacious and proud!
To my country I owe life;
It will owe its liberty to me.
(La Muette de Portici.)[2]

To profess to be a great and savant politician, I
have never cared and never will care. In truth to
perfect such a métier, would it not be necessary to
be more pitiless than a professional hangman and
torturer? The latter only torment the body; by
contrast, politicians torment the body and the
soul, and are thus the true and perfect demons of hell.
(Philippe Bouclelier, *History of the Breton Wars*.)[3]

---

1 Policarpa Salavarrieta (1795-1817), nicknamed "La Pola," was
the name attributed to a spy executed for treason by the Spanish
Royalists during the Spanish American Wars of Independence, which
were re-intensified after the end of the Peninsular Wars that ravaged
Spain before the fall of Napoléon I. This is another story illustrating
Berthoud's blithe disregard for matters of historical accuracy when
featuring real individuals in his fiction.
2 *La Muette de Portici* [The Mute Girl of Portici] is an 1828 opera by
Daniel Auber, with a libretto by Germain Delavigne and Eugène Scribe.
3 This reference is fictitious.

ANTONIO was lying down beside Polycarpa; when he woke up, the young woman was still asleep, her head supported on a bare arm, her breasts veiled by the beautiful black hair that fell in voluptuous disorder.

Leaning over, the young man respired for some time, in silence, the warm breath that Polycarpa's parted lips exhaled. Then he deposited a kiss on one of the beautiful Colombian woman's brown shoulders; she raised eyelids over laden with languor and amour. "Antonio, my Antonio . . . !" she murmured; and, throwing her arms around her lover's neck, she repeated: Antonio, my Antonio . . . !"

"I have to go; it's necessary for me to leave you," he replied, in an emotional voice, while he slowly disengaged himself from the soft grip that retained him. "Polycarpa, my love, I have to go."

She sat up, gathered together the long tresses or her hair, and her arms, falling back, enlaced her Antonio again.

"Stay, oh, stay longer, stay in your lover's arms; never leave me, never! Let me rest my head again upon our breast; let me contemplate our sparkling eyes again, and the white teeth that your smile reveals."

"And Santander?[1] The independents?" the young man replied, weakly, who yielded nevertheless to Polycarpa's intoxicating sensations.

She tore herself from his arms; her gaze became animated, and her modulated voice became graver and more energetic.

---

1 Francisco de Paula Santander was a military leader during the war of independence of 1810-19, and subsequently became acting president of Gran Colombia.

"Antonio, you have to go! Hurry up! Culpable that I am! Listening to my love when my country, when liberty, demand you! No, not one more kiss, not one more smile! Go, this instant, Antonio! When Santander has received Gregorio's dispatches, when he knows how easy it is to retake Bogota, then and only then will you be embraced by my caresses and your forehead reddened by my kisses. Adieu!"

Antonio drew away, and the young woman, from the height of her balcony and for as long as possible, followed him with her gaze veiled by tears; she wept then, because no one could see her.

He had disappeared a long time ago, and she was still there, motionless and staring. The brocade of a few Spanish officers who stopped to gaze at her extracted her from that reverie.

"Insolent fops," she murmured, closing the balcony violently. "Wait for my Antonio to return, and our gallant words will be repaid for what they're worth, a dagger-thrust in the left side. Strut, lift up your heads overladen with plumes; in two days, Santander will come back with his army; in two days your corpses will be lying in the streets of Bogota, and the flag of independence will be fluttering over our towers, presently debased by the folds of our ensigns."

As she spoke those words, a young woman, her companion, irrupted into the apartment. "Antonio! Antonio! A prisoner! The sentinels are bringing him to the viceroy!"

An icy frisson ran through all Polycarpa's limbs; her legs buckled beneath her; vertigo troubled her sight.

Without saying a word, she threw a mantilla over her head; she hid a stiletto in the pleats of her dress and went to the viceroy's palace amid the crowd that Antonio's rest had assembled.

He was in a broad and vast hall. The prince and two other officers were interrogating the young man. He was responding proudly, without anxiety.

It was almost all over; it only remained to deliver the sentence, and the judges were deciding it in low voices.

Then Polycarpa cleaved through the crowd and walked boldly straight toward the viceroy.

"You're about to commit an injustice," she said. "Antonio isn't guilty. For love of me, he took charge of a message, but he didn't know that the papers enclosed in that box were for Santander; he thought they were letters addressed to my fugitive father. For I'm the daughter of Salavarieta, one of the six brave men who hatched a plot last year to assassinate you. He alone escaped the murderers of his generous accomplices."

"She's lying! She's lying!" cried Antonio.

"Why do you want to die in my stead, when I alone am guilty; when I've dragged you, without you suspecting it, into the abyss? Viceroy, I swear to you, I attest it by the holy Madonna, Antonio did not know what papers he was carrying."

"Oh, don't listen to her: her love is leading her astray. I took advantage of her sleep to set forth. Poor girl! She didn't even know that I'd gone!"

"You're lying, Antonio! You're lying, lying, I tell you!"

At this noble dispute, a murmur of sympathy spread through the spectators, in spite of the presence of the Spanish soldiers who were guarding all the avenues, and forming a living wall behind the tribunal.

The viceroy pretended to be moved.

"Antonio," he said, "your youth and the love of his young woman, touch me. You merit death, and you'll receive it instantly if I don't grant you mercy; listen, I want to grant it to you . . ."

Polycarpa uttered a cry of joy.

"That's on one condition," the prince continued. "Name the author of that letter to me, and I'll return your life and liberty."

Antonio smiled disdainfully and kept silent. After waiting a few moments for a response, the viceroy pronounced the sentence and ordered that it should be carried out immediately. After that, he took the Colombian woman aide.

"Young woman," he said, "save your lover. Confess to me now, in a whisper, the names he is obstinate in not pronouncing; no one, I swear to you on the salvation of my soul, will know where I heard them, and I'll return Antonio to you."

She turned her head away, and began to weep bitterly, wringing her hands.

"Speak, speak, hurry! Here, look: the soldiers are loading their weapons. They're advancing, surrounding him, taking him away. Poor insensate! To what false heroism are you sacrificing your lover? There's still time—name me the cowards who are letting him perish in their stead."

Polycarpa parted her lips as if to speak, but she only uttered a confused sound, and then cried: "Opprobrium to Antonio's lover, opprobrium to Salavarieta's daughter, for having conceived such a thought!"

One of the viceroy's counselors approached him and whispered something to him.

"You're right," replied the viceroy. "Take her to the place of execution; she'll be free to ransom her lover, even when the weapons are aimed at his breast."

She was dragged away, fainting. In accordance with the viceroy's orders, the preparations for the execution were only made slowly. They were not yet concluded when the crowd saw the young woman arrive; it was suddenly thought that she had obtained her lover's life, and cries of "Mercy! He has mercy!" rose up from various places.

At those cries, Antonio raised his head and took off his blindfold. Polycarpa was beside him; at the sight of her, a violent despair burst forth.

"I don't want your mercy; I don't want it. Woe is me! Woe is me! I've loved a wretch unworthy of my love! Oh, why didn't I die a few moments sooner? I would not have known Polycarpa a denouncer!"

She came to him, and held out her arms to him, but he did not even want to look at her.

"I'm worthy of you! I haven't talked! They don't know anything," she proffered, effortfully.

"Bless you, my Polycarpa! Bless you, daughter worthy of your father, and of your lover! Come to my breast once more . . . now, I can die!"

They were separated. The rifles were aimed at the condemned man's breast. The officer, his sword in the air, looked at Polycarpa; she was praying fervently.

"There's still time!" he cried.

Suddenly, the young woman tottered, fell, and was covered with blood. She had stabbed herself.

The officer made a movement with his sword, and it was all over.

Polycarpa was not yet twenty years old, and her lover was six months older than her.

The Room In The Inn
A French Story
1825

Now, listen attentively, and you'll remember
when necessary what I'm going to tell you; luck is
a slippery eel, hard to grasp, which flees the hands
that grip it, and leaves them emptier than if they
had not held the fallacious fish.
(Eustache Pierret, *Moral Instruction on the Human
Passions.*)[1]

Massoud, after having drawn to the bank with
great difficulty the nets that he thought to contain
an enormous fish, only found therein a heap of
stinking mud.
(*The Thousand-and-One Nights.*)

The mocking phantom, with its light wing
Deceives the extended arms that try to seize it,
Leaving nothing in its stead but bitter dolor,
And then repentance.
(Héloïse Pennequin, *Epistle to a Sister.*)[2]

---

1 Fictitious.
2 The poet Héloïse Pennequin is belatedly mentioned in the obituary

THERE is no afternoon more tedious than one spent in a room in an inn when it is pouring with rain and one does not know a single person in the town one is in.

Can one sit down? A hard, uncomfortable armchair, higher or lower, narrower or broader than the one in which one usually nestles, is inconvenient, and renders the capricious reveries of the imagination impossible.

If one has a whim to write, the desk is not perfectly level; the narrow table-top does not permit the elbow to be braced there, in order that the left hand can support and gently warm the forehead; the ink is thick, the pen squeaks, the paper wobbles.

Is there the means to conceive or to express a single idea?

Then one searches vainly around one: the wallpaper with large interlacing flowers, the gilded frames hanging from long ribbons, the family portraits that seem to smile. If the gaze strays toward the windows, they only perceive inanimate and unknown objects through the panes.

Alas, not even the resource of sleep remains, for the fatiguing ennui of I know not what physical malaise aggravates I know not what irritable agitation; one gets up, one sits down, one paces, one stops, only to sit down again, to get up again, to pace and stop again.

At least, that is what I experienced, some five years ago in the inn of the Sign of the Cross, forty leagues from Paris,

section of the *Mémoires* of the Societé d'émulation de Cambrai as having died young in 1816, but was almost certainly an invention of Berthoud's, whose notional existence originated in this quotation; a eulogistic mention of her talents in his subsequent account of the legends of Flanders was reproduced in several other volumes published in the late 1830s.

during a sojourn of twenty-four hours in a small town near Orléans.

Finally, not knowing to which object to direct my imagination, I went, in despair, to place my forehead against the muslin curtains that two small tringles extended over the four lower panes of the window; in that position, I started watching the rain that was falling, bouncing on the pavement, flowing away in broad streams.

But the coarse muslin was imprinted on my forehead, in little red grooves, with an almost painful itching, the broad mesh of its fabric. Abruptly, in my chagrin, I tore the curtain away.

It fell, crumpling up, and let me see a few words engraved on the widow, doubtless with the aid of a diamond:

JULIE AND CASIMIR
4 September 1819

At that moment, my hostess brought me dinner.

It must be said that the good woman, a witness to the ennui that was agitating me, had gone to great lengths to procure me the means of distraction.

She had assembled on my table all the books she had in the house: an incomplete volume of *Florisa, or Virtuous Love*; two other poor novels at six sous a volume, and *The Terrible Montbard, the Exterminator.*[1]

I had not been able to read four pages of them.

In her eagerness, she had even borrowed from her neighbor, a blind fiddler, the most atrocious violin, of which I

---

1 These two books do not exist, but the Marquis de Montbard is a character in Honoré de Balzac's early pseudonymous novel *L'Héritière de Birague* (1822).

would nevertheless have made use to stave off ennui and pass the time—but the instrument lacked two strings, and no replacements could be found in the little town.

The good woman did not know what saint to turn to in order to dissipate the sadness of my physiognomy and stifle my yawns.

When she saw me contemplating attentively, with a sort of interest, the two lines engraved on the window pane, she smiled, and deposited on the table the faience plates with which her hands and arms were laden.

"Oh, my good Monsieur," she said, advancing toward me and sitting down, for the burden was heavy and the staircase quite steep, "Oh my good Monsieur, those two weren't bored, like you, I can assure you. They were, however, very unfortunate. It's a story I can tell you. Just let me collect my memory for a moment."

She passed a brown and wiry hand over her suntanned face, and got ready to speak.

"It was some years ago; it was the first year that I had the inn; a young man and a woman arrived here and came to lodge in my house.

"I spent a week trying in vain to discover the reason for which they'd come here. Shut up in their room until nightfall, they only went out to take a long walk; then they came back without speaking to anyone; anyway, they were very exact in paying me what they owed me at the end of the week.

"One Sunday, the young lady came down, in accordance with her custom, to give me my money. Then she asked for charcoal, and went back up to her room. I thought I observed that her eyes were red, as if she had been weeping a great deal, and I was all the more convinced of my idea when they didn't go out for a walk that evening.

"My husband and I had scarcely been in bed for an hour when a post-chaise stopped at the door of the inn. You can imagine that we didn't have to be asked twice to get up.

"Quickly, we ran to open up. Saving your respect, I had taken the time to put a skirt on and throw a scarf over my shoulders.

"It was a monsieur, who seemed dangerously wounded, for his head was covered in blood; it was a sickening sight. One of his domestics—he had three—told me that he had fallen from the carriage on the road.

"The difficulty was putting him to bed somewhere. You know, Monsieur, that there are only two decent rooms here: ours, which wasn't yet sorted out at that time, and the one where you are.

"Come on," I said to my husband, "those two young people won't mind, I'm sure, lending their comfortable room and their excellent bed for one night to a respectable individual wounded so badly; I'll go ask them.

"Holy Virgin, my dear Monsieur, when I opened their door I almost fell over. I only just had time to go out and lean against the wall.

"They had set fire in the middle of their room to a great pile of charcoal, and by the blue light of that charcoal, I saw the poor children lying there, motionless and as pale as corpses.

"I opened a window and called for help. My husband, the stranger's domestics and the stranger himself came running, I shouted so loudly.

"When he came in, the stranger cried: 'My son!' and collapsed himself, as if dead.

"When the young man came round and began to open his eyes, his father pressed him in his arms; his domestics surrounded him.

"He looked round in astonishment, and then turned his head away.

"Then the monsieur gestured to us all to get out.

"The next day, all three of them set forth in the old monsieur's post-chaise, and I would never have been able to get to the bottom of such a curious story, for they paid me generously, but without explaining anything of the previous night's scene.

"Fortunately, the postillion who had brought them had got into the good graces of the father's valet. I don't know how he did that, for the valet was as insolent as a lord, and treated me as if I were the least of the humblest servants.

"To get back to my story, this is what the valet told the postillion:

"The young man had fallen in love with a young orphan girl who had no money at all; the father had opposed their inclination.

"Then they had fled to hide a long way from their homeland, in my inn, and when they had nothing left to live on, they decided to kill themselves.

"Fortunately, their father, who thought they were in Paris and was going there to look for them, arrived in time to save them from such a misfortune.

"Touched by their despair his time, he forgave them, and promised to marry them, which I'm quite sure that he did."

My hostess' story had almost moved me, and took strong possession of my young imagination. That evening, in the room in the inn where the events related by me by my hostess had courted, I transcribed the pages that you have just read.

✳

Two years went by, and I had completely forgotten the lovers and their adventure.

One evening, I was invited to a soirée at the home of one of our celebrated painters. When I went to greet the artist, I found him arguing with a man of grave and pensive appearance; marriage was the subject of their conversation

The painter was sustaining, ardently, that without love there can be no happy union.

His adversary was establishing that such marriages could only be unhappy.

"Woe," he exclaimed, after long developments, "woe betide the insensates who seek in such a union the reality of their fantastic dreams of happiness and tenderness. Woe betide them, for, soon cruelly disabused, they will wring their hands in despair and curse their fatal error!"

"Monsieur," I replied to him, "I can cite you two persons who, I'm sure, would combat your paradoxical reasoning victoriously." Then I told him the story of the room in the inn.

It moved the artist greatly. "Well, Monsieur?" I asked.

"Well," my adversary replied, "scarcely married for a year, your unfortunate young man will have deplored his father's weakness; disappointed by the misalliance of the social position in which he found himself, deprived of the fortune he would have acquired by an appropriate union, by the dowry that he had the right to expect from a wife, he will have vegetated all his life.

"Alas, he will have been subject to even greater evils, even more real.

"Soon, the romantic amour of the two lovers, their intoxicating ecstasies, will have been succeeded by satiation, indifference, coldness and disgust. Who knows—perhaps they are seeking today in other affections the chimeras that they believed they would find in their foolish union? That, yes, that is the existence of your Casimir and his companion!"

"Do you know the heroes of that adventure, then?" asked the painter, surprised—for I had not said what names were engraved on the window-pane.

The man to whom the painter had addressed the question did not hear it, or pretended not to hear it, for he went to a gaming table without replying. A few moments later a young man came to inform him that his wife wanted to leave.

He was playing then, and that information caused an unequivocal expression of ill-humor to spread over his face.

"Uncle," the young man continued, "if you want to stay, I'll take my aunt home."

"Go on, Alfred," he replied.

And the young man, joyfully, ran to a pale woman who, more than once during the soirée, had exchanged tender gazes with him. He gently pressed the arm that came to lean on his own, and I was able to observe that the arm returned his embrace.

The mistress of the house saluted the lady who was leaving with an amicable inclination of the head.

"Who is that lady?" I asked her.

"Madame Casimir de Beausencourt."

The Madrigal
A French Anecdote
1672

> And the main reason is that I'm its author.
> (Molière, *Femmes Savantes*, Act III)

APPARENTLY, the conversation had been very tender, for the Duchesse de Ventadour did not think of withdrawing the hand that the Duc d'Enghien was covering with kisses, and she made no objection when, in a fine transport, the young prince got down on his knees.

Suddenly, she tore herself from his arms and ran to the window.

"A carriage! It's him! It's him! We're doomed! How can we avoid his gaze? Oh my God, my God! I'm doomed! He's going to come up here . . . I can hear him . . . this cabinet...here! Here! Go in! Hide!"

She locked the door of the cabinet and took out the key, which she deposited in her bosom and let herself fall into an armchair, trying to disguise as best she could the disturbance that was agitating her.

At the same moment, the Duc de Ventadour,[1] foaming

---

1 The Duc de Ventadour in 1672 was Henri de Lévis (1596-1680), who had a successful career as a soldier before taking holy orders

with rage, irrupted into the apartment, where he started pacing back and forth, his fists clenched and his hat pulled down over his eyes.

"Damnation! Double damnation!" he swore, energetically. Then, taking hold of his hat, he launched himself violently toward the mantelpiece, where there was a candlestick and two figurines; the porcelain images fell to the floor and shattered into a hundred pieces.

That fine exploit did not soothe the Duc's wrath, but seemed to redouble it.

For anyone except his wife it would have been amusing to see, behaving so dementedly and blaspheming wholeheartedly, the odd little hunchback of whom Bussy-Rabutin[1] has left us the portrait: "Aesop, who is represented to us as ugly," says the author of the amorous history of Gaul, "was an angel compared with the Duc de Ventadour; for he has the stature of a dwarf, a horrible nose and lips, and to complete the depiction, a kind of perpetual foam emerges from the latter, and from the other a substance that little children often pick. If one examines the rest, it is worse still, if that is possible: he is humped before and behind, with arms each shorter than the other, and as for his legs, one cannot see them without being afraid."

and financing Jesuit missions. Historical accounts of him bear no resemblance to the character depicted here. At the time, Duc d'Enghien was a courtesy title used by the eldest son of the Prince de Condé; in 1672 that would have been Henri-Jules de Bourbon (1643-1709) son of the great Condé, who was said to be ugly, brutal and insane—probably not the person Berthoud had in mind.

1 Roger de Rabutin, Comte de Bussy (1618-1693) does indeed relate an anecdote about the Duc and Duchesse de Ventadour in the section of his memoirs entitled "La France galante," but it is not this one and it refers to the wife of Louis-Charles de Lévis (1647-1717), who bore a much stronger resemblance to the Duc described in Berthoud's story but only inherited the title when his father died.

That strange little body would have given anything in the world for the Duchesse to give him the slightest excuse to get carried away and take out on her the anger that transported him, but she knew the man, and in any case, as she believed that the Prince's clandestine visit was the cause of all that racket, she kept quiet and refrained from breathing a single word.

"Damn! Double damn! Triple damn!" the Duc went on, stopping in front of her and folding his arms. "It's necessary to say that I'm on a fine footing at court! Damn! To escape the ridicule that's being heaped upon me, it only remains for me to bury myself on one of my estates." Uttering a frightful oath and placing his hand on his sword, he added: "But it won't be said that I'll go without taking vengeance. Those who have caused it will pay dearly for it!"

The Duchesse shivered in all her limbs, for it seemed to her that she was already receiving the mortal blow.

"God's blood!" Ventadour went on, becoming more and more animated as he fixed his flamboyant gaze upon his wife. "I admire your fine composure. One might think that all this is nothing to you!"

Immediately, the poor lady began mentally reciting her *in manus*.[1]

"I'm the laughing-stock of the entire court, ridiculed by the King himself! And for whom? For a low-bred individual, some pedant of a poet!"

The Duchesse let her breath out forcefully, for at those words she sensed that an enormous weight had been lifted from her breast.

---

1 *In manus [tuas, Domine, commendum spiritum meum]* is the beginning of the prayer translated into English as "Into thy hands, O Lord, I commend my soul."

"Who is he, then, and why such despair?" she asked, delivered from the rudest anxiety that she had felt.

"Can you imagine that Benserade[1] read, yesterday evening, when the King was about to go to bed, the dedicatory epistle of the work that His Majesty had printed so richly at the royal press."

"I know: Ovid's *Metamorphoses* in rondeaux.[2] Madame de Luddres, who mingles with intellectuals, mentioned it to me the other day."

"Everyone is ecstatic about the thing! The King overbid everyone else's praises, and wanted to have a copy of the Dedication; others imitated him; I did as everyone else did, although, to tell the truth, these things do nothing for me. Here, read it—this damned piece of paper is the cause of my chagrin."

The Duchess read, aloud:

"Dedicatory Letter in Rondeau, of my book, to Monseigneur le Dauphin.

To Monseigneur, Monseigneur le Dauphin.
As I know that you are inclined

---

1 The poet Isaac de Benserade (1613-1691).
2 Author's note: "This bizarre work is a 471-page quarto; it is made up of 232 rondeaux, each illustrated by an engraving by Sébastien Leclerc and Chauveaux; it emerged from the presses of the Imprimerie Royale, and was designed by Sébastien-Mabre Cramoisy, His Majesty's printer and director of the Imprimerie Royale; every time the engravers had to represent an Orpheus they put a violin in his hands instead of a lyre. The rondeau cited in this story is one of the least ridiculous; however, Benserade enjoyed, during the reign of Louis XIV, in the time of Racine and Molière, the reputation of a distinguished poet!" The work in question was published in 1676, later than the date attributed by Berthoud to his story, but prior to Louis-Charles' inheritance of the title of Duc de Ventadour.

To leaf through any book that one dares
To dedicate to you, and as in all things
You give evidence of a fine and exquisite taste,
I follow my bent, and the order of destiny
Which tells me: "Go, take in fine morocco.
Your rondeaux made on the Metamorphoses
  To Monseigneur."
Look upon them, Prince, with a kindly eye;
Preserve them from that mortal venom
By which envy infects verse and prose.
In a few words, that's my letter closed;
And a humble servant, to the end,
  To Monseigneur.

"That's pleasant, and well-turned."

"Well, damn it! Such a memory makes me seethe with anger. We were waiting for the King to chase a red deer. Poquelin,[1] Racine and that fop Despréaux were chatting together in the embrasure of a window; I took it into my head to show them Benserade's rondeau. It was the Devil, I believe, that gave me the idea of doing such honor to those petty individuals, who certainly ought not to be seen in the king's palace with the cream of those of noble birth.

"Look, Messieurs," I said to them, "you're fond of versifying; here's something prettily turned, with which I ought to regale you. I started reading the rondeau. Racine lowered his eyes, Poquelin formed one of those sad and dubious smiles typical of him, and Despréaux asked me brazenly who was the author of such a wretched rhapsody.

"'Damnation!' I cried. 'You'd do well to improve on it. You doubtless deem yourselves higher than the noblest in

1 Poquelin was Molière's real name.

the realm, and the King himself, who praised this rondeau a great deal yesterday evening."

"'I'm a better judge of poetry than the King,' replied the impudent rhymester.

"Oh, if it hadn't been for respect for the place where I was, I would have broken the fop's bones, but I did my best to contain myself and, turning on my heel, I went to tell the story to La Ferté, who expressed his indignation.

"A few minutes later, chamberlains announced His Majesty. The King's physiognomy expressed good humor, and he deigned to converse with Biron, d'Aumont and me. 'Messieurs,' he said to us, after various remarks, 'it's necessary that I consult you about a madrigal on which I'd be glad to have your opinion.'

"'Your Majesty couldn't have fallen better to have a good one,' I replied, 'For here's Sieur Despréaux, who was boasting just now of being a better judge poetry than Your Majesty himself.'

"'And he's surely right, Ventadour,' the King replied, smiling.

"Blood rose to my face. To make me such a reply! And to encourage the insolence thus . . . of whom? A dauber of paper! But the King, so severe to the nobility, tolerates that rabble to the highest degree; he laughs at the remarks of a Despréaux, but he's just exiled Tilladet for knocking down a bailiff who had dared to seize his carriage!

"My embarrassment was extreme, as I told you, and the King, excited by Biron and other pasquins of the court, continued in these terms: 'So, you dabble too Ventadour, in judging poetry? I wouldn't have believed it; well, listen, I pray you, to this madrigal, and see whether you've ever seen one so impertinent. Because people know that I like verses, and they bring me all kinds. Here, Racine, read it aloud, so that everyone can hear.'

"'On my honor, sire,' I exclaimed, when Sieur Racine had finished, 'Your Majesty divines everything very well; it's true that that's the most stupid and ridiculous madrigal I've ever read.'

"The King started laughing. 'Isn't it true that the man who made it is a conceited ass?'

"'Sire, there's no other way of putting it.'"

At this point, the Duc was seized by a further fit of despair; he struck out violently with his fist, and resumed pacing precipitately.

"Well?" said the Duchesse.

"Well," cried the Duc, tearing out his hair, "the King told me that he was the author of the madrigal, and that he was delighted that I'd spoken of him so honestly. There was, as you can imagine, a general burst of laughter. Biron, Vardes, Châteauneuf and even La Ferté, who had just shared my anger against Despréaux so forcefully, heaped me with gibes regarding my good taste; the King sank into his armchair, and had a great deal of difficulty suppressing a noisy hilarity that drove me to despair.

"'Come on, Messieurs,' he says, trying to resume his gravity. 'Let's go chase the deer.'

"'I thought the hunt was over,' murmured that Biron, who never refrains from kicking a man when he's down. 'Hasn't your Majesty just put a stag at bay?' Damn it, Madame, I don't attach much importance to what that buffoon says, but if you ever give rise to such remarks . . . ! Everyone left for the hunt, but I climbed into my carriage and came back here, in despair and beside myself."

Madame de Ventadour did her best to calm her husband down, and, when she had succeeded in getting him out of her apartment she ran to open the door to the Duc d'Enghien. With the aid of an adroit soubrette, he made his escape without a hitch.

Almost from that day on, the Duc d'Enghien became the intimate friend of the Duc de Ventadour, and everyone marveled at it, for the little hunchback, generally despised, was a ridiculous object of amusement for all. Six months later, however, he became cold, disdainful and surly once again toward Ventadour, for he was a very haughty seigneur, and proud of his title of prince of the blood.

Insomnia

A Neapolitan Story

1750

"Oh, if you knew the evil I have suffered!"
(Shakespeare, *King Lear*.)

OH, how long a night is, a night without sleep, a night
in France, a night in winter, when the tempest is
howling, as it does, and hurling cold swirls of snow against
my shaking windows! Will it not be granted to me henceforth to sleep, a gentle and profound slumber, a slumber
that refreshes my blood, and which frightful dreams don't
render more baleful than a burning insomnia? If I only
could drive away the memory that is always there before
me, which is drying me up and killing me! If I could only
become once again as happy and calm as I was in Naples!

Naples! Oh, if those who boast to me about their France
could see her! If they quit their cold cities where, in order
to sleep, it's necessary to load oneself with more garments
than are needed in Naples to dress an entire family! If they
found themselves in the evening on the Môle, in the Via
Toledo, or Kiapa![1] I would smile at their surprise at the

---

1 The reference to "Kiapa" is slightly enigmatic, but probably refers to
the Via Chiaia.

sight of such a marvelous spectacle, a spectacle such as their gaze has never admired.

To begin with, one sees nothing but a strange confusion of men, women, children and carriages: an enormous mass, in which innumerable lanterns float and scintillate. One hears a deafening medley of voices and cries. There are thousands of marching feet, thousands of rolling wheels, crossing paths and screeching on the lava pavement, which they pulverize. One might think they were the roaring waves of the sea, which heap up, separate, collide and draw together again, confounded, before fleeing again.

Malediction! That's where I saw her for the first time, where my eyes followed the light carriage that drew her away, where I said: "She must be mine!"

In vain, sage friends repeated to me that she was Paola, the coquette Paola, the sister of the poor Roman cavalier Pietro de Monte Nuovo. "It doesn't matter! She must be mine!"

And the next day, I had shaken Pietro's hand, and he had sworn to me: "You shall be my brother!"

I saw her every day, and when I fixed the gaze of inflamed eyes upon her, she lowered hers languidly, blushed, and raised them toward me again tenderly. When, mad with love, I said to her: "Paola, my Paola, I love you!" she abandoned her hand to my kisses, and a vivid emotion caused the undulations of her bosom to hasten.

I was happy! Oh, no saint ever savored the joys of a sweeter paradise; no predestined soul ever slaked itself with delights more ineffable!

Eternal damnation! At those memories of a lost happiness, lost forever, a horrible rage constricts my heart, causes my breast to heave. That despair chokes me. My fists clench convulsively . . .

I quit her, drunk with tenderness. A letter was handed to me by a stranger; it told me that a man penetrated into Paola's room every night. I ran to Pietro's house; he read the fatal piece of paper. Without saying a word, we buckled our sword-belts, and hid ourselves near the perfidious woman's widows.

By the Demon! Her treason is real! Someone calls: "Paola, the rope-ladder!" She throws it; he climbs up . . .

Vengeance! I hurl myself on his traces; he disappears into the obscurity, and I find myself in the midst of Paola's relatives . . .

Twenty daggers are pointed at my breast; I'm called perfidious, coward, traitor, suborner!

"No!" I cried. "It isn't me who's perfidious, it's her, it's not me who's a suborner, it's the man who introduces himself into her room every evening."

"Oh, with what calumny the wretch punishes my weakness and my amour!" Those are Paola's words, as she pretends to faint.

"Your brother, your brother Paola, tell the truth! He too knows your crime: ask him whether I am a suborner."

At that moment, distressed valets bring in a corpse. I recognize Pietro. The word vengeance is repeated around me. A frightful vertigo and an inexpressible anguish stun me, overwhelm me, strike me with delirium . . .

After that, everything that happened appeared to me to be a bad dream, in the midst of which it was impossible for me to act, to think. I saw whirling around me a chapel, a priest, a woman, men, daggers . . . and when I recovered consciousness, Paola was lying by my side.

Uttering a cry of horror, I hurled myself away from that infamous bed; I ran to the door. A ship received me, and I fled Naples and Italy forever. I left Paola my property, my treasures, everything I possessed in the world. That was the price of treason, the price of adultery, the price of her brother's murder. May his blood fall back on the head of the culpable!

Oh, if it were only possible to deliver myself from such a memory! If I could, just for one night, sleep peacefully, without frightful dreams! For a night is so long . . . a night without sleep, a night in France, a night in winter, when the tempest is howling, as it does, and hurling cold swirls of snow against my shaking windows!

The Baptism Of A Bell
A Flemish Story
1820

She has passed like the grass of the field! In the
morning she flowered, with what grace you know;
and in the evening, she was withered and trampled
underfoot.
(Bossuet, "Funeral Oration for Madame Henriette.")[1]

HOW comfortable one is, in the morning, in a vast
soft armchair beside a crackling fire, before a little
round table on which is a lamp whose yellow radiance
gleams on a few volumes of Rabelais, Montaigne or Walter
Scott. How good it is, oh, how comfortable it is! One is
enveloped by a warm and voluptuous atmosphere; a fresh
and calm blood circulates in the veins. One experiences
I know not what physical wellbeing, which disposes the
imagination to a delightful release, a fantastic mixture
of memories of the past, present enjoyments and future
projects; it is an ideal existence that changes the location

---

1 The reference is to Jean-Bénigne Bossuet's funeral oration for
Henriette d'Angleterre (1644-1670), daughter of Charles I of England
and briefly wife of Philippe I, Duc d'Orléans, the brother of Louis XIV.
He was known at court as "Monsieur," so she became "Madame."

at every moment, reproducing itself in a thousand various forms and giving rise to the most bizarre, the sweetest, the most burlesque, the most touching, the most impossible and the most enchanting reveries; it is a drama in the manner of Shakespeare, a drama that progresses from a cemetery to a ballroom, from a kiss to a massacre. A child, one agitates a rattle; then, suddenly old, one meditates; one shivers amid snow, one sits down breathless under a fiery sky; then, there are the mystical transports of amour, abstract philosophical theories, narrow calculations of interest, profound meditations, infinity, eternity; a great thought gives rise to a risible sketch, and from the most ludicrous nightmare a sublime emotion springs forth.

How painful it is to extract oneself from the imaginary to return to the real, to quit one's vast soft armchair, the lukewarm atmosphere of one's study, to crouch down in a rude cart! If only its light canvas tent could provide protection against the north wind, or if, at least, fresh green foliage and fields of yellow wheat undulating like waves were offered to sight during the journey! But the red and desiccated leaves have fallen from the branches to strew the ground, from which icy whirlwinds sometimes lift them up; and the gaze can extend as far as it is able, but only perceives brown plains methodically furrowed by the plow.

Then again, nothing is more contrary to the caravans of the imagination, nothing hinders one more from mounting one's hobby-horse, as Sterne put it, than physical malaise, when cold is burning the eyes, reddening the face and dolorously gripping the stiffened limbs. If I had been able, at least, to avoid the harsh jolts that caused me to ache all over! But broad and muddy ruts, and then a cold rain, held me captive in the vehicle.

I was sad and discontented. I would have given a great deal to have refused the invitation that my childhood friend, the worthy Anselme, had sent me to attend the baptism of a bell destined for the church of which he had been curé for ten years.

A cry of joy that was heard when the carriage stopped, two large hands that pressed mine, two eyes shining with tears of pleasure, compensated me amply for the petty tribulations of my journey. Within a minute, I was carried rather than led to a blazing hearth; I was sat down before a table laden with my favorite dishes; and the good, the excellent Anselme, sitting facing me, was contemplating me with a gaze delectable moved by the sight of a cherished friend, a friend of childhood.

Soon, we found ourselves in the midst of memories of college, and we passed all our comrades in review, wondering: "What's become of him?"

And the good Anselme, who, in his peaceful retreat, had remained ignorant of the world and was not disabused of any of the tricks of a fervent and virtuous imagination, still entirely under the illusions of his youth, was astonished on learning of the very different destinies of those among whom we had lived as brothers for a long time.

While we were amazing one another, laughing together and becoming fonder, an antique clock chimed ten; it was necessary for us to separate. Anselme left me in order to make preparations to fulfill the duties of his ministry, and said that he would meet me at the church.

"It's Madame Caroline who's the godmother of the bell," he told me, as he went out.

It was not the first time that Anselme had mentioned Madame Caroline to me; the name was in all his letters;

admiring epithets always escorted it. I found it quite natural that the simple and good priest should wax ecstatic about the wife of the only rich landowner who lived in the village, so the emphatic manner in which Anselme, in quitting me, pronounced Madame Caroline's name did not produce a greater effect on me than the eulogies I had already read.

By virtue of I know not what puerility of self-regard, it was only after having examined attentively the Gothic stained glass windows of the church and the picturesque crows assembled against the railings of the choir that I directed my gaze toward the principal group.

Oh, how right Anselme was to laud Madame Caroline!

She was a young woman with beautiful black hair, large blue eyes full of tenderness, a fresh and pure complexion, an angelic and radiant physiognomy such as happiness alone can give. Her figure announced that she would be a mother in a matter of days—a mother for the first time—and her husband was there, next to her; by the emotion in his gaze, I understood that he was able to appreciate the angel that he had by his side.

From then on, all the good people kneeling around the altar, the embalmed and diaphanous clouds of incense, the mystical light of the candles, the veiled young women, and the wreaths of flowers with which they were covering the bell, all lost their charm and vanished from my sight; I no longer saw anything but the celestial creature who only interrupted her fervent prayer to dart amorous glances at her husband.

After the ceremony, Anselme came to say to me: "We're dining at the château."

I shivered with joy, and hastened to accompany my friend. To remember what he said, at length, while we walked, would be impossible for me; my ears heard the words, but my imagination paid no heed to them.

When we went into the drawing room, Madame Caroline was sitting at a piano; leaning over the back of her chair, her husband was listening silently. When she saw us, she stopped playing; I would have given anything in the world to hear, for a few seconds, the tone of that sweet voice.

As happy as any man ever was, Madame Caroline's husband felt the need to talk about his happiness. We had only been together for a quarter of an hour when we understood one another; united by a kind of intellectual freemasonry, we were chatting effusively, like two old and intimate friends.

He was rich, he was loved, he was about to be a father; he could do good, a great deal of good; so, not a single somber idea was offered to him for the future; everything appeared to him to be cheerful, fortunate, delightful. When he pronounced his wife's name, a pure and soft smile parted his lips; when he talked about the child that was about to be born, a radiant and indescribable expression blossomed in all his features.

Playful, naïve and tender, Madame Caroline joined in with that merry chatter. Never in my life have I had a more delightful meal . . .

When it was necessary for me to leave, I felt sad and uneasy. I was cordially invited to come back four days hence; you can imagine that I accepted gladly.

"So much the better," said Anselme. "You'll hear my bell ring; it will be in position."

Having returned home, I found myself agitated by a secret anxiety and a painful melancholy; in addition to that, I felt prey to I know not what need, that I could not have defined; everything around me seemed empty and deserted. I accused my bachelor independence, previously so precious in my eyes, of dryness and isolation.

Four days went by. The frost had rendered the roads practicable; I departed on foot to go to the château.

I could still only make out the little steeple of the church imperfectly when the plaintive sound of a bell began to ring; without any reason, my heart was gripped by sorrow. I hastened my steps.

Everything was in disorder in the presbytery; Anselme dissolved in tears. "It's to announce the death of Madame Caroline that the bell is ringing for the first time," he exclaimed, throwing himself into my arms. "She died this morning, giving birth to a stillborn child. Her husband collapsed under those rude blows; I've just left him dying himself."

I returned home bleakly, enumerating fearfully all the chances of happiness on which the unfortunate man, now so much to be pitied, had been counting the day before.

A year after the events I have just related, on returning from a long voyage, I was in haste to see Anselme, and I set out for the presbytery. On the way, I heard the sound of the bell, and its ringing added further to the bitterness of the sad memories to which I had delivered myself.

I asked a child clad in his Sunday clothes why the bell was ringing.

"Oh, Monsieur," he said, "it's for the wedding of Madame Caroline's husband."

The Stone Cross
A Spanish Story
1824

"Is that him? No, it's only the rustle of the foliage."
(Shakespeare, *King Lear*.)

THE crowd emerged from the cathedral of Saint
Sebastian and spread out in noisy and animated groups
over the steps of the temple and the Piazza di Castillo.

It was a spectacle that only Spain can offer, that picturesque mixture of bizarre and gracious costumes: monks
with shaven heads marching gravely beside pretty peasant
girls; the latter, playful and frivolous, getting ahead of the
most hasty. It was marvelous to see those charming young
women, as youthful and cheerful as Figaro's Suzanne, lifting up the long tresses of hair that descended over their
shoulders coquettishly, and folding their semi-naked arms
over an elegant corset, whose brown color formed with
a white skirt one of those contrasts so dear to Spaniards.
Beggars assembled in bands, enveloped in dirty mantles,
holding out filthy hands to receive the alms ceded to their
importunities and the dread inspired by their hideous appearance. Then there were men enveloped in their dark
hooded capes and large berets from which long curls of hair

escaped; and señoras with black or white veils; and elegant youths clad in the French fashion; and foreigners, whose pale and delicate complexion provided a contrast in the midst of all those brown and passionate physiognomies.

Léonora went through the crowd rapidly; she did not even notice that all eyes turned toward her in admiration, and all the young men leaned toward their friends' ears to whisper: "See how beautiful she is!"

In fact, no señora was as able as her to throw a light veil over hair blacker than the blackest fabric; none could dispose with as much grace the embalmed flowers that hung down over a pure forehead and add their brightness to two shining creole eyes. At each of her hasty steps, her short and narrow dress betrayed voluptuous forms and allowed a glimpse of a foot of delightful smallness, uncommon in Spain.

But what do the gazes and admiration of the crowd matter to her? A mysterious hand has slipped a note into hers; pretending to readjust her veil, she deposits the imperceptible scroll on a breast palpitating with amour and anxiety, and hastens to reach the country house that she occupies at the extremity of the outlying district, not far from the sea.

There she reads the precious paper, rereads it and covers it with burning kisses. It only contains a few words: *Midnight, at the foot of the stone cross.* But a cherished hand, which trembled with emotion and could hardly guide the pen, has traced those words, sweet precursors of a rendezvous: a final rendezvous, for Fernando is leaving the beautiful land of Catalonia tomorrow, perhaps forever.

And even if he were not leaving it, would the unfortunate lovers be able to see one another again? They have scarcely succeeded in deceiving the jealousy of Don Merando, retained in Madrid for a month; they could only meet at long intervals, by dint of ruses, audacity and peril; tomorrow he will come back, and will not leave again; tomorrow, his piercing gaze will no longer turn away from Léonora.

How slow the hours preceding a rendezvous are to pass! How difficult it is to feign a calm and profound sleep, when the anguish of doubt, dread and expectation send a burning, agitating fire coursing through the veins!

Those whose unquiet surveillance she fears have never yielded to sleep so belatedly! Never has silence taken so long to establish itself in the country house! Finally, however, she can no longer hear anything. Everything is mute, everything is asleep. Hastily, she puts on a few garments, and, enveloped in a large cloak, she races to the stone cross.

Fernando is not yet there.

It is the first time that he has not arrived at the rendezvous first. Why shiver with terror? Midnight has barely sounded. Then again, surely, Fernando's friends have come to say their farewells; they've retained him or a few moments more. Poor young man! He's cursing that fatal constraint . . . oh, how Léonora's kisses will compensate him when he arrives!

The clock of the metropolis chimes one o'clock . . .

It chimes two . . .

It chimes three . . .

It chimes four . . .

Fernando had not yet appeared!

It is impossible for human speech to express the anguish experienced by Léonora during her long wait.

Dawn was beginning to break; a few peasants were already appearing in the fields; Poor Léonora got up from the cross, at the foot of which she had been kneeing, her hands joined, as if the chaste Madonna listened to adulterous prayers.

"Oh," she murmured, despairingly. "I shall never see my Fernando again."

"He's at the rendezvous!" cried a terrible voice. It was the voice of Merando, Léonora's husband.

And in her terror, the unfortunate woman tried to embrace the stone cross with her weakening arms...but she recoiled, uttering a scream. The cross was covered with blood, and the mound had been freshly dug.

The Violin

A fragment imitative of the German

1826

"He's my friend, my only friend my consolation!"
"I'll give you six francs for him."
"Here he is, for I'm hungry; but I no longer have
anything in the world to love me."
(Owen, "The Blind Man and his Dog.")[1]

"MONSIEUR, there's an excellent violin for sale."
Six months before, the young man had set aside
the sum that would serve him to procure the instrument
he so desired; for six months, on awakening, he had been
dreaming delightfully of the pleasure he would experience
in making an excellent Cremona violin speak under his
bow.

The words of his domestic, however, caused him a disagreeable sensation.

It is true that his two feet were resting warmly on the
fire-irons; it is true that, his eyes fixed on the hearth, he
was plunged in the kind of reverie that is as pleasant as it
is vague, in the semi-somnolence of the mental faculties

---

1 Not an actual quotation, although one of John Owen's sermons did
make reference to the utility of a blind man's dog.

produced by the quietude of the mind and the wellbeing of the body.

It was, therefore, with an ill humor of sorts, firmly decided to find the offered violin detestable, that he said: "Let me see it."

The man whom the domestic had brought appeared to be about sixty years of age; not a single patch soiled his threadbare garments; his face expressed an insouciant bonhomie. He placed the black wooden case that he was holding on a table, took a little key from his pocket, and, after having lifted the instrument from its case, he sighed, passing the worn sleeve of his frock-coat over the shiny wood of the violin—after which, he presented the instrument with a smile that mingled sadness and satisfaction.

"Is that really a Cremona violin?" the young man asked, in the disdainful tone that one affects when one wishes to depreciate an object.

For his only response, the old man picked up the instrument and drew sounds of a great purity therefrom.

The young man was convinced of the violin's merit, but he persevered nonetheless in his refusal to buy it.

"It wouldn't suit me," he said.

Then the old man started gently replacing the violin in its box of black wood. While he was occupied in that task, a large tear trickled down his brown cheek.

That tear stirred the young man's compassion; he became discontented with himself, as if he had done something bad; nevertheless, by virtue of I know not what stubbornness, he let the old man lock the case, put the key back in his pocket and take a few steps in order to leave.

Already, he was trying to forget the large tear that he had seen; already he was trying to resume the pleasant reverie of a little while before, when he heard the old man's footfalls coming back.

"Monsieur," he said, "it's just that I need money."

There was so much unhappiness and supplication in the manner in which he pronounced those few words, that the young man felt moved to tears. For a moment, he almost asked the old man to pardon his harshness, and offer to pay him double the violin's value, but a false shame held him back.

There was nothing but embarrassment in his voice when he asked: "How much do you want for it?"

"I'll leave that to you," replied the old man, and, which a hand tremulous with emotion, he hastened to open the case again.

"I don't do business like that; tell me what you want for it."

"Monsieur . . . it seems to me that it's worth . . ." He named a figure.

It was less than half the real value.

At any other time, the young man would have blushed at taking advantage of the distress of an unfortunate, but there are days when one is atypically stiff and surly.

"That's too high. I doubt that it's worth that. I can only give you . . ." He named a figure.

The old man darted a melancholy and complaisant glance; then he said, sadly: "Oh, Monsieur is too knowledgeable to value such an instrument so slightly."

It must be said, to the young man's shame, that he was more sensible to that miserable flattery than to the old man's tear; the fear of not being reckoned a connoisseur put an end to his miserly underestimation, but, as I said, he was under a bad influence, and that influence suggested another ploy to him.

"I'd like to give you the price you're asking, but in your turn, it's necessary for you to buy this violin from me; I'll pay you the difference in price."

A sigh of resignation and a nod of assent were the old man's response.

Shame pricked the young man, and prevented him, this time, from over-valuing his own violin.

Without making any complaint, without saying a single word, the old man acceded to everything the young man wished. After that, he left, bowing very low, walked as rapidly as he could to the door of a house of undistinguished appearance, and went up to the fifth floor.

Then, sitting down at the edge of the bed where a sick and aged woman lay, he spread a number of five-franc pieces over the coverlet.

The invalid put her hands together in surprise and blessed the good Lord. "My love, where did you get so much money?" she asked, joyful and relieved.

The old man did not reply; he began to play the violin. Internally, nevertheless, he was joyful and afflicted at the same time, because his wife was unaware of the great sacrifice he had made for her, but also because she owed that fortunate ignorance to her poor taste, to the lack of finesse in her hearing, to her incapacity to distinguish—her, the wife of such a fine musician—a poor fiddle from an excellent Cremona violin.

The Killer
A French Story
1825

"In that fashion, then, a man, without having
courage, is sure of killing his man and not being
killed?"
(Molière, *Bourgeois gentilhomme*.)

The good young man could not imagine how, the
sins not being on his side, the shame of them was.
"But the laws of honor!" the cry came from all
directions. "Wretch, you're doomed if you don't
satisfy them!"
"I'll satisfy them, then."
(Saintine, *Jonathan the Visionary*.)[1]

I HAD heard the cavatina from *Il Barbiere di Siviglia* sung
many a time. Never, until that day, had the delightful air
been understood, either by me or the singer. But her, the

---

1 *Jonathan le visionnaire, Contes philosophiques et moral* (1825, in two
volumes) by X. B. Saintine is a collection that has much in common
with Berthoud's in the wide range of its settings and its habit of
employing headquotes for each item (authentic in Saintine's case),
but the stories are considerably longer and more elaborate, and their
morals less replete with disenchantment.

Signora Camilla, oh, what an expression she gave to it! How she revealed the soul of thoughts and sensations that remained unperceived by anyone but her—her, a young woman with big blue eyes, and a tender and mischievous smile.

To begin with, it is a protestation of naïve, solemn, profoundly felt love, a protestation of Spanish love; after that, and insensibly, the mischievous and infantile nature of Rosina gets the upper hand; for those grave thoughts, even when passion produces them, cannot preoccupy the head of a frivolous sixteen-year-old for long. Then come the fantastic caprices of light and bantering lines; she laughs at her guardian, she rejoices in escaping from him, and thanks to the tricks of her imagination, wretched and under lock and key, here she is singing about joy and liberty!

There was a young Italian next to me who could not take his eyes off the cantatrice.

No breath escaped his parted lips; tears glistened in his eyes; the ineffable intoxication of his pale face expressed more than enthusiasm; it was love.

And when she had finished the cavatina, while transports were bursting forth on all sides, Camilla darted a furtive glance at him. He was loved as much as he loved.

Oh, how I envied his happiness! For one must be so happy to hear a thousand voices saluting the woman one loves! One must be so happy, on looking around, to see nothing but attentive faces, cheeks inflamed by delight; and then a sign from her, a sign that no one else understands, a sign that says: "That glory, it's yours, it belongs to you like all that I possess, it belongs to you as Camilla belongs to you!"—and then the memory of confused words of love, of languorous smiles, white and semi-naked arms embracing tenderly . . .

Oh, how I envied his happiness! Me, alone in the world, who has no one to love me . . . no one.

To the young man's right was a stranger who, since the beginning of the opera, I had cursed silently more than once. There was throughout the man a repulsive mixture of inquisitiveness and bad taste; sprawling on his banquette, he was rubbing elbows with his neighbors, and, doubtless gorged on drink—for a dense redness circled his eyes and expanded over his cheeks—he continually troubled the spectacle with brutal reflections made in a voice that was almost loud; several times he had provoked a disapproving "Shh!" but without paying any attention to it.

Entirely given over to his emotions, Camilla's lover had not noticed all that discourtesy, but when the scene remained occupied by Bartolo and the worthy Basile, he gently pushed away his neighbor's elbow, the discomfiting fashions of which he had noticed for the first time.

I don't know what the other said, but I saw the Italian's eyes light up and his cheeks become crimson.

However, he kept silent.

Emboldened by so much moderation, his antagonist made a threat and raised his hand. He was challenged; the Italian struck him in the face.

"Let's go outside!" they exclaimed, at the same time.

As they drew away, a cry emerged from the stage; then I saw the young man shiver, and hesitate, with tears in his eyes; but his adversary turned his head to see whether he was being followed, and he marched on.

I cannot explain the interest that Camilla's lover inspired in me. It was at that point that I followed him to discover the outcome of the scene.

Two men of rather nasty appearance accompanied the

brutal stranger; the Italian was alone, and darted anxious glances around him.

"You're a foreigner, you have no witness," I said, going forward. "I'll serve you."

He extended his hand and shook mine; I understood from that grip how desperate he was.

After having obtained weapons, we traversed several solitary streets and emerged from the town.

There was the most beautiful moonlight I had ever seen; the sky was pure and calm, the air imprinted with a voluptuous freshness. There was I know not what irony of wellbeing and sensuality therein that rendered me even sadder.

Having reached a terrain appropriate for combat, the stranger took off his coat tranquilly; he rolled the sleeves of his shirt up to the elbow, carefully examined the sharpened foil, and put himself on guard like a fencing-master, smiling. What horror possessed me at the sight of that smile!

At the first pass, the Italian fell, his breast run through.

He tried to speak; the blood prevented him from doing so; he tried to make a sign; the convulsions of death prevented him from doing that.

"Camilla! Camilla!!" I said to him, for I had understood his final thought.

I thought I felt his hand press mine, and then he stiffened, and it was all over. In the meantime, the man who had killed him wiped his bloody weapon and chatted with his companions.

"Help me," I said to them, in my trouble. "Help me to carry this unfortunate somewhere where he can obtain help."

The assassin looked at him as an old physician looks at a patient; he interrogated the pulse of the cadaver, and said: "Let's go, let's go! He has no need of help; he's dead."

They left me alone with their victim.

I felt full of fear and anxiety; I did not even know the name of the man who lay at my feet; I did not even know to what hands I ought to return the bloody corpse.

As I was looking around aimlessly, I saw the moonlight glinting on the silver clasp of a wallet. It was the Italian's. It had fallen out of his coat during the preparations for the combat. I opened it.

It contained a portrait of Camilla and a letter addressed to Signor Paolo Frienzi; I read it; it was a love letter, the first he had received from her, which a hand full of emotion had dated that very day.

You will understand what my sensations were on reading the tender and happy words of the young woman, at night, next to the corpse of her lover.

Some peasants passed by, going to market with a cart; I persuaded them to transport the Italian's remains to the town. When he arrived, I informed the law of the night's sad event and I went to Camilla's house.

Pale, and in a horrible resignation of despair, she understood as soon as I spoke what I had me to tell her; she listened to me without interrupting, and only spoke when I had finished.

I sought in vain in her motionless features for something of the previous evening's Rosina; it was no longer her; it was vengeance personified.

"His name! His name!" she said, finally.

"I don't know it," I replied.

"His name!" she repeated, throwing herself toward me. "His name! Tell me! I want to know! Tell me!" She held a stiletto to my breast.

I seized her arm and turned it away. "Heaven is my witness that I don't know!"

"Forgive me, oh, forgive me . . . you who saw him die, you who received his last breath, you so generous to him!" Then she murmured: "It doesn't matter. I shall find out!"

Four years after that event I made a journey to Naples. One evening I went to La Scala; *Il Barbiere di Siviglia* was playing.

Rosina appeared. Rosina was Signora Camilla.

I shivered, and by virtue of a mechanical movement, I looked for Paolo Frienzi beside me.

His murderer was seated on the banquette on which I was sitting!

Like me, Camilla suddenly caught sight of him, for an exclamation from her interrupted the cavatina, which she was then singing—but her emotion disappeared immediately, and her voice had never appeared to me so ravishing and bold.

That made me feel ill. Her, singing that air, in front of the assassin!

I had to leave the theater, for I could not bear such a proof of insensibility. I set about wandering around Naples, and when I returned close to La Scala, the crowd had just finished coming out.

Suddenly, at the corner of a street, a woman, running, bumped into me. She raised her head, recognized me and uttered a cry: "He's avenged!" she said—and her hands, which gripped mine, were holding a stiletto still wet with blood.

The Actress
A French Adventure
1826

So that's how one loves!
(André Chenier, *Elegy* XXVIII.)[1]

THERE are moments in life when I know not what vague sadness fatigues an anxious agitation. It must have something to with physical impatience, nervous agitation produced by the dubious whistle of a brushed fabric or the mordant screech of a file. A frivolous contrariety, a wound inflicted on self-esteem, those are usually the causes of that mental irritation. Ashamed of finding oneself afflicted by such miserable trivia, discontented with oneself and others, one experiences an insupportable isolation; one feels an imperious need for consolations of sentiment, and not words, of the affectionate caresses of which women alone possess the secret, and know how to soothe and mollify the dolors of the soul so well. Oh, how relieved one would be if, taking refuge with one of those cherished beings, one could only bury one's head in her bosom and shed tears there freely!

1 The poet André Chenier (1762-1794), a victim of the Terror, became a hero to the members of the French Romanic Movement, hailed as an important precursor.

173

Such was the mental condition of Léopold, a young sublieutenant in the hussars garrisoned in a town in the Midi; gambling losses, reprimands from his colonel, and a few sarcasms from his comrades had rendered him unhappy for the rest of the day, for Léopold only received a modest pension from his father, then exhausted, and he was amply endowed with that irritable susceptibility, the consequence of an ardent imagination and a good opinion of himself, which one does not lack at the age of twenty-two.

He had sought in vain to extract himself from the disagreeable memories that were tormenting him; the proof of that was evident in the books scattered around him; but as one is no more free to set aside one idea and devote oneself to another than to make one's stomach digest well when it refuses to fulfill its functions. Léopold's ideas remained permanently there before his imagination.

A curse on the position in which fate has placed me! he thought. *Restrained by the exigencies of an endless hierarchy of superiors, surrounded by frivolous and spiteful comrades, why can I not deliver myself from such servitude? Insensate! For the pleasure of sporting a moustache and hearing a long saber dangling at my side, I've foolishly disdained the peaceful existence I could have found in my father's house, in the bosom of lucrative employment! Isn't the least of his clerks more fortunate than me? He's nailed to a desk all day but, good God, is my wearying, uniform idleness any less annoying? Making soldiers maneuver for I don't know how many eternal hours, standing guard, spending the rest of the time in a café, wasn't that my day yesterday, my day today and my day tomorrow?*

Why didn't I listen to my father's sage advice? Who can tell? Perhaps I'd already be married . . . married! On returning home, I wouldn't any longer find that solitude that kills me: a benevolent smile, an amicable world, would greet me on my arrival, and my forehead would expand if it were furrowed by care . . . Never alone with myself; intimate conversations, full of abandon, delightful! An emotion responding to each of my emotions! A lively, solid, understood, shared affection! Joy everywhere, amour everywhere. Nothing desolate, nothing indifferent! That, oh that, is the happiness that I've lost by my own fault!

Léopold, a soldier, envied the existence of the tradesman he had once disdained; as a tradesman, Léopold would not have failed to envy the existence of the soldier, embellished in his eyes by the illusions of regret. Alas, happiness is too often for the man who does not have it! "He goes forth ever-yearning," as Montaigne says, "for the good things he cannot have, instead of settling for those he has."

"What the devil are you doing there? Are you asleep?"

That loud exclamation of a youthful voice, full of merriment, suddenly interrupted Léopold's mental philippic.

"A plague on you, my dear," continued the sublieutenant who had just come in. "We'll arrive too late; the performance will have started. Poor Victorine! She'll be utterly nonplussed if, contrary to habit, mine isn't the first face she perceives when the curtain goes up."

Mademoiselle Victorine was an actress, Monsieur Gustave's mistress.

In regiments of hussars, one is not usually very discreet in matters of amorous intrigues, especially intrigues of the wings, so Gustave gave no thought at all to hiding his liaisons with the pretty soubrette.

He walked all over town with her; in the middle of performances he exchanged winks with her that were not unintelligible for anyone; his greatest pleasure was to see all the eyes of the spectators directed toward him, all the faces with expressions of bewilderment, and the equivocal smile excited by a scandal that one dares not criticize overtly. Young, rich, from a powerful family, the scatterbrain found it extremely piquant to stare in the face what he called bourgeois prudery. Without the scandal, he might have left Victorine after a week, but it had lasted for more than six weeks, because people were clucking about it all over town.

During the performance, Gustave had a whim to go meet his mistress at the theater. "Come with me," he demanded of Léopold.

Léopold hesitated.

"Oh, that's right!" Gustave went on, laughing. "It's necessary not to compromise oneself!"

Léopold did not hesitate any longer; the fear of ridicule stifled his reluctance, and he followed Gustave, trying to imitate, in places that were entirely new to him, the ease and aplomb of his comrade.

While they were both chatting with Victorine, another actress, Coraly, came cheerfully and unceremoniously to join in the conversation.

That conversation caused Léopold an extreme surprise; he could not get over it; it was not the brazen discourse of courtesans; it was a mixture of pleasantries, undoubtedly amusing but not licentious, an exchange of witty remarks, fortunate expressions, delicate and mischievous comments.

Never, above all, had anyone shown such wit as Victorine's cheerful companion; never had anyone seized with more tact even the most imperceptible ridicules; never had anyone attacked them with a more pitiless gaiety.

Victorine, Gustave, Léopold, everything that happened to be in the theater, was harassed by the pretty satirist. Even the prompter, a fat and unkempt man scared by smallpox, received his fair share and, leaning against one of the wings, forgot, while listening to Coraly, to go back to his hole and give the signal for the second act.

Léopold was delighted, intoxicated. It was with difficulty that Gustave dragged him away from the stage and back into the auditorium.

Throughout the rest of the performance, Léopold could not take his eyes off Coraly. The next day, the first person she perceived, on going in for the performance, was the young officer from the previous day. She greeted him with a smile that filled Léopold with joy.

From then on, he avidly sought out every opportunity to find himself in Coraly's company; he never quit the wings. The more he saw of her, the more he wanted to see her; his passion acquired new strength every day. However, he dared not tell Coraly that he loved her madly. In vain, all day long, he heard his comrades talking about the facile successes obtained by them among the population of actresses. An insurmountable timidity prevented him from speaking. Twenty times he was ready to do it, twenty times a convulsive contraction sealed his lips. He promised himself incessantly to be bolder, but at the sight of Coraly all his fine resolutions vanished, and the poor young man could only look at her and smile.

Finally, one evening when she had welcomed him with a marked benevolence, after a long conversation in which the ravishing creature had been more delightful than ever, Léopold took her hand passionately and murmured a few incoherent words, Coraly responded with a loud burst of laughter, and Léopold, with a fiery blush on his cheeks, went away confused and desperate. He spent all night without closing his eyes, cursing his disappointment, his maladroit timidity, Coraly's burst of laughter, and envying the brazen assurance that was worth so much good fortune to Gustave.

Finally, when daylight began to appear, an incomplete, burning, agitated drowsiness, the result of depression and fatigue, gradually took possession of him. He was not asleep; he was not awake; fantastic visions whirled in his dazed imagination; his faculties, half-suspended, floated in a strange vagueness, and I know not what anguish squeezed every fiber of his breast dolorously.

In the midst of that confusion of ideas, that nightmarish disorder, he believed he heard the dubious accents of a voice that was not unknown to him; they drew nearer; they became more distinct; it seemed that someone wanted to come in, that his domestic was refusing them entry. The door opened abruptly. A young man precipitated forcibly into the chamber; he fell into an armchair and burst out laughing. During that joyful convulsion his hat fell on to the floor; long tresses of black hair fell over his shoulders.

"Coraly! Oh, Coraly!" cried Léopold.

Six months...how that short space of time can change a man's fate! Six months have gone by. Two of the most ordinary of life's events, two of those that occupy the vulgar for an hour and are forgotten—a young cousin's fall from a horse and the devastating apoplexy of an aged uncle—have rendered poor Sublieutenant Léopold a millionaire!

In the midst of a dust cloud, four horses are drawing his post-chaise; the postillions are stimulating them, their whips in the air; that splendid and almost regular sound, the gallop of horses and the rattle of wheels, the jolts of the carriage, the landscape that appears to be fleeing, rapid and dazzling, incessantly renewed, past the window; ardent thoughts, a fortune in which he can hardly believe, the ardent pleasures that await him on his arrival—all of that produces in Léopold a tumultuous inebriation, delirious transports. The carriage is flying; it is too slow for his liking. As if he could hasten it, he agitates, gets up, falls back, only to get up again, curses the postillions, flatters them, insults them, and promises them money.

Perhaps he is paying too much for the joy of seeing Coraly again a few moments sooner? Coraly, from whom he has been separated for four months! Coraly, from whom he has received so many proofs of love! For, when he was poor, when his improvident negligence and his father's parsimonious prudence had reduced him to contracting debts; when he had to submit to the insolent persecutions of impatient creditors; when they were about to divulge his shame and is distress, what generous friend gave him the means to appease them, and save his gravely compromised reputation? She was far from being rich, however; to procure such a considerable sum, she had had to sell her jewels, everything precious that she possessed, even clothes!

He had only found that out afterwards. Oh, certainly, if he had known then all the generosity, all the delicacy of such a sacrifice, he would never have permitted it. Good Coraly! Now he can recompense her worthily for so much love, so much virtue; it's necessary that she renounces the theater; it's necessary that she come traveling with him in Switzerland, Italy, and Germany; he wants to flee for her an egotistical, narrow society, prejudices that can only compromise their tenderness.

After long voyages, they will come to inhabit some delightful and unknown redoubt; there, peaceful, happy, sufficient for one another, they will spread happiness over everything that surrounds them. Beneficence in one of Coraly's virtues; how many times he has seen her covertly deposit rich alms in the hand of an unfortunate who dares not beg! And that old actress, wretched, without bread, without shelter, who as weeping one evening at the theater door . . . he will remember it with emotion as long as he lives . . . Coraly emptied her purse for her; and it was necessary for everyone else to contribute to her good deed. Woe betide anyone who did not accord a gift to the playful solicitor's smile A bitter sarcasm punished him immediately; self-esteem and dread opened purses of which avarice had never resolved to undo the strings.

But now an austere and somber daylight succeeds the morning light that was just reflected, dazzling and gilded, from the glass of the window; the wheels cause a heavy drawbridge to resonate over which they are passing between two high towers; then the carriage traverses long solitary streets . . .

It stops.

Léopold leaps to the ground.

"Coraly? The residence of Mademoiselle Coraly?"

Everyone knows the dwelling of the public's favorite actress; a street-porter offers to take him there.

The happy young man climbs the stairs rapidly, bumps into a door without a key, then listens: a sleepy voice replies. It's not hers. Oh, the damned porter has made a mistake.

Those gross accents are not unknown to him; they belong to the prompter.

Where, then to find a guide at this hour, to Coraly's lodgings.

Of course—the prompter!

Léopold knocks again; the semi-naked prompter comes to open up, and recoils, stupefied.

A burst of laughter emerges from the bed.

"Léopold, here! What a pleasant surprise!"

The Gypsy Girl
A Catalan Story
1829

> Everything is changed for me far from the homeland!
> Even time, time itself, no longer has an even flow;
> The cold days of winter prolong their duration;
> Summer has only long nights . . .
> Exile is the greatest of evils.
> (Madame Dufresnoy, *Alcée*.)[1]

THERE is no more beautiful place in all the world than Catalonia, Catalonia with its Pyrenees that raise their snowy white summits, scarred with precipices, all the way to the clouds; Catalonia, on the rocks of which the roaring waves of the Mediterranean break.

Its plains are fields of wheat, its marshes rivers, its hills vineyards, olive groves and orange groves; its mines of marble and iron. Ask a bold diver what rich coral is hidden under the waves that bathe the shores of Catalonia!

Oh, don't breathe for a day, only for a single day, the lukewarm and voluptuous air that one breathes there; don't raise your gaze toward the deep azure of its beautiful

---

1 Fictitious.

sky; lazily lying in a boat that is drifting slowly with the insensible current of a river, don't contemplate, on either bank, the groups of young women with dark eyes and slim waists, in short and tight dresses that design ravishing figures; don't listen to their songs; turn your eyes away when they form the petulant dances that make one shiver with amorous desire. Oh, believe me; for after that, a memory full of regrets, a sad and languishing illness, like homesickness, will come to squeeze your heart and fill your eyes with tears.

And yet I am far, far away from beautiful Catalonia, the mountains where I was born, where my father died, where my daughter . . . my daughter . . . ! My dagger has avenged her! Three days and three nights, lying prone on a solitary rock, eyes watchful, a finger on the trigger of my rifle, I waited for her murderer. He came; he fell; he writhed in the dust; his convulsive hands furrowed the sand; blood spurted from his breast.

During the hour that his death-throes lasted, I stayed there motionless, contemplating my vengeance. Afterwards it was necessary to flee, like a miserable assassin, robbing travelers like a coward, for their laws—their justice, as they call it—offer for the head of a father avenging his daughter the same price that they give for that of a brigand!

If people knew what wealth a miserable Andalusian has stolen from me by his execrable cunning; if they knew all the evils that weigh upon old gypsies, instead of looking curiously at my unfamiliar garments and my bronzed face, instead of pointing fingers at me and murmuring: "He's a refugee, he's a murderer," perhaps someone would offer me a friendly hand, saying with compassion: "Son of a gypsy woman, you are greatly to be pitied!"

Oh yes, I'm greatly to be pitied! And once, I was happy, in the evening, when after unfastening the white veil whose folds enveloped her head, my daughter, my Peppa, threw back her long black hair over her shoulders. After that, she knelt at my feet, she put her two hands in mine, she fixed her large attentive eyes upon me, and then, laughing at my serious words, she suddenly fled to go and climb some very high rock.

From the threshold of my cabin, I called to her, agitated by I know not what fearful joy; I was glad of her agility and the grace she deployed in those perilous pleasures, and trembled nevertheless that they might become fatal to her. But the delightful child, without listening to me, laughed, clapped her hands, bounded over the rock, and then started to sing some Bohemian song, one of those songs only known to our race, which ought to accompany a light and passionate dance. At each of Peppa's gestures, fugitive reflections of pale light sprang forth round her; it was the moonlight that had just illuminated one of the broad silver rings with which her bare arms and legs were laden, in the gypsy fashion.

While I contemplated her, in a trace of delight and terror, she suddenly launched forth, and I scarcely had time to fear that her foot might slip on posing on a spur of rock, that her hand might lose its grip on the frail bush that suspended her in mid-air when my daughter was already hugging me in her arms, offering her fresh brown cheeks to kisses.

Such had been her games one beautiful autumn evening when she came back into my cabin and sat down beside me.

"Do you know, Father, that Don Fernando de Gemellas, Doña Bianca's fiancé, arrived a little while ago at the castillo of Melposo. He's come from Seville. It's a beautiful thing to see his carriages, his horses, his mules and all his domestics! They're not, like our Catalans, dressed in a simple striped jacket and short trousers that leave their alpargata-shod legs bare. A silken net envelops their hair, which is much more graceful than the red cloth bonnets of our mountain peasants. Their rich velvet jackets are overlaid with braid; they have broad brightly-colored belts, elegant gaiters and vast cloaks.

"But if you had seen the majestic features of their master, Father! He saluted is fiancée with a sad and thoughtful expression. I can understand why the young man is sad, though; he'd never seen the woman he has to marry; it's a marriage made by their parents; how can one be joyful, Father, marrying a woman one has never seen, even if she's a great lady, the owner of ten castillos like the one at Melposo, and more beautiful than Doña Bianca, who isn't at all?"

All evening, she talked to me about Don Fernando. The next day, she went out very early in order to go to the castillo. She was sure of being welcome there, for everyone loved the little gypsy girl, so pretty and playful.

"Goodbye," she said to me. "I'm in a hurry to see Don Fernando's beautiful carriages again."

I started to smile at her childish urgency. *A fortunate age*, I thought, *at which the thought of a little splendor causes such keen and innocent joy!*

Insensate! Why, oh why, didn't I force her to stay with me? Why didn't I lock her in my cabin, and forbid entry to it, with my rifle on my shoulder? One of Don Fernando's valets, one Pedrille, would not have put his indecent arm around her virginal waist and would not have dared to say: "Be the concubine of a valet."

Poor weak child! What could she do against that robust scoundrel except utter plaintive cries? Alas! And me, comfortably couched a long way away, in my cabin, sleeping profoundly. Someone other than her father came to protect her!

It was Don Fernando; he came running as fast as his horse could carry him. At the sudden sight of Pedrille, who ran away abruptly, the animal reared up. The unsaddled rider fell and struck his head against a spur of rock.

When the domestics who were following their master at a distance arrived, Peppa had already dressed the young señor's broad wound; his head was resting gently on her knees; her veil had been torn up to staunch the blood and envelop Fernando's head in a bandage. When he recovered consciousness he shook Peppa's hand to thank her, and his men carried him to the castillo.

The next day, Pedrille appeared at the door of my cabin. I seized my rifle to lay him dead. I wish to God that Peppa had not deflected my carbine, whose bullet went whistling to embed itself in the trunk of an orange tree. My Peppa would still be alive; I wouldn't be alone in the world with no one to love me.

Pedrille had come on his master's orders to beg the pardon of the person he had outraged in such a cowardly fashion. She received him disdainfully, and he went away.

A fortnight went by, during which a strange change took place in the young woman's character; from being cheerful and playful, she became pensive and sad; I often surprised her with large tears in her eyes, and the one whose sole joy I had once been then seemed to fear my presence.

There was no mistaking such symptoms; Peppa was in love. A young woman rarely confides amorous secrets to her father, even when she cherishes him as Peppa cherished me; I therefore resolved to spy on her secretly, and discover by that means who as the object of her tenderness, and whether he was worthy of my daughter.

If he isn't worthy of her, I thought, *we'll leave my peaceful hut; if necessary, I'll resume the errant life of gypsies, even if, like so many of them, I have no other resource on which to live than shearing mules . . .*

But I wouldn't be reduced to that. I had buried a sum of six thousand ducats in my cabin, and it could, with the price of my hut, allow us to live for ten years. God would do the rest.

We would therefore travel together for some time; then we would settle down in some other part of Catalonia. My Peppa would soon become placid and happy again, for at fifteen, there's no love that can resist absence and distraction.

My surprise equaled my despair when I discovered that Peppa was having frequent meetings with Pedrille. All my blood boiled with indignation. How could a gypsy girl be smitten with an Andalusian valet, a coward who only had courage enough the insult feeble young girls?

I slid furtively behind a bush; I lent an ear to their conversation. Pedrille was speaking in a respectful tone, and it wasn't about himself that he was talking.

"Don Fernando can't see you again today," he said. "He's ill, and besides, to leave his room would compromise your secret. As for receiving you at the castillo, it's even more impossible; Doña Bianca already has too many suspicions of her fiancé's infidelity.

"Take this letter, Señorita, it will plead better in favor of my master than a poor valet; it will let you know the plan he's made to be his dear Peppa's forever."

With those words he dropped a letter at her feet and disappeared.

A slight sound was heard; Peppa picked up the letter, hid it in her bosom, and I saw her walk precipitately toward my cabin

When I returned, she was sleeping profoundly; I didn't have the courage to wake her, and I put off until the following day warning her that the love of a great lord is fatal for a poor creature like her, and that it was necessary to renounce those sweet girlish illusions.

Let her be happy tonight, I thought, *and let the despair and tears only commence tomorrow for the poor unfortunate girl.*

It was well into the night before I was able to go to sleep.

Suddenly, I woke up with a start; oppressed by a presentiment, I ran to my daughter's bed. My daughter had disappeared!

A letter she had left on her bedside table begged me to pardon her for her flight. *Don Fernando*, she wrote, *is going to marry me secretly, tonight, and take me to Andalusia right away. There, Father, once the anger of a powerful family is appeased, you'll rejoin your Peppa, to witness her happiness.*

I ran toward the castillo in order to snatch my daughter away from her seducer, if there was still time, for would a proud Andalusian lord ever marry a poor Bohemian? He could only want to seduce her.

Halfway along the road, I thought I recognized my daughter's voice. I headed in the direction from which he cries were coming. In the moonlight, I saw Peppa; she was half-naked, her hair scattered, a fiery redness in her face, her eyes wild. She didn't recognize me . . . she lay there, stupid and plaintive, in her father's arms.

Her incoherent speech, her insensate words, finally told me the frightful plot of which she was the victim. Fernando's letters were made up; Pedrille had fabricated them. She had thought to hold a beloved spouse, Don Fernando, in her arms, and it was on the wretched Pedrille that she had lavished her embraces and her amour.

She languished for two more days, prey to a burning and delirious fever; then she died without having recovered her reason for a moment, without having addressed a single word to her father, who was weeping beside her.

I cut her black hair and put it in my bosom; then the body was confided to the earth with the ceremony customary among gypsies. When it was all over, I picked up my rifle.

You know the rest.

That's why I left Catalonia, the most beautiful country in the world, forever.

Agib
or, Wishes
An Arab Tale
Year of the Hegira 523; 913 of the Christian Era[1]

> Happiness is the horizon of the desert; having
> arrive breathless at the summit of the mountain of
> sand where he thought he would reach it, the
> traveler despairs in suddenly perceiving the
> immense extent that recoils before him; then he
> looks back and bitterly regrets the places he has
> quit.
>
> (Almozar.)[2]

FOR three days, the angel of death had kept the point of
his fatal scimitar suspended over the mouth of Caliph
Ebn-Alnalchar.[3] The vizier and the emirs were prostrate

---

1 The year of the Hegira begins its count from 622 in the Christan
Era, so this calculation of equivalence is extremely inaccurate
2 The quotation is fictitious, but Almozar is a character, described as
"the Linus of the Persians," in a poem by Charles Hubert Millevoye,
published posthumously in 1823.
3 Author's note: "Orientals believe that the angel of death keeps a
scimitar suspended over the mouth of a sick person, from the point
of which three drops fall; the first takes away the use of speech, the
second forces the soul to emerge, and the third initiates the corruption

before his royal bed; some promised the divine prophet to make a pilgrimage to Mecca and kiss the black stone of Mount Arafat;[1] others tore their garments, and seemed to be striving to hold back sobs that burst forth regardless. The people filled the mosques, for the Cadi's staff meted out justice to those who did not pray for the commander of the believers.

But when the exterior terrace of the palace suddenly glittered with the light of a thousand torches,[2] the inanimate body of Ebn-Alnalchar was left under the guard of a few eunuchs, and the viziers and the emirs, surrounded by an immense crowd, ran to the castle of Alamut,[3] where, in accordance with custom, the Caliph's brother Schach-Alled had been locked away.

Raised in that sad prison by an old nurse, the pueng[4] had aborted the seed of valor in Scach-Alled's heart; so, when he heard the joyous "Allah!" that was repeated on

---

of the cadaver. As soon as a dying man expires, the Mohammedans empty all the pitchers that there are in the house, for fear that the angel might have washed his scimitar therein."

1 Author's note: "Mount Arafat is near Mecca. In the principal temple is a small square edifice in which a black stone is sealed, an object of the veneration of Arabs. See Pococke, *Specimen hist.* Reland, *de reliq. Moham.*" The former reference is to Edward Pococke's *Specimen historiae arabum* (1649); the latter is to the Latin version of Adrien Reland's *La Religion des Mahométans* (1721).

2 Author's note: "When a Persian reaches the last moments of life, torches are placed on the exterior terrace of his habitation, to alert passers-by to pray for him."

3 Author's note: "Alamut signifies 'castle of death.' It was situated in the Manzanderan, the ancient Hyrkania.

4 Author's note: "A liquor composed of poppies, nux vomica and hemp-seed. The Indians make use of it for State criminals or pretenders to the throne, to render them imbecilic and stupid. See Chardin vol. IV p.20." The reference is to Jean Chardin's record of his voyage to Persia and the East Indies, published in 1686.

all sides, he ran to hide under a sofa, trembling. Extracted from that refuge, pale, distressed and dying of fear, he was saluted as Caliph. In vain, however, it was repeated to him that his brother was dead; he begged those who surrounded him not to risk his life by putting him at the head of rebels.

Gradually, however, he recovered a measure of confidence, and that confidence became a pride devoid of nobility and an ignoble joy when he saw the people prostrating themselves as he passed by. Like a child in haste to move the springs of a new toy, Schach-Alled incessantly gave those surrounding him ridiculous orders, and woe betide anyone who did not hasten to carry them out, for the wrath of the imbecile Caliph was as terrible as his power.

After having taken possession of the magnificent palace, the abode of the commander of the believers, Schach-Alled was taken to the seraglio; there, he was presented with a golden bowl full of rose-water, after which perfumes of aloes were brought in a cassolette sparkling with gemstones; he perfumed his beard and garments, and received the scented water in his hands, which he then passed over his face.

He was introduced from there into the hall of festivities; it was an alabaster dome supported by a hundred columns of white marble; the bases and the capitals were ornamented by gilded animals and birds. In the midst of his standing courtiers, Schach-Alled sat down beneath a magnificent brocade awning and a table was set before him laden with large vases of porcelain, crystal, jasper, jet, porphyry and agate. In vain, however, slaves presented him with the most exquisite dishes; they only excited his disgust.

"Vizier," he said, ill-humoredly, "all this doesn't sharpen my appetite like my nurse's stews; if I'm not hungry to-morrow, you'll be impaled." Then, abruptly curling up in the corner of the sofa, he said: "Come on, you've boasted about your amusements—relieve my ennui."

Scarcely had he spoken than fifty richly-dressed dancing-girls came into the hall, singing; fifty musicians accompanied them. Some extracted the sweetest sounds from the Persian flute, the hautboy and the lute; others balanced light tambourines in their hands, and flashes sprang from the gong agitated in their midst by six black men of gigantic stature.

Then the young women entered into the rhythm, with crimson, gold and azure scarves in their hands; sometimes they enlaced those dazzling fabrics in light draperies, and became a vision of a swarm of houris in the midst of the clouds and fires of the Orient; sometimes they drew apart, came together again and were confused, before drawing apart again.

But the music slows down; the seductive odalisques stop and form a semicircle; one of them comes forward; her black hair falls in perfumed waves over her white shoulders; her smile is soft, her gaze distant; at the merest glimpse of her semi-naked breast one shudders with lust. She moves timidly, her eyes lowered . . .

Suddenly, a young dancer runs toward her; on seeing him, to launch herself forth like a timid gazelle at the sight of a hunter is her first impulse. He flies in her pursuit; sometimes his arms seem to enlace her slender and graceful figure, but already she is far away; sometimes he pretends to succumb to fatigue, and, while the imprudent female smiles at her triumph, he brushes her light garments.

Gradually, however, her flight becomes less rapid, and her gaze often returns to the handsome dancer; she still flees, but regretfully. Finally, she stops; her hand no longer pushes away her lover's hand; their ardent sighs fuse, their lips meet; and their passionate dance retraces all the transports of amour.[1]

"And you call that amusement?" said Schach-Alled, yawning and stretching his arms. "By Mohammed, I've never experienced such tedium. I spent my time very differently at the castle of Alamut—what beautiful tales my nurse told me! I dreamed about them all night long, and I couldn't finish my ablutions soon enough, in order to hear her marvelous stories recommence. But she's dead, and I'll never find anyone who knows such beautiful tales!"

"Commander of the true believers," the vizier replied, "your sublime brother liked to hear the old Emir Hassan relate the adventures of which he had been the witness, or learned from his father Ali, known as Moukeded because of his wisdom and profound knowledge."

Schach-Alled made a sign, and the vizier came back shortly thereafter, accompanied by Hassan.

He was an old man of venerable aspect, and while he struck the carpet on which the Caliph's feet rested with his forehead, the latter said to him: "So, you have the pretention of being a good storyteller? I'd like to hear you, even if I only get the satisfaction from it of seeing that you're not, in that regard, comparable to my nurse. I don't expect you to be any good; for one thing, every storyteller marvels at

1 Author's note: "See Chardin, Pococke, Galand, Eug. Archimandrite, Émelin, Voyages vol. III; Reberstein, in his German work on the lands between Kur and Tereck, etc., etc." These references, like all the others attached to the story, are appropriated from Conrad Malte-Brun's *Geographie universelle* (1803).

his stories, and secondly, you've never heard my nurse; but we'll see. At any rate, begin, and above all, don't be as monotonous as the cries of the Imams when they announce the hour of prayer from the height of minarets."

Hassan prostrated himself again, and began the following story.

"Caliph Haroun-al-Raschid had the custom of going through the streets of Baghdad disguised as a merchant, having no one with him but Mesrour, the chief eunuch, and Giafar, his principal vizier. Apart from the fact that he often had surprising adventures, he was thus able to see for himself whether justice was rendered exactly by the cadis, and the plaints of the people reached his ears, for that illustrious caliph was penetrated by the wise maxim that the truth is enveloped by seven veils, and that it is necessary to tear them away to see all its features.[1]

"One evening, while traversing the Bezestein,[2] he heard groans being uttered. They were coming from a tent where a lamp was burning, and by the light of that lamp he saw through the canvas a young Persian with a pleasant face, but whose pallor and depression seemed to announce imminent death. An old man sitting beside him presented him with a cup that the young man pushed away with his hand.

"'Oh my son, my dear Agib,' said the old man, 'why this despair, the cause of which I'm unaware? On the last day of the moon of Saphar you embraced me tenderly and said that you were the happiest of mortals; we have scarcely reached the moon of Gemmadi, and you want to die! Oh,

---

1 Author's note: "Saadi." (i.e., the thirteenth-century Persian poet.)
2 Author's note: "A Bezestein or bazaar is a kind of fair in which all the Arab merchants come together."

if, at least, I knew where this frightful chagrin is coming from, but you're obstinate in keeping silent. Agib, Agib, don't you love your father any more?'

"'Oh, Father, do you want to know your unhappy son's deplorable secret?' Agib replied, in a faint voice. 'A fatal passion is consuming me; and even if you possessed the treasures and the power of a vizier, you couldn't give me Zhera.[1] One day, when I was in this tent, she came in with two eunuchs and asked me for silken fabrics.[2] In order to judge the fabrics better, she lifted her three veils, and I stood there motionless with admiration at the sight of her celestial beauty.

"'After that, an unknown burning fire spread through my veins; the image of the beautiful odalisque followed me everywhere; sleep no longer closed my eyelids, and I experienced an indescribable disturbance and agitation incessantly. Two days went by. What was my joy, my intoxication, when I saw her entering my tent again! Deceiving the vigilance of her black guardians, I dared to address a few words to her covertly, and, lifting her veils, she showed me a smile that filled my heart with bitterness and joy.

"'Emboldened by that mark of benevolence, I placed in the folds of the fabrics she had bought a grape-seed, and pieces of charcoal, ginger and alum, wrapped in yellow silk.[3] Anxious, agitated and trembling, I waited for her re-

---

1 Author's note: "Zhera signifies *flower*, and *ornament of the world*."

2 Author's note: "'In Turkey, women are not locked away as harshly as some writers have led us to believe; on the contrary, they enjoy their liberty to a high degree; although in the bosom of slavery, they have a way of going out in disguise that is very appropriate to favour gallant adventures.' *Letters of Lady Montagu.*" The reference is to the letters of Lady Mary Wortley Montagu (1689-1762), and is in accord with her observations, if not authentic.

3 Author's note: "In the symbolic language of Orientals, these various

turn with an impatience and a dread mingled with I know not what hope. I finally glimpsed her at the entrance to the Bezestein. Oh, how my heart palpitated! What a cruel anxiety I experienced! Zhera advanced slowly, and passed before my tent without looking in that direction, but when my despair was about to burst forth . . . O joy! Her hands dropped at my feet a black tulip with inflamed corollas.[1] But Father, her grim guardians had doubtless perceived our secret intelligence; since that moment, Zhera has not reappeared in the Bezenstein, and life is unbearable to me without her, and only the angel of death can terminate my suffering!'

"'Mesrour,' said the Caliph, 'who is this Zhera whose beauty inspires such a violent passion in that young Persian? I didn't know that there was an odalisque of that name in my seraglio. Go find her and bring her to Agir's tent.' He added, with a visible joy: 'Giafar, my nocturnal excursion hasn't been wasted. May it please Heaven that Mohammed permits me to fulfill thus the desires of all the faithful believers in my empire!'

"'That desire is worthy of Haroun-al-Raschid,' replied the wise vizier, 'but the human heart is insatiable, and all your sublime power would not be able to satisfy the wishes that the most wretched inhabitants of Baghdad never cease to form. Agib himself, as soon as the first illusions of his amour have dissipated, will abandon himself to other desires . . .'

---

objects signify: *My secret desire is to reveal my love to you. I have only seen you once, and my heart belongs to you; but I shall bow down like a wilting flower, while you blossom in the soft warmth of prosperity, if you do not deign to reply to me and cure the ills I am enduring.*"
1 Author's note: "A black tulip, in the symbolic language, means: *I share your love, and I languish in your absence.*"

"'Giafar,' replied Haroun, 'at this moment you are not showing your accustomed wisdom, and I want to prove it to you. Zhera, you say, will not be sufficient for Agib's happiness; well, I shall spread the radiance of my power over him, and I shall prove to you that the benefits of Haroun-al-Raschid can make it impossible for the son of a merchant to desire anything more.'

"The Caliph had scarcely finished speaking when Zhera suddenly came into Agib's tent."

The Emir interrupted his story to say: "To depict the happiness of the two lovers is beyond my abilities, and . . ."

"And you're right not to do it," said the Caliph, yawning. "Your tale, Emir, is in bad taste. You're not putting anything marvelous into it, and you haven't yet said a word about divas, sorceresses, or even the admirable roc, without which no story can be amusing. Oh, my nurse's tales were very different. Finish your story, though; I'd rather hear it than that stupid music of a little while ago, and if you're as boring as that, one can at least fall asleep listening to you."

"Toward the beginning of the moon of Zilcalde," the Emir continued, "Haroun-al-Raschid and Giafar were wandering through the Bezestein again, and the Caliph remembered the young Persian, all of whose desires had been fulfilled by his generosity. Even if one is a caliph, one is always flattered by the superiority one obtains over others by proving to them that they are wrong, and Haroun steered the vizier adroitly in the direction of Agib's tent.

"He was on a sofa next to Zhera. 'Soul of my life,' the beautiful odalisque said to him, who does that somber cloud of cares envelop your forehead? Has Zhera ceased to please you?' And tears fells from her charming eyes, which she attached to Agib. The latter reassured her with tender caresses. 'Light of my gaze,' he replied, 'I swear by Mohammed that you are as dear to me as the shadow of the sidrach[1] and the aspect of the most beautiful houris; you appear to me as beautiful as the gracious stem of a lotus softly swayed by the south wind, but—shall I confess it to you?—since you have been my wife, I regret being only a simple merchant, and I could not help feeing envious a little while ago in seeing an Emir pass by, surrounded by the pomp of his rank.'

"The Caliph withdrew abruptly, without lending his ear any further to Agib's discourse.

"An hour later, a troop of janissaries, preceded by an aga and two cadis, surrounded Agib's tent; he was dressed in a caftan, and all those present prostrated themselves at his feet and saluted him with the title of Emir. Agib thought he was the victim of a dream sent by the angel Maimoun, but when he had been taken to the feet of the Caliph and then put in possession of a magnificent palace, he surrendered to joy and, pressing Zhera in his arms, he cried: 'Oh, nothing is any longer lacking to the happiness of the Emir Agib.'

"The new Emir was cheerful, witty and clever; admitted to the intimacy of the sovereign commander of believers, he had the gift of pleasing him, and Haroun often sat him down next to him in the middle of the royal sofa, to hear his ingenious sallies and his delicate and piquant repartee.

"One day, the Caliph was astonished by the sadness that covered his favorite's face. 'Agib,' he asked him, 'why are tears glistening in your eyes, while a forced smile parts

---

1 Author's note: "The voluptuous arbor in the shade of which Mohammed enables houris to rest."

your lips? Speak: I order you to make the cause of your dolor known to me.'

"'Sublime Caliph,' cried the Persian, falling to the ground face down, 'I'm an ingrate unworthy of your generosity; you have spread your benefits over the son of a merchant and, forgetting his obscure birth, he groans at being obliged to render to the vizier the honors that, in his pride, he ought to owe to you alone. A little while ago, an aga, before all the grandees of our court, told me harshly to prostrate myself at the sight of Giafar; and even though he is your right eye, tears of chagrin bathed my visage.'

"'Well, if he is my right eye, you shall be my left,' the Caliph replied. 'Get up, Vizier Agib, and share the power of Giafar.'

"Agib showed himself to be not unworthy of the power with which Haroun had invested him; he rendered justice itself, and anyone who dared to solicit him with presents in hand was punished by the staff as an infamous corrupter. Giafar did not take long to appreciate the noble qualities of the new vizier, and was bound to him by a close amity. Something unexpected! Two ministers were seen not seeking one another's mutual destruction, only rivaling one another in zeal to support the magnanimous intentions of their sublime master.

"One day, the Caliph was talking familiarly with his viziers; the conversation turned to happiness, and Agib sang the praises of a quiet and retired life. 'Oh,' he said, 'Happy is the man who possesses in is retreat a pleasant mediocrity; happier still if numerous children do not oblige him to contemplate the future with anxiety, and if jealousy, the inseparable companion of a young and beautiful wife, does not drive repose and peace from his heart!'

"'That happiness,' said the sultan, 'is not, I agree, the one that you savor, but after all, Agib, in Baghdad there is only me above you; you share my power, and that lot is a happy one.'

"'Happy!' replied the vizier. 'Happy! Can one be happy in the midst of a court, where an avid and deceitful crowd strives to tip the scales of justice that you have confided to me; when the dread of losing your favor, of rendering people unfortunate, torments me night and day? Oh, if happiness can exist, it is not among viziers that it's necessary to search for it; I repeat: it is in the humble dwelling of the peaceful and obscure merchant, whose repose is never troubled, either by the anxieties that his family cause him, nor by jealousy, nor by the cares and torments that attach themselves to the insensate who abandons himself to the seductions of ambition!'

"'Agib, that is precisely the lot that you enjoyed three years ago,' cried the Caliph, 'and you wanted to die then in order to escape the situation that you now covet with so much ardor. Oh, Giafar, Giafar, you were only too right; humans are insatiable, and when they no longer know to what object to direct their desire, they turn it back to those they have quit, which they curse the great Allah then for having imposed it on them.'"

"Emir Hassan," said Scach-Alled, on waking up, "when one takes it into one's head to attach such a suffocating moral to a tale, one does not come to narrate it before our royal sofa, and you merit my making an example of you that will frighten the tedious, the most redoubtable of the scourges that can approach caliphs. But as there is no torture greater for a storyteller than to inform him that he tells stories poorly, and as he would prefer, I believe, to pass for a dishonest man than a fool, our sublime clemency will grant you mercy.

"If, however, while dozing, I understood correctly three of four words seized at hazard, it is not the case that your moral is entirely askew. I will even tell you that I, who am speaking, am not without regret for the Castle of Alamut; for one thing, I heard tales there whose inimitable merit I appreciate far more now that you have involved yourself in telling them; and secondly, my nurse, being alone with me, did not seek to put herself further forward in my good graces by seeking to cause others to lose them. There is not a single one of you, on the contrary, in the day that I have been Caliph, who has not boasted to me of his merit and fidelity, while painting all others as infamous traitors worthy at least of the staff and the stake. But whether you're wrong or right, a moral is still a moral, and it's too bad to want to make one by causing people chagrin, when one only ought to seek to amuse them."

Then, uttering a great sigh, he added: "Oh, my poor nurse, you told very different tales!"

Alice

And the evils that endure, and the evils one suspects,
And those that I have sung, will not prevent anyone
From loving as they loved before.
(Émile Deschamps, "Conclusion")[1]

A LICE was the daughter of a poor country minister.
She was eight years old when her mother died; at
twelve she was an orphan.

The only relative that remained to her in the world,
Miss Abigail Lawton, a retired seamstress in the city, took
Alice into her home, making a great issue of the extreme
charity she was displaying in not putting her brother's only
child in the orphanage.

No benefit was ever more dearly bought, for little Alice
had to satisfy the demands of a shrewish, eccentric, exacting
old woman, and the angelic resignation, loving character,
gentility and precocious intelligence of the poor girl could
not find any mercy from Miss Abigail.

Alice worked from dawn to dusk, and if, stealing a few
moments' relief, she took refuge in her little room to read

---

1 Émile de Saint-Armand Deschamps (1791-1871) was one of the
early leaders of the French Romantic Movement; with Victor Hugo he
founded the periodical *La Muse Française*. "Conclusion" was included
in his collection *Études française et étrangères* (1828).

a page or two of an old edition of *Pamela*,[1] the sole legacy that she had inherited from her father, Miss Abigail immediately came to throw her out again, protesting against the "lady-like airs" that her niece was putting on.

"Isn't this," she said, in the harshest voice that had ever been heard to screech in the city, "a fine occupation for a girl who doesn't have a farthing? Learn to earn your daily bread with your arms, for I won't live forever, and when I'm gone you'll soon have dissipated the savings that I've had so much trouble amassing. Who'll feed you then?"

At these unjust reproaches and gross outrages, Alice shed many bitter tears, which it was necessary for her to strive to conceal, for they would have occasioned a further diatribe. Without saying a word, she went back to work.

Constrained to the most servile tasks, to the most repulsive work, Alice never let slip a murmur, but not because Miss Abigail's persecutions had produced in her the kind of indifference that might have rendered such an existence tolerable; the extreme pallor of her physiognomy and her habitual sadness revealed how profoundly she felt the misfortune of her situation.

Two years had gone by when an old naval officer came to lodge in Miss Abigail's house. Touched by Alice's sad situation, the old man became her friend, and thanks to the protection of Sir John Clapperstuck, the orphan's fate became a little more tolerable.

The former long-haul captain was a learned man; he took great pleasure in cultivating Alice's fortunate disposi-

1 Samuel Richardson's work was very popular in French translation, especially *Pamela; or, Virtue Rewarded* (1740), which provided a key model of the kind of "moral fiction" to which the cynicism of Berthoud, Janin and Petrus Borel—not to mention the Marquis de Sade—provided conscientious opposition.

tions; his pupil's rapid progress filled him with joy. Miss Abigail often shook her head, murmuring, on seeing her niece wasting her time, as she put it, with the old mariner, but she dared not complain too loudly, because the captain had sworn that, if his pretty protégée were harassed, he would immediately leave Miss Abigail's house and take lodgings at the other end of the street with Miss Southey.

Now, Miss Southey was the owner of a well-stocked lingerie shop, and had established a redoubtable competition with Miss Abigail. There was no sacrifice that the latter would not have made rather than lose a guest like the captain—a guest who was sometimes visited by lords. If she had ever seen their carriages stopping outside Miss Southey's boutique, she would have fallen ill with chagrin. Alice, therefore, spent all her recreational time with Sir John.

Glad to receive testimony of affection that reminded her of the days when she had had a father, Alice loved the old man with all the abandon of her age, and surrounded him with the most tender cares and most delicate kindness. The captain often said, with tears in his eyes, that the child would fill his final years with happiness.

Alice was eighteen when the venerable old man yielded his last sigh peacefully, in her arms.

For her, everything then became sad, bitter and empty again. Miss Abigail had counted on the old man making her his heir, but he did not bequeath anything to her or to Alice but trivia of little value. That disappointment returned all its original bitterness to the old woman's character—a bitterness further augmented by the chagrin of seeing the captain's room remain unoccupied for a long time.

Finally, a young man from Exeter presented himself as a tenant for the late Sir John's apartment. Teddy Wolsey did not take long to get into his landlady's good graces; he was a young medical student, jovial, tidy and studious, and extremely polite to Miss Abigail. He soon acquired a considerable intimacy within the household; nothing was done without asking his advice, and if the old woman had a fit of ill-temper, Teddy's cheerful remarks were able to dissipate it and restore calm and gaiety.

Gradually, a pleasant intimacy was established between Alice and Teddy; the young woman yielded to the vague and indecisive sentiment that she was beginning to feel, without seeking to examine it closely. She knew that the affection she had for Teddy was not the same as that the captain had once inspired in her, but because the mixture of sweet languor and melancholy pleasure that gradually took possession of her entire being did not give rise to any alarm, she was already in love with the young man before she had given any thought to explaining the nature of her new sensations.

Imagine her terror when, one evening, she saw Teddy come home covered in blood, with a wound on his head! Oh, what a horrible despair clutched her heart when the doctor who was summoned examined the wound for a long time, silently, and sadly shaking his head. Imagine her anxiety when, that night, sitting up with the invalid on her own, she interrogated the feeble palpitations of his heart, dreading that she might feel it stop!

For eight days and nights they trembled for the life of the injured man, and for eight days and nights Alice kept vigil by his bedside; she scarcely closed her eyes for a few minutes from time to time in order to sleep, and her slumber was so light that, at the slightest moan, she would be standing over the invalid, offering refreshing beverages to his burning lips.

Finally, they ceased to fear for his life, but it was necessary to surround him with long, attentive, persevering care. When the doctor announced that, Alice was distressed to earn that Teddy had a long time still to suffer, but was gladdened by the thought that she would be close to him for a long time yet.

With what a mixture of modesty and tenderness she rendered him the kind and gentle cares that only women are able to offer so affectionately! He never had time to formulate a desire; she was already offering whatever he was about to request; she interpreted his vaguest gaze reliably.

One evening, she had helped him to sit in an armchair, and, as her hand placed the pillow that was to sustain the convalescent's head, Teddy took that hand in his stiff fingers and raised it to his lips. A fiery redness, and then a sudden pallor, covered the poor young woman's cheeks in turn, and she had to lean on the back of the chair, having become unsteady on her feet.

Teddy put his arm around Alice's elegant waist; he tried to speak, but, too emotional, could scarcely proffer an exclamation. They both kept a long silence, and that silence was delicious, for Alice's pretty head rested on Teddy's shoulder; their hands were entwined, and the young woman's tears fell one by one on to the convalescent's knees.

Then their lips met, and they swore to love one another forever.

Afterwards, they set about making long and pleasant plans for the future, and confiding to one another the most secret thoughts of their souls. Alice told Teddy about the chagrins she had suffered since her mother's death; then, her eyes bathed in tears, with a celestial smile, she said: "I shall be very happy now."

He drew her gently to his bosom. "My Alice! My Alice! We shall soon belong to one another. When my mother knows that she owes her only son's existence to the tender care of my Alice, she'll leave Devonshire and come to call you her daughter."

The three months of the convalescence went by so quickly for the two lovers that they were struck motionless by surprises when the doctor said to Teddy: "Nothing more is needed now to render the cure perfect than to go and breathe the air of your natal county. You can support the fatigue of the journey; I've written to tell your mother the good news, and this is her response—she wants you to leave the day after tomorrow."

He left.

Unfortunate children! Large tears formed in their eyes, and they threw themselves into one another's arms, sobbing. "Oh no!" Teddy exclaimed. "I don't want to leave you!"

"What about your mother?" poor Alice murmured, affecting a firmness that was far from real. "How disappointed she would be."

He left, and only four days had gone by when a letter from Teddy arrived to console Alice and render the isolation in which her friend's departure had left her less frightful.

Tomorrow, he wrote, he was going to confide his love and the promise he had made to marry Alice to his mother.

Two days later, another letter arrived, and Alice opened it with a hand agitated by hope and anxiety. Misfortune! Teddy's mother had forbidden him even to think about a marriage so disproportionate. "But," he said, "I'll keep my promise. I'm going to leave for London in secret; we'll go to Gretna Green, and a marriage will be made there by the Scottish blacksmith, without which I'd have nothing else to do but die."

On reading that letter, Alice shed bitter tears, but she did not hesitate for an instant.

"My Teddy, I have only you in the entire world to love poor Alice, and Heaven is my witness as to how dear you are to me, but I would rather lose your tenderness than buy the name of your spouse at the price of the remorse that such a disobedience would cost you. Let us defer, my Teddy, a marriage that could not be happy, since it would be a bad deed; and let us hope for the future."

Such was Alice's reply.

And she was well-rewarded for so great a sacrifice, for every week she received letters from Teddy expressing the greatest tenderness; as she read them she thanked heaven for having blessed her because she had listened to the voice of duty.

Alas, Teddy's letters soon became less frequent and less tender. Then they stopped altogether.

Six months went by.

It was evening. Sitting in his study, beside a large fire, Teddy was formulating dreams of marriage and happiness; but the image of Alice was not, alas, associated with those future projects. A young miss with blue eyes, a dowry of a thousand pounds sterling and, perhaps even more than that, the numerous and lucrative clientele of his fiancée's father, the celebrated surgeon Olbarn—such were the ideas caressing Teddy's imagination. In becoming Miss Olbarn's husband, he would clear at a single stride all the discouraging hindrances that a young debutant in the healing art must overcome; protected by his father-in-law's name, associated with his work, he would effortlessly acquire a reputation and the abundant advantages that would flow from the acquaintances that he would make in London.

A sudden groan made him tremble; he raised his head. A woman, Alice, was standing before him, pale and hardly able to stand.

At the sight of the unfortunate woman, alas, one sole dread agitated the ingrate Teddy's heart: the dread that Alice's unexpected arrival in Exeter might trouble his marriage to Miss Olbarn.

And when, making an effort, she advanced toward him, and her lips, contracted by a convulsive movement, tried to pronounce a few words, he said to her, harshly: "What are you doing here?"

A cold sweat was streaming over the unfortunate woman's brow. She uttered an inarticulate groan. Despair had annihilated all the faculties of her being.

Teddy went outside, precipitately, for a few moments. The night was dark and the street was deserted. He went back in, took Alice by the hand, and led her away silently. She did not offer any resistance, but numbly allowed him to take her wherever he wished. They walked for a long time, and when they had arrived at the road that led to London he put a purse full of money in Alice's hand and abruptly fled.

There's an inn a short distance away, he said to himself. *She can spend the night there, and go back to London to-*

morrow. *It's a violent remedy, but what else can I do, in the circumstances?*

Soon, the agitation caused to Teddy by Alice's unexpected arrival gave way to a profound depression, the common result of an extreme determination. Alice's presence, the cruel manner in which he had treated the unfortunate woman, now appeared to him as a bizarre and deceptive dream; he would not have believed it, if the remorse of his sin had not weighed heavily upon his heart.

He made the greatest efforts, in vain, to snatch himself away from the ideas that were stabbing him; he gathered all the faculties of his soul, in vain, to concentrate, as before, on his dreams of ambition. Alice alone, always Alice, remained in the forefront of his thoughts. A burning fever circulated in Teddy's veins; a circle of fire gripped his head . . .

He got up, and repose became an intolerable fatigue to him; he walked, and his limbs, worn out by an unaccountable lassitude, obliged him to fall back into the armchair that he had just quit. He tried to read, and forced his eyes to scan the pages, but it was without the characters translating themselves in his imagination; and his hands turned the pages mechanically, without any other idea replacing the one that was obsessing him: *Alice, Alice.*

No sleepless night had ever been longer or more dolorous.

At about two o'clock in the morning someone hammered on the door. He pricked up his ears. Could that be Alice—Alice returning? Oh, this time, he would listen to her pitiful cries; this time . . .

The knocker rapped again; a hoarse voice made itself heard. It wasn't her. No, he knew who it was.

He opened the door, and let in two men of sinister physiognomy; their ferocious smiles were a horrible parody of the satisfaction of a merchant seeking to talk up the merchandise he is offering.

"Oh, for this one you'll have to pay no less than fifteen guineas—we've paid more than two-thirds of that."

"Yes," his companion added, "it cost us dear."

Teddy paid the two men the money they were demanding; then they deposited, on a long table, a burden whose form it was difficult to discern, because it was wrapped in a vast sheet, and the only lamp that was lit in the apartment was giving out very little light.

When the two men had gone and he had closed the door on them, Teddy unwound the cloth; it enveloped a corpse, the black and disfigured features of which were half-covered by a mask of pitch.

"They've murdered her!" cried the young man, shivering with horror and indignation. "Oh, those villainous resurrectionists! I'm going to denounce their crime and demand vengeance for it!"

He brought the lamp closer in order to try to identify the victim.

It was Alice.

Prestige

May Our Lady aid me, good sire! A tattered
rag instead of an entire mantle of new fabric!
(Père Mathias, *La Querelle des Chevaliers*.)[1]

My daughter is young, she is pretty;
And her mother has trained her
In economy since childhood.
I'm rich, it's true, but I have many children;
It's time I married her off.
(S. Henry Berthoud. *Le Projet de mariage*.)

IT was four o'clock; the sea, leaving the shore dry, was
only audible as a dull murmur, and only a few waves
were perceptible, still swaying on the edge of the horizon.

The greatest activity reigned in the port of Dunkerque;
troops of fishermen, their baskets on their backs and their
nets in hand, wearing their skirts of thick red cloth rolled
up to their knees, were advancing barefoot in the midst
of the hardened sand that the ebb-tide had uncovered;
their confused and singular cries mingled with the racket

---

1 The citation is fictitious, but it probably relates to the Père Mathias
featured in Berthoud's story "Saint Mathias the Hermit," one of the
items in his collection of legends of Flanders.

of carts, the oaths of mariners in their various languages, the plaintive and rhythmic songs of sailors unloading ships, and other confused noises. Cabin-boys in tarred hats, tradesmen, foreigners, women wrapped in the gray or black mantillas known locally as "capes," and others elegantly dressed in fashionable costumes, were moving around the harbor, crossing paths, forming groups, moving apart, advancing on to the jetty; and the rays of the setting sun displayed their ruddy light through the furled sails, rigging, flags and masts that rose up in all directions.

Picturesque as the spectacle was, it did not attract the slightest attention from a young man who was making his way along the harbor precipitately.

I should think not! All his sensations were absorbed by one of those ardent and unrestricted joys that arrive so rarely in life to dilate the breast of a young man, although it suffices, in order for it to happen, that he is young and in love.

Far from noticing the effects of the light, Paul, for that was his name, did not even think about looking where he was going. That would have been a good idea, however, for on two occasions he attracted energetic protests, and he finally found himself in the arms of someone who demanded in a phlegmatic tone, with an unequivocal English accent: "Paul, have you gone mad?"

"Sydney, my friend, you, here? I thought you were in London. It's my good angel who's sent you! Oh, I'm the happiest of men!"

After that beginning, which a professor of rhetoric would have called an exordium *ex abrupto*, Paul linked arms with the friend that he had encountered in such an opportune fashion, and set about telling him the cause of his joy. Nothing befits and animated conversation like a precipitate pace, and Paul dragged his listener along so rapidly that the latter exclaimed: "God damn it! Don't you know that I've got a bullet lodged in my leg?"

That interjection slowed Paul's march for a few seconds; even so, he gradually resumed his hasty pace, and when they both arrived at the hotel where Sydney was staying, the islander's face was covered with sweat.

"My friend," he said, stopping with an entirely British gravity, "I see that felicity is at least as loquacious as misfortune. You've asked for Mademoiselle Tréa's hand in marriage; her father, Monsieur Vandermoudt, has promised it to you. Thank God: there, in one sentence, are your confidences of five quarters of an hour.

"Personally, I left London the day before yesterday and Calais this morning. My business affairs will keep me here for two weeks. I'm going to have dinner; will you join me?"

Paul accepted, laughing, talked about nothing all through dinner but Tréa, the charming Tréa, and would not give Sydney a rest until he had consented to be introduced to Monsieur Vandermoudt. Sir Edward Sydney finally gave in, and after having retired to a room whose door he took extreme care to close, he emerged again dressed with an elegance and taste that the most committed dandy would not have disavowed.

Sir Edward might have been forty years old. At first sight, his distinguished bearing, teeth of admirable whiteness and regularity, beautiful blond hair and graceful manner produced the favorable impression that disposes people to great benevolence. It was only after a more attentive examination that one discovered a discordance in his gaze and bizarre effects that lingered.

Furthermore, he expressed himself in French with great facility, albeit with a certain hoarseness and awkwardness in his pronunciation. The limp occasioned by the wound in his leg was hardly noticeable, perhaps not even lacking in a certain grace, and, far from harming him, reflected upon him the interest that a soldier's wound almost invariably produces. Let us add, too, that the wound in question was not his only one, for he experienced some difficulty in making use of his right arm, the hand of which remained constantly covered by a glove.

The portrait of Mademoiselle Tréa will not be as long: an only daughter, a spoiled child, delightful caprices, and a whimsicality that might drive a husband to despair or render him the happiest of men; nourished on novels like all the young women of the province, and in consequence, excitable; incorrect in judgment and imagining the ideal type of happiness in the features of a cavalry officer with an epaulette and medal, whom every sentry salutes.

At any rate, she was allowing herself to be married to Paul without regret, but without joy, saying to herself: *He's a nice fellow who loves me as much as he's capable of loving—which is to say, very gently—and with whom I'll find a negative kind of happiness.*

The rank that gave Tréa's father his consideration and his fortune were only secondary; according to the conventional expression, it placed him among the well-to-do bourgeoisie and nothing more; the young woman's vanity felt flattered when Paul, with a solemnity unaccustomed for him, introduced, first to Monsieur Vandermoudt and then to Mademoiselle Tréa Vandermoudt, "Colonel Sir Edward Sydney of Sydney Hall."

Sir Edward's distinguished manners, which made a contrast with Paul's blunt and bourgeois manners, initially inspired in Tréa a kind of suspicion of herself and respect for Sir Edward; she did not indulge that evening in her customary chatter, a delightful profligacy overflowing with mischief and candor; she maintained a certain reserve, and replied timidly.

It was a major occasion for her, when Sir Edward arrived the following day on his own. Paul had left that morning on important business, which would keep him absent for at least a month.

On the one hand, she did not want to appear silly, and on the other, she could not overcome the impression of superiority that Sir Edward made on her; she was flattered to be associating with a man of his rank and merit, and yet the man in question imposed himself upon her in the most cruel fashion.

There was in Sir Edward's character that exaltation that, far from being incompatible with experience and disenchantment, is rather the companion of them, if not the consequence.

Utterly smitten with the Tréa's grace and naivety, he had promised himself the previous day that the charming creature would not be Paul's. Rich, powerful and accustomed to satisfying his slightest whim, Paul's departure served his purpose marvelously; it was up to him to do the rest. He set to work with the confidence of a man whose experience and intelligence guaranteed success, and the wariness of a lover who is very much in love and who is staking too much on success not to be afraid of failure.

The colonel had observed, without seeking to destroy, the impression of superiority that he had made on Tréa; far from being unfavorable to his plans, it was to serve them. He showed himself to be so witty and so amiable that Tréa felt attracted to him by a gentle charm that would temper, but without diminishing, the sentiment she experienced of the colonel's merit.

The next day and on the days after that, Sir Edward continued to surround Tréa with the most assiduous attentions. However, he never mentioned love; he did better than that: he let her see that he loved her.

It was necessary to lead Paul's fiancée insensibly to renounce the man to whom she and her father had granted the right to her. That was a treason that would go against and revolt the young enthusiast's romantic ideas, and such a rupture would be bound to cause a scandal. All the small town gossip! To have fingers pointed at one, to be subjected to sarcasms and mealy-mouthed atrocities!

The colonel read Tréa's mind. He therefore continued his skillful seduction, always putting himself, by indirect means, in parallel with Paul; that was to establish his value and to denigrate, perhaps doom, the man who, although younger, admittedly, did not possess any of Sir Edward's brilliant qualities.

Even so, he would never have triumphed if he had not dissipated the ideas of treason to which Tréa's romantic character was opposed, making them disappear beneath generous sentiments.

Naturally melancholy in his character, he took advantage of that disposition. He allowed it to be glimpsed that a profound chagrin was consuming him. That somber despair, about which he never uttered any complaint, inspired that tender interest in the young woman which, quite different from pity, only differs from love by an imperceptible nuance, and whose effect is all the more sure because one is less wary of it, and the mystery in which its attraction is clad.

The progress of that sentiment was rapid in Tréa, but it was necessary to hasten it further, because Paul was going to return, along with the forgotten scruples and the shame of saying to his face: "I love someone other than you, whose wife I have promised to be."

The opportunity for a decisive struggle presented itself the next day. The colonel was alone with Tréa. Tréa yielded with charm to one of those conversations which relaxation, confidence and a tenderness as-yet-unadmitted or concealed render so delicious.

The subject turned to happiness; she cited someone as an example of a happy man.

"Happy!" he said.

"Yes . . . there are many who are said to be happy."

"And yet, if one knew that they were suffering, perhaps one wouldn't want to change places with them, at the price of the softness of luxury, the glamour of rank and the glory of renown. Perhaps one wouldn't want to, if one had to sleep on straw and eat black bread.

"I knew a man whose lot everyone envied; amiable, it was said, learned, a great name, and rich enough to satisfy the vastest desires. He was, however, very unhappy. There was no ostentation or exaggeration in his dolor; he allowed himself to drift in the midst of life's pleasures, insouciantly, without receiving any beneficent impressions therefrom.

"An atrocious and prolonged dolor numbed his moral faculties, as it can dull the physical faculties, except that the latter are sometimes cured, the former never can be. He loved, he was beloved; a woman had sacrificed everything for him: happiness, the past, the future, conscience! He was worthy of such sacrifices. He was worthy, because he did not regard love as a frivolous struggle of pleasure and vanity a duel in which one deploys cunning, which one refines with skill, and after which one departs cold and indifferent.

"To love, to unite oneself with another for life, in spite of misfortune and despair, he for her and she for him: that was what he understood by love; that was what she understood by love. Poor fools!

"She belonged to another, and he knew of their love, and cruelly avenged himself for his misunderstood rights. She had only given her friend a tenderness that he alone could understand, that he alone could inspire; it did not matter; she belonged to another, body and soul; her thoughts, imagination, desires and dreams all belonged to another. That other claimed them. He claimed them by virtue of the pact she had signed, as a poor girl devoid of experience whose parents had guided her hand.

"He proposed to the unfortunate—the man whose story I'm telling—either exile for him or opprobrium for her. Opprobrium for her! The world would have laughed at that fall as at the fall of an angel.

"He exiled himself.

"For five years, only two people in the world knew where he had taken refuge: a sure friend and her.

"Finally, she became free again; the pact that bound her to another was broken, for death alone can break such a pact. And he received a letter that said: *Come back; I can be yours.*

"Yours! What, together! Always together! No longer to be apart, no longer to await as a boon letters sent at long, uncertain intervals—letters, not from her but from another, saying: *I've seen her; she loves you and is weeping . . .*

"Yours!

"Together now, together forever, arms entwined, lips seeking one another out!

"To admit his love to the entire universe; to say: *I surround you, I protect you with my tenderness!* She is mine! I am hers. She is my wife. She will be the mother of my children. Oh, what delight, children! To see them born, to be gripped by new bonds. Children who will love me as much as she loves me, whom I will love as much as I love her.

"'Come on, come on, faster! Here's gold, press your horses, hurry up!'

"No distance was ever crossed with as much urgency as the two hundred leagues that separated him from her.

"He arrives, he runs. 'Where is she?' He's stopped; people try to speak to him. 'Let me go! Let me go! Her! I want no one but her!' He shoves them all away, moves them aside; he succeeds in reaching her. There she is!

"She's asleep. Next to her is the crucifix before which, yesterday, she prayed for him, for now she can pray for him; her love is chaste and virtuous.

"He dare not wake her; her sleep is so pure, her beautiful face is relaxed with so much grace.

"How pale she is! There are the traces of what she has suffered for him—for she has suffered a great deal, suffered as much as a woman can suffer; despair, anguish, opprobrium . . . and all that for love of him!

"In his arms! In his arms! It's necessary that he press her in his arms!

"Her cool lips . . . her closed eyes . . ."

"Dead!"

"The unfortunate man!" cried Tréa, violently moved by the story.

"Oh yes, very unfortunate," said Sydney. "Very unfortunate . . . for, after ten years of despair, after having thought his heart broken forever and incapable of love, the unfortunate fell in love again . . . with an angel like her. But that one, who could have made him forget all his sufferings, that one, who could have made a heart withered by despair palpitate with joy again . . .

"Treá, she loves another! Another will possess her!"

With both hands, he covered his eyes.

The young woman allowed her head to fall upon Sydney's breast, and hid her face therein. And he gently picked up a hand that she abandoned to him, and covered it with kisses and tears.

A few moments went by.

"Tréa," he murmured, then, emotionally. "Tréa, my Tréa . . . "

Trembling, joyful, troubled, she raised her eyes tenderly toward him . . .

An exclamation expired on her lips; her cheeks paled and tightened.

Sydney's mouth was wide open, open as no human mouth ever opens; convulsive efforts were reddening his face, his expression was strange and staring. He looked like a vampire ready to feed . . .

Sydney ejected the young woman from his arms, and ran out.

He came back almost immediately, a smile on his lips. Joy, he claimed, had caused him to experience a violent convulsion, but the fresh air had sufficed to cure it.

Soon, and gradually, his grace and amiability dissipated the terrible impression that the bizarre incident had produced; he ended up causing it to be forgotten by means of

222

gentle pleasantries, which he gradually transformed into tender words and passionate protestations.

The following day, at dawn, Sydney went to Paul's house as the latter was getting down from a carriage, had a long conversation with him, left him, and went to meet him again an hour later outside the town, armed with pistols and accompanied by two witnesses and two domestics.

At the first shot, Sir Edward fell; a bullet had broken his left leg, the leg that was already wounded. He was seen to crumple at knee height, the heel forward.

Paul fled, and the witnesses hastened around the colonel, but he wrapped himself up in his cloak, obstinately refused their help, and had himself taken away by his domestics in a carriage that was waiting a short distance away.

A courier was sent to London during the night by the colonel, and as soon as he returned, the servants marveled to see their master quit his bed and go to see Tréa's father, without limping any more than he had limped before the duel.

A fortnight later, the marriage took place of Sir Edward Sydney, colonel and baronet, and Mademoiselle Tréa Vandermoudt.

The newlyweds left immediately for London, to the great regret of the idlers and scandalmongers of Dunkerque, the sort of people who thrive in little towns and for whom gossip is the greatest joy—except, of course, for the pleasure of spreading a slander.

For a year, Tréa has been Sir Edward's wife.

To bear his name, to be his, she has sacrificed everything, including her own conscience and the pledge made to another, and left everything, including her father and the beautiful land of France.

She is unhappy! In buying that name at such a price, she believed that she was buying happiness; alas, she has only bought two things to which she had never given any thought: rank and fortune.

Tender and sweet caresses, words of love murmured and repeated by lips so close to one another that they quiver with the warm vapor of their confused breath . . . never to be apart . . . two in one . . . that, oh, that was the happiness of which she had dreamed with him!

Instead of that, a mysterious and inexplicable constraint! One would think that he is afraid of being broken by her hugs, devoured by her kisses!

Spending nights alone, far from her, in an apartment that no one but he enters, has ever entered! Never, for him, a spouse who sleeps peacefully in his arms, murmuring words of love; never, for him, the awakening of a spouse whose dreams and sensuality have left her white shoulders bare and her breast palpitating!

Always a desperate reserve, always stripping love of its sweetest prestige, its most intoxicating charms, repressing voluptuousness to the point of outrage!

He has just left her; he has just retired to that apartment whose mysteries he alone knows, that apartment that Tréa cannot open either with supplications or tears.

What are the mysteries that unfold there?

Already too much that is strange and menacing surrounds her: that fixed and satanic gaze . . . that horrible convulsion, that gaping vampiric mouth, which she saw one evening . . . that mortal wound miraculously cured . . .

Why that hidden life? Without being superstitious, Tréa cannot help believing that there is something supernatural about it.

But let what comes of it come! There is too much despair, too much doubt, too much anguish. She is his wife; she has the right to penetrate where the sacred title that she holds on the part of Heaven and the law is perhaps being outraged . . .

She gets up, she takes a step . . . and then, frightened of what she wants to do, she stops . . .

At length, she arms herself with all the resolution of which she is capable, and marches with slow and unsteady steps to the door of the mysterious apartment.

There, she hesitates again.

She leans over, she listens: not a word, not a movement, not a sound!

She is about to draw away when the moon, suddenly emerging from behind a cloud, causes a key to gleam. A key! He has forgotten to take it out.

She can go in.

Hesitation and anguished twitches take possession of her again.

Finally, she turns the key; she pushes the door slowly; she goes in.

A profound darkness . . . no other sound than the breath of her mouth, and the palpitations of her heart.

If she dared to lift the thick curtain over the window! She reaches out her hand; the fabric yields, falls, and the moonlight inundates the fantastic apartment.

Then a slobbering voice threatens; then a bald and naked head looms up, a bald head, one of whose eyes is nothing but an empty hole; a bald head, whose flaccid cheeks dangle to either side of a jawless mouth; a bald head, the rightful complement of a mutilated trunk to which only one arm and one leg remain . . .

Now, she is mad.

The Painter Ghigi

I have never understood very clearly,
in a satisfactory fashion, how some
people can cut a man's throat as if he
were a pig, and pay no heed to their
crime after committing it, while
others suffer horrible remorse.
I have referred in vain to differences
in nervous organization, to differences
in education; it has remained evident to
me nevertheless that remorse, like disease,
destroys some people while leaving others
untouched.
(D.-M. Fabien,
De l'Organisation morale de l'Homme, ch. VII.)[1]

HAPPY is he who feels no remorse! If he throws himself on his bed, he soon abandons himself to a refreshing and peaceful sleep; he does not pant in the grip of a nightmare; he does not wake up with a start; he does not dart wild glances in all directions.

He does not yearn for daybreak as a blessing; and during the day, he does not have one implacable idea, and once

---

1 Fictitious.

alone, a frightful phantom that attaches an insupportable gaze to him, which never lowers the accusing finger extended toward him.

He does not reply in a brusque tone to the loving words of his young wife; he does not push away his child, who comes to kiss him; he is not irritated by his noisy games.

He has no remorse!

People envy me my renown and my glory: it is a crown of red-hot iron that burns my head, and which I cannot tear off.

People envy me my palazzo, my villa, my domains, my carriage, my horses: I would give them all, I would give everything, to whomever could take away my remorse.

But that is impossible, alas. No, that is quite impossible, for I have done everything to rid myself of my remorse.

I have never been able to do it!

I have knelt in a priest's confessional; I uttered such sobs there; I struck my breast there with such despair that the man of God said: "My son, there is no sin that cannot be redeemed by such great repentance."

I spoke; the priest fled.

After that, young artists sometimes demanded why I was pale, why my lips never wore a smile any longer. "Come with us; a secret pain is eating you away, but there is no pain that joyful orgies cannot cure; come to lewd songs repeated in chorus; come to wine that will intoxicate, to semi-naked women who will intoxicate even more; there—that is what you need!"

I followed them, and when their speech became noisier; when, tottering, they were rolling on the grass in the arms of their mistresses, I drank, I drank, and I drank more, for

I said to myself: What joy! I shall be like them! I shall no longer have reason!

Alas, wine has no drunkenness for me.

Once, I saw a hermit who lived far away from men; he boasted to me of the calm he had found in his retreat, and I ran away into a desert.

I prayed, in vain; I imposed the greatest austerities upon myself, in vain; I tore myself with blows of the disciplinary lash, in vain: there, always there, my execrable idea!

I was told that women have marvelous secrets to render peace to those who have lost it; that no one in the world knows how they are able to put dolor and despair to sleep; I was told that, cradled in their arms, with one's head laid on their bosom, one becomes placid again, devoid of remorse; that they purify and enable forgetfulness.

I married Marianna, an angel of beauty, tenderness and love, the most celestial of creatures who ever murmured intoxicating words in a man's ear.

Her caresses make me feel sick; they are killing me; I have no response to make but gestures of refusal, indifferent, harsh words.

She calls me Ghigi.

Ghigi, Ghigi! Always and everywhere that execrable name!

Romans, foreigners, my wife, my son, always Ghigi, always Ghigi!

If they knew how much it hurts me, what daggers they're showing me, what muffled death-rattle they're causing me to hear!

For I'm not Ghigi. Antonio Ferragio is my name. Ghigi is a name I've stolen, a name in which there's ingratitude, treason, adultery, theft and murder!

Oh, if there were no Hell, if death were oblivion, how immediately I would die!

But a life without end, a life of eternal punishment, a life in which I always hear that name: Ghigi! Ghigi!

Never can my head, never can my soul conceive an idea with which that name is not alloyed; it has become inherent in my nature; it torments me; for me, it is a necessity. And now that I'm alone here again, alone in the midst of darkness and silence, tell me how it is that I find, in writing ideas that drive one to despair, a horrible pleasure, a torment that Hell does not have; tell me how an imperious force is attaching me to this table, is making this pen move.

Oh, may you never experience remorse!

There was once a time when I never experienced remorse myself. I was a young man then, with a slim figure and black curly hair, a young man who abandoned himself with delight to a precarious and nonchalant life. Pleasure was my great, my only affair: I enjoyed the present moment, and never had a care for the quarter-hour that would follow it, much less for the next day.

One night, one single night, arrived, however, to change my destiny, and make me the most rascally and miserable of men.

I had spent a part of that fatal night in debauchery; my head heated by wine, I was wandering aimlessly in the ruins of Palermo with a friend when we encountered a senora escorted by two cavaliers. "I'll wager," I cried, "that I can lift the veil of that unknown beauty!"

"I'll help you," replied the madman who was accompanying me.

229

That cost the lives of two men—one of the cavaliers and my friend were killed.

In the meantime, I lifted the señora's veil; it was the governor's mother.

"Antonio Ferragio," she said to me, "your head will expiate my brother's death."

Where could I find refuge? Already, sbirri were running in response to the senora's screams, those implacable screams that never ceased naming Antonio Ferragio.

I fled aimlessly, and when day broke, I was alone a few leagues from Palermo, on the shore of the sea.

I let myself fall on to the sand, in a stupid torpor produced by fatigue and despair. I resolved to wait there for the fate that I could not escape. For I could not deny my murder; one of the victims had recognized me. I could not leave the country; I did not have a sequin. I could not find a refuge; anyone who had given me shelter would have perished with me.

A man, still young, passed by on horseback. Seeing me pale and unmoving, he thought that I had been robbed and stabbed by thieves, and came to help me. His questions and his pity wearied me. "Leave me alone," I said. "I've murdered the governor's uncle."

"Climb up on the rump of the horse with me," He said. "I'll give you a safe hiding-place where I defy the governor to find you."

My death was inevitable, death on the scaffold! Imagine what I experienced in hearing those words, which gave me hope! I leapt on to the horse, and after riding for three hours, we arrived at a villa of meager appearance.

The interior of the villa matched its exterior: poor walls with no wallpaper—but they were partly covered by paintings worthy of a celebrated master.

Then the stranger said to me: "I have your secret, and to reassure you as to my fidelity, I'll give you mine. You've heard mention of the Neapolitan painter Ghigi, whom some say has been dead for ten years and others say has gone to Mexico. I'm Ghigi.

"After having studied my art for a long time in foreign lands, I returned to Naples, where no one recognized me, for I was an orphan, and fifteen years of absence and traveling have changed me considerably. I was nevertheless about to take up residence in Naples and devote myself to works of art, when I saw the young daughter of Count Rienzi, when I succeeded in becoming Paola's lover.

"Then all my plans changed; I liquidated my fortune, abducted Paola and, fleeing the vengeance of a noble family, we came to seek refuge in Palermo under assumed names. I bought this villa, where I live a happier existence with Paola than I can say.

"Yes, the mystery that surrounds us, never being apart from one another, living only for one another, cultivating the art that I adore—unknown, it's true, but also without being harassed by envy—all extends over our existence a peaceful, inexpressible charm. I've exchanged glory for happiness, and the deceptive amity of men for Paola's love; not a day goes by when I do not bless Heaven!

"I've revealed to you what no one in the world knows, other than myself and Paola; you can see now that your refuge is safe."

Wretch! I destroyed that happiness, destroyed it irredeemably! Oh, Ghigi, how have I repaid you for your kindness!

My idleness and my solitude in that retreat set my Sicilian blood on fire. One day, beside myself, I took the sleeping Paola in my arms. She was mine.

Attracted by the poor woman's screams, Ghigi came running to take revenge. A dagger-thrust laid him at my feet.

Then I thought I heard infernal laughter; I thought I heard a voice whispering in my ear: "Leave for Rome with Ghigi's gold; take his paintings. Say: 'I'm the painter Ghigi; I've come back from Mexico.'"

Yes, it was the Demon that gave me that advice, for what man could conceive such a sin? Yes, it was the Demon; I felt his burning breath exhaling into my ear!

But that woman! Ghigi's body . . . he might yet revive; his tongue might speak; his hand might write . . .

A delirious rage, a fiery vertigo took possession of me . . . and when I recovered my reason, I was aboard a ship whose cannon was saluting the port of Nettuno, and I was sitting on a crate that contained all of Ghigi's paintings.

Arrived in Rome, I exhibited a few of the paintings; I said that I had painted them. Soon, the name of Ghigi was being repeated enthusiastically; his paintings were snatched up. I had glory; I became rich, and the intoxication of glory and fortune stunned the memory of my crime; it sometimes came back, at long intervals, to persecute me, but the whirlwind of pleasure and prestige stifled it.

I thus had, for nearly ten years, a kind of happiness.

I had sold all my paintings except for one, representing a Madonna nursing her son; Prince Borgia saw it, gave me a considerable sum for it, and immediately had it transported to his gallery. The painting was not covered by any veil during the journey, and, gripped by admiration, a crowd soon assembled around the masterpiece and started following it to the prince's gallery, saluting wildly the name of Ghigi. The excitement went so far as to require me to participate in that improvised triumph and follow the painting in the prince's uncovered carriage, in the midst of enthusiastic shouts.

There were so many people that a cart carrying a victim to execution could not get past; it was a mute beggar who, driven by need, had stolen a loaf of bread. At the sight of me, and hearing the name of Ghigi, he stood up, extended two mutilated hands toward me, tried to say a few words with his severed tongue . . . and fell back in despair.

It was Ghigi.

Oh, may you never feel remorse!

The Enjoyments Of Death
A French Anecdote
1825

> Vagabonds, vagabonds
> Are happy folk;
> They like one another.
> Long live vagabonds!
>
> A palace's splendor strikes you,
> But ennui makes you groan there;
> One can eat well without a tablecloth,
> One can sleep well on straw.
>
> Vagabonds, vagabonds
> Are happy folk;
> They like one another.
> Long live vagabonds!
> (P.-J. de Béranger, "Vagabonds")[1]

SCARRON, in his *Roman comique*,[2] paints the most humorous picture of the kind of life led by a troupe of traveling actors: the witty Cul-de-Jatte has grasped nature

---

1 "Les Gueux" [Vagabonds] (1812) by Pierre-Jean de Béranger.
2 Paul Scarron's *Roman comique* [Humorous novel] was published in two parts, in 1651 and 1657.

in essence so well that his picturesque buffoonery, like the comedies of Molière, still rings true in our day, except that his colors are a little too garish. Let us also say, to acquit our conscience entirely, that it would be necessary to smooth over forms that are too jagged, and rejuvenate certain details of mores that have become obsolete.

He would still be the same man, but he would have changed his doublet and hose for a frock-coat and trousers.

At any rate, I don't know of any way of life more joyful, more diverting, riskier, more varied and more fecund in incidents than the existence of the little nomadic troupes that exploit the provinces: today rich and saluted by applause, tomorrow flat broke and booed, but always cheerful, always mocking fate, hastening to devour the provender it supplies, laughing at its rigors and flicking a finger at cares; vagabond and prodigal, charitable and failing to pay their debts, as idle as monks, as voluptuous as Neapolitan women, it is a mixture of vices and good qualities, of reason and folly, unknown elsewhere. There is something in those folk of Montaigne, Rabelais and Gil Blas.

Two or three years after my return to Paris, where, God knows how, I had fulfilled the intentions of my father, who had sent me there to study law, I was gripped by a passion for the history, so rich and poetic, of Flanders. In my enthusiasm I resolved to visit on foot even the smallest townships in that beautiful country. To stop in very place made illustrious by a memory; to wander through vast halls where the shades of warriors once revisited; to sit down on the ruins formed by the oratories of beautiful chatelaines; and, in the evening, by lamplight, beside a peat fire, to hear some villager recount a legend whose events had transpired in the very place where they were being related—that was a delightful project; that was joy for the head of a twenty-year-old, for an enthusiast who shivered in every limb at a poetic idea.

Let's go, let's go! It's necessary not to put it off for a day. Six hundred francs in my purse, four shirts, quills and pencils in my pocket, and off we go!

There was only joy and enthusiasm the first day; the next, I had blisters on my feet, I could not have been more weary, and I suffered beyond all expression from the lack of the petty advantages that one enjoys at home without thinking about them, of which it is necessary to be deprived to perceive their worth.

So, I found myself in a wretched room in a poor inn, not asleep sprawling in my soft and vast armchair, but wedged narrowly in a hard wicker chair, when a voice started to sing the air from *Il Barbiere*, "*Largo al factotum della città*." Only a partition separated me from the singer, and from the very first notes I recognized the voice of a law student, formerly my commensal.

"Théophile!" I cried.

The door opened, and we were in one another's arms.

"By what adventure . . . ?" I asked him.

"By what hazard . . . ?" he said, at the same time.

As we couldn't both continue talking at the same time, I told him first about my expedition and its objective. In exchange, he said to me, gravely: "I'm an actor—the *Martin* of a very good troupe that sings opera, plays comedy, bawls melodrama and excels in vaudeville. We even have tragedies in our repertoire. We're just about to leave to play *Le Barbier de Séville* four leagues from here. I have a place for you in the carriage; you can come with us, and we'll bring you back tonight."

And he dragged me away.

Right away, I found myself shoved into a carriage, between Théophile and the prima donna, who squeezed a very pretty soubrette into the other corner; facing, were the *base-taille*, the *Colin* and the *Trial*:[1] the *Trial*, a funny fellow if ever there was one, with a deregulated and facetious imagination, a veritable La Rancune of twenty who had never conceived a rational idea, and whose conversation was as amusing as it was profligate. A pupil at the École de Médecine, he had found the means of consuming in Paris, in two years, a very tidy fortune, after which he had enrolled in a troupe of actors in which he took everything as it came, laughing at everything and making a game of poverty.

A fine voice had convinced the *basse-taille* to quit a sergeant's stripes for the finery of the stage; the *Colin*, the son of a businessman, smitten with an actress, had quit everything for her; as soon as nothing remained to the poor young man, she had left him flat. As for Théophile, corroded by debts, he had embraced the condition of actor with the objective of enraging his family, who no longer wanted to pay them. The soubrette was a child of the game, the daughter of an ex-duenna. As for the prima donna, I never found out exactly what kind of misfortune had determined her comic vocation.

In half an hour, I found myself treated as if I were one of the troupe, and the conversation had brought me up to date with all the petty intrigues and gossip that are never lacking in that society. Their laughing-stock was a

---

1 These terms appear in numerous lists of players reproduced in French playbills of the 1820s, when they were evidently in common usage to describe different vocal registers.

former orchestra conductor, a boastful Gascon, conceited and cowardly; by dint of relating the poor man's arrogant impostures and making fun of him, heads became heated, and it was proposed to put his courage to the test when they came back that night, after the performance. The project was greeted with unanimous approval; roles were distributed, and oaths were made to preserve the utmost secrecy.

What was resolved was done, and after the performance, when supper was finished, during which more than one champagne cork had been popped—for the takings had been good—we set out for the neighboring town where the troupe's headquarters were.

It was about midnight. The caravan only consisted of two carriages and a cabriolet belonging to the orchestra conductor. A means had been found to break something in the harness of the latter vehicle, with the consequence that we left before the poor conductor, while he was doing his best to repair the perfidious damage.

He finally set forth. Having covered half the distance of his journey, in a little wood, he suddenly heard whistle-blasts departing and responding. Four brigands raced forward, stopped the horse, threw the musician into the mud and robbed the vehicle, not without trampling the poor man underfoot. Far from putting up the slightest resistance, he dared not even whimper. I can believe it: there was a broom-handle there decked with a cloak and hat; the wind agitated that grotesque mannequin, and at every rustle of the cloak, the unfortunate Gascon thought he saw an arm being raised to strike him.

Afterwards they talked to one another in a mysterious and frightening fashion. The orchestra leader as lifted up, stripped to his chemise, hoisted into the cabriolet and wedged in stifling fashion between two thieves. A large blindfold had been placed over his eyes beforehand.

The vehicle departed at a rapid trot, and the two brigands embarked on the following dissertation—you can easily imagine whether the victim was at ease during such an exchange.

"Let's resume the thread of our conversation, Doctor. You were saying, when this animal arrived to interrupt us, that death is not an evil."

"Far from it," replied a harsh and gruff voice, "for Montaigne relates what he experienced when he nearly died, and I have his own expressions present in my memory: 'It seemed to me that life was only holding on to me on the edge of my lips; I closed my eyes to help, it seemed to me, push it out, and took pleasure in stretching myself out and letting myself go.'"

"That, Doctor, explains why Saint Paul also says, somewhere: *Mort lucrum est.*"[1]

"Socrates, Seneca and Petronius took pleasure in prolonging their death-throes. Pacha Ahmet made the executioner who was to strangle him promise to allow him to savor death by relaxing the cord from time to time. A highwayman who was hanged and taken down from the gibbet before he had rendered his soul, recounted, when he had returned to life, that he had seen a great fire and then very beautiful hills. One can read in Bacon the story of another gentleman who had tried to hang himself, and who had similarly seen, without experiencing the slightest dolor, a fire resembling a vast conflagration, then a thousand magnificent colors blue and pale; he testified to the greatest chagrin on sensing himself taken down, and

---

1 The phrase, meaning "death is profitable," is actually from a commentary on the epistle to the Philippians, not the actual text.

regretted the marvelous spectacle of which he had been deprived so much that he hanged himself again the following day. Let us cite, in support of my opinion, Doctor Darwin, who in his *Zoonomia*,[1] in the chapter *Orci timor*, treats the fear of death as an absurd dread. Cyrus, Plato, Socrates, Cicero,[2] Ovid, Lucretius and Napoléon[3] only saw death as a gentle sleep. Finally, Tiberius replied to a man who asked him for a prompt death: 'Do you think, then, that we are reconciled?'

"The physician Béard, in his work *Du Physique et du Moral de l'homme*,[4] section LCXXV, tried to prove that life and pain continue for several hours in a decapitated man; it's a paradox, as Lélut demonstrates in his *Examen anatomique de l'encéphale des suppliciés*."[5]

"That's a curious dissertation, Doctor, and I rejoice in having for a colleague in brigandage a man as erudite as you. You've convinced me so strongly by the accuracy of your reasoning, that I want to offer you in exchange the practice of your theories: we've robbed this worthy man; let's give him in exchange the delights of hanging; let's

---

1 Erasmus Darwin, *Zoonomia* (1794)

2 Author's note: "*Emori nolo, sed me esse mortuum nihili aestimo*. Cicero *Tusc. Quaest.*, I, i." ["I don't want to die but I don't care about being dead"—attributed by Cicero to Epicharmos]

3 Author's note: "'Death is only a dreamless sleep.' *Mémoires de Constant*, vol. I p. 183." The memoirs in question were those of Napoléon's valet, Louis Constant Wairy, published in 1830.

4 The reference is actually to Pierre-Jean-Georges Cabanis' *Rapports du physique et du moral de l'homme* [Reports on the Human Body and Mind] (1815), but there are secondary references to an elusive quotation of that work by a physician named Béard.

5 Louis-Francisque Lélut's monograph detailing his *Examen antomique de l'encéphale de cinq suppliciés* [Anatomical examination of the brains of five guillotined men] was first published in 1929, and attracted a great deal of comment in 1830.

suspend him from a tree; we can take him down in half an hour, and he can recount his emotions."

Then two enormous hands started to untie the unfortunate orchestra-leader's tie, and, in spite of his plaints, a rope was put around his neck.

Then the sound of hoofbeats was heard; the two brigands leapt out of the vehicle; the cabriolet moved off, and stopped a few moments later.

The orchestra conductor waited a long time before daring to move. Finally sure of being alone, he risked removing his blindfold. Imagine his joy—he was at the door of his inn!

He got down from the cabriolet, and arrived pale at tottering in the room where we were waiting for him with great impatience. He was surrounded and questioned; and when a glass of wine had enabled him to recover somewhat, he recounted his misadventure, but embellished with a vigorous defense, two brigands killed by his hand, and a band of at least a hundred thieves. He had nearly had to yield to force.

Bursts of laughter contracted all faces. His garments and violin were thrown at the feet of the orchestra-leader. The Trial, the former physician, started to falsify his voice, which he rendered harsh and discordant; the other thief was Théophile.

The musician wanted to fight a duel with us, but he finally allowed himself to be calmed down, thanks to the intervention of Mademoiselle Justine, the kindly soubrette.

The worthy Gascon told me the next day, in confidence, that it had cost the lady dearly to calm a wrath so legitimate, which threatened to be fatal.

I smiled.

I could have burst out laughing.

The Day after the Wedding

There are good marriages; there are no
delightful ones.
(La Rochefoucauld, *Maximes*.)

Alas, neither reason, nor imagination, nor
intelligence, nor the heart can render
happiness; I understand that now.
(*Lettres d'amour*.)

Cologne, 25 September 1820.

SO, my dear Frédéric, you are abandoning me at the
moment when, according to your advice, I have to
sacrifice my most cherished errors to reason!

You're leaving for Mexico!

If, at least, your letters had been able, once a week, to
continue to encourage me, to persuade me, to make me
persevere . . . but alas, they'll only reach me henceforth at
long intervals! No more fixed day to receive them, no more
desirous waiting for the post! Immense seas will separate
us; you'll be living in another world!

It's no longer letters that I'll be writing to you; it's a
journal that you'll receive, God knows when . . . perhaps
never . . .

If you knew the courage it required for me to break the links that bound me to Madame Narscheid! Poor Louise, who sacrificed to my love her future hopes, her conscience, her domestic joy, and her reputation!

I admit it: twenty times, during that last meeting, I felt close to renouncing my marriage to Fraulein von Reistadst.

Yes, Frédéric, I would have done it; but, after fits of the most frightful despair, Louise suddenly armed herself with a resignation that I no longer had. "I love you more than my happiness," she said. "Be happy, Édouard, since you can be, with someone else."

Then, after that, without saying another word, she went to collect everything that had come to her from me, and threw it all into the fire.

Frédéric, I bought very dearly, that evening, the happiness that you promised me in a marriage of convenience! What interior peace, what wellbeing of fortune, can be worth the love that I'm losing, Louise's love? It was surrounded by perils, by despair, I know, but it was burning, devoted, sublime.

Poor fool that I am! Look, there's my imagination running away with me again!

I shall not see Louise again; her husband arrives this evening, and, as you know, my mere presence in Cologne can move him to the most frightful fits of jealousy; since the discovery of one of my letters to Louise, four years ago, he's capable of anything.

I'll leave at daybreak for Aix-la-Chapelle, and I shall finally see my wife.

✳

Aix-la-Chapelle, 26 September, 3 p.m.

I've just seen her; she's a pale and rosy-cheeked young woman; a great freshness, beautiful blonde hair, an ingenuous smile. Her name is Fanny.

Her parents made a big occasion out of our meeting; they introduced me to my fiancée with solemn ostentation.

It's a singular thing to find oneself among so many unknown people, that I'll be calling brother, sister, father, mother and wife tomorrow!

My wife! A lover who will lavish the most tender caresses; the only one it will be permissible to love henceforth; a faithful friend in happiness as in adversity; a companion from whom death alone can separate me! And I've never seen her before today! And it's tomorrow that she'll become my wife!

You're wiser than I am; I recognize the superiority of your reason over mine; you judge things with a much greater justice than I can contrive; you love me as much as one can love a friend, and it's you who have proposed to me, have advised me, who have made this marriage possible.

Frédéric, I need to remind myself of all that; I need that, for otherwise it won't be tomorrow that she'll become my wife.

The same day, 6 p.m.

I've just had a long conversation with her, after supper. Her ideas seem to me to be more solid than extensive; her imagination is as pure as a virgin's, her soul as affectionate as that of a young woman who has never been parted from a good and wise mother. She has had a prudent education, and has been brought up in great principles of economy.

The conversation has done me good; yes, my friend, I'm beginning to understand that you were right: a calm, placid, uniform happiness without the slightest shock; peace, repose, a good wife who surrounds you with kindness and tender attention; a fresh and naïve smile always ready to form at your first words; a delicate hand that prepares and presents the beverage when fever burns you and your breast is oppressed . . . It's not Louise; it's not the ideal, impossible happiness of which I once dreamed; but it's real happiness.

Yes, the conversation with Fanny has done me good; yes, her smile has calmed my unbearable agitation.

Frédéric, were you telling the truth?

27 September, 4 a.m.

I've slept, Frédéric, slept peacefully until now; yes, I'm going to be happy.

Yes: until now, I had not sought happiness where one might find it, and, blasphemer that I was, I said: "There is no happiness."

A young woman as beautiful and pure as the angels; her innocent caresses, her ineffable tenderness; and then, soon, children who will tighten the solemn bonds more narrowly; children who, with their dear little voices, will cause the delightful name "Father" to resound in my ear, in my intoxicated soul.

✳

28 September, 6 a.m.

The virgins of Heaven do not have her purity; the fiery cherubim do not have her tenderness! Oh, Frédéric, Frédéric, I'm happy, happy forever, and I owe that happiness to you.

She's getting dressed at present, and then we're going to take a long walk in the countryside that surrounds us. Frédéric, Frédéric, we'll be alone, alone with nature and its sublime beauties; we'll exchange sensations in a glance, a smile, the pressure of a hand. Frédéric, my friend, do you comprehend fully the happiness that I possess? Tell me, do you comprehend?

✳

15 October, same year.

I'm alone in my room, lying down. Is it a dream I've had—a horrible dream? Oh, if it were only a dream!

Madman that I am, it can't be otherwise; such misfortune isn't possible; no, no!

Can you imagine that I dreamed that I was going for a walk with my young wife, with Fanny; I'd never seen a more beautiful sunrise. That's because I'd never seen the sun rise while my Fanny was giving me her arm.

We were on the bank of a river. Suddenly, I saw something floating in the water, something indistinct . . . it came closer . . . a woman's corpse . . . Louise!

Oh, what a dream! What a frightful dream!

I don't know what I experienced at that moment: a convulsive rage set all my limbs ablaze and trembling; my eyes could no longer see; my ears were deafened by an execrable ringing . . .

I seized, I clutched tightly, obstinately, something warm and delicate; then I felt a flaccid weight fall upon my breast and slide to my feet with a dull sound.

Then people surrounded me; they were uttering cries of horror; I struggled against those numerous men; they tied me up and took me away, through an immense crowd.

And I saw two female corpses on a stretcher that was being carried in front of me: Louise and Fanny.

Oh, what a dream! What a frightful dream!

My God, what an impression it has made on me! I've just looked in the mirror; I saw myself livid, emaciated.

But everything around me is in chaos, broken, strewn with debris . . .

My clothes! They're no more than tatters!

Iron bars on my windows! Enormous bars at the door!

Ah . . . it wasn't a dream! It isn't a dream . . .

The Curate's Story
1830

> If one reflected seriously on the harm that the
> most honest and gallant man does, insouciantly,
> simply out of self-esteem, it would be enough to
> make one the most incurable misanthrope.
> (Jérôme Bonnier, *History of the World*.)[1]

MY young cousin Jules is a charming fellow: well-
dressed, with fine curly hair and large dark eyes that
sparkle.

I can't describe the interest I experience for that young
man, whose confused desires are becoming more distinct
and more imperious every day, whose seventeen-year-old
imagination is seething with poetry and amour; he's happy,
but suffers burning needs, mysterious impulses that make
him shudder: a vague sadness, an unknown felicity to
which he aspires; frissons under a woman's gaze; a modest
and libidinous blush at voluptuous stories—and then, in
the midst of all that, schoolboy sallies, the repartee of a
mischievous child. Isn't my young cousin Jules a charming
young man?

Very preoccupied, he came to my home the other day,

---

1 Fictitious.

threw himself into an armchair, and, putting his elbow on my desk, he covered his face with his hand.

"I wish I were like Charles," he murmured, not so much to talk to me as to express the idea that was dominating him.

That exclamation troubled me, for, of all young men, Charles is the last I would recommend as a model to my young cousin.

"How lucky he is! How lucky he is!" Jules went on, warmly. "As many mistresses as he wants! The most intractable can't resist him; he has four at this moment!"

"Is it out of delicacy or modesty that he boasts of them?" I asked, laughing.

Jules' cheeks turned scarlet. "I'm his friend," he replied, in a tone of injured pride. "He confides his secrets to me."

I had engaged the attack poorly, and I immediately moved my batteries. "You've seen very little," I said, with feigned indifference. "Have you encountered in his house the good Ambroise, the worthy curate, our comrade at college?"

"No, cousin."

"I'm sorry about that. I fear that the excellent man might be ill . . . the cruel emotion that he has experienced lately . . . doubtless Charles has told you about it?"

"No, on my soul!"

"So, young cousin, he has secrets from his confidant. I shall be less reserved than him. I'm not sorry, moreover, that hazard has given me the opportunity to tell you the story; I've noticed, Jules, that Ambroise' soutane and the hair flattened behind the ears do not always earn him the regard you ought to show him; when you know my story, that will no longer happen, I'm sure.

"Last week, at Charles' house, a few of our comrades from college got together; I was among them. The conversation was becoming more than free when Ambroise appeared. He could scarcely stand up. We surrounded him, concerned; we inquired as to why he was suffering—for we love Ambroise, my young cousin, and we respect him so much that we would think ourselves culpable if we afflicted him, or even offended his prejudices—he's so good.

"'If you knew,' he said, 'what a sad scene I've just witnessed! A young woman dying of languor, a poor young woman of eighteen!

"'Her grandmother came to request my ministry two days before she died. No one had had the courage to tell the individual the sad situation she was in; it was necessary to charge me with such a duty. You don't know, you others, how heart-rending that is.

"'When she saw me, she uttered a cry of distress: "Oh, Monsieur Curate! Monsieur Curate."

"'She turned her head away, and did not want to look at me any more.

"'My eyes were full of tears. "My child," I said to her, I haven't come to afflict you."

"'But she wasn't listening to me. "Die! I don't want to die! I'm not as ill had people think. No, I'm not as ill as that. You've been misinformed. I can still live. Yes, I can live! I wanted death, but now that I've seen it, I want to live. I shall live! The doctor has promised to cure me. He's promised me, and he knows better than anyone!"

"'I had a great deal of difficulty calming her despair. It was necessary for that to use pious lies, and assure her that she would get better, that she wasn't in any danger. But for not being in peril, ought you to tremble at the sight of a priest's robe?" I asked. "Ought you for that to defer your reconciliation with God—God who holds life and health in his hands?"

"'She raised her head again sharply. "God can cure me! Oh, yes, Monsieur Curate, he'll cure me, isn't that true? You'll pray for me. If you knew how frightful it is to think that one is going to die . . . !"'

"'I was silent momentarily, because my sobs would have burst forth.

"'Having recovered from my emotion, I succeeded gradually in leading her to confess—poor unfortunate child" She had only committed one sin in her life, and even that sin was the work of another rather than her own.

"'Living alone on her needlework with her old grandmother, she would still be happy and full of life today, but a seducer promised her love until the tomb, and swore to marry her; ignorant of the world and its traps, she believed him. Reduced to despair by the prompt abandonment of the man she loved, she fell ill.

"'Fatal and futile precautions taken to hide a pregnancy; the curiosity of the world for her sin; lack of work, poverty and then death—that's the rest of her story.

"'Poor creature! She died making every effort to live; she died regretting it despairingly. And yet she didn't curse her seducer once. When I exhorted her to resignation, she replied: "Yes." But when I said to her: "It's unnecessary to forget him, no longer to love anything on earth," she reanimated her dying voice to reply: "That's beyond my strength; I shall always love Charles!" For, like you, his name was Charles.'

"That resemblance of names, Jules, produced a dolorous and almost convulsive effect on our comrade. He went pale, and, standing up, said with a forced gaiety: 'Come on! Ambroise is softening us up with his stories as he softens up old devotees from the pulpit.'

"Is it necessary to confess it, Jules? For a moment, I was tempted to believe that Charles was the seducer about whom Ambroise was talking, but I've never known him to have a mistress whose name was Fanny."

Jules opened his mouth as if to utter an exclamation, but then controlled himself and remained silent. I pretended not to notice his disturbance.

The story I had told left a profound impression in Jules' generous soul, and since that day, he no longer sings Charles' praises to me.

Nevertheless, I observe sadly that my young cousin has lost none of his envious enthusiasm for him, and, perhaps without meaning to, is applying himself to copy his gait, his manner of dressing and his slightest mannerisms.

It's true that Fanny's seducer is extremely elegant, and that Ambroise is a poor priest rather negligent in his deportment. Unfortunately, it is only too true that advice and example acquire all their influence from the man who gives them. Depravity preached by a brilliant man, alas, is bound to hold sway over the severe morality preached or practiced by an unprepossessing man, who has nothing that self-esteem can envy.

The Hunchback[1]
A Spanish Story
1633

That is, however, true; it is for themselves alone that
people act.
(Luiz Velez, *El Diablo Cojuelo*.)[2]

Chapter I
Of the misadventure that happened to Mendoce Perez.
The kind of man the hunchback was.
Where and how he made Mendoce's acquaintance.

TWO travelers, one mounted on a mule charged with
an enormous valise, the other allowing his beautiful
Andalusian horse to walk at will, were slowly following the
road that leads from Cal-del-Penas to Calatrava. The former
wore a livery less rich than elegant, and the scarlet net that
contained his black hair beneath a small embroidered hat

1 This story was one of several items that Berthoud published in Émile
de Girardin's pioneering fashion magazine *La Mode*, in 1831. It was
also translated into English that year for publication in the New York
Mirror. Girardin subsequently hired Berthoud, in 1834, to edit the
"family magazine" *Musée des familles*.
2 *El Diablo cojuelo, novela de la otra vida* (1641) by Luis Velez de
Guevara.

added further to the naturally unprepossessing expression of his physiognomy; his master, enveloped by the folds of a vast cloak, seemed entirely absorbed in the melancholy thoughts to which he had abandoned himself.

It was the end of autumn, and yet the sun was still darting its uncomfortable rays forcefully, so that the valet's gaze often went toward an inn that was perceptible about a hundred paces away, and the mule, either because it felt the whip or by virtue of an instinct natural to those animals, recognized the place where a pittance of oats awaited, and suddenly broke into a trot. The horse followed its example, but the other scarcely seemed to notice the change of pace.

"Señor Mendoce Peres," said the valet, stopping outside the inn, "since your departure from Val-del-Penas, you have not taken any nourishment; trust your faithful Pedro and pause here momentarily." And, without awaiting his master's response, he leapt down from his mule. Mendoce imitated him mechanically, without any reply.

"Come on, come on, our joyous host," cried Pedro, on going in, "serve this young cavalier the best you have, and don't forget to enable us to make the acquaintance of a jug of the Val-del-Penas wine that is said to be so good."

Those words, reeled off emphatically, did not produce the effect that they would unfailingly have had in any other circumstances; observable in the inn were the trouble and confusion that the unexpected arrival of an important stranger brings in its wake: the hotelier, in a shrill and piercing voice, was giving two bronzed serving-girls and a tall fellow in rags contradictory orders, and a child sitting in the corner of the hearth was getting ready to turn the spit, while the hotelier was attaching a pullet to it that he had metamorphosed into a capon, of which the feathers and debris, still bloody and lying on the floor, betrayed the recent murder. He interrupted that occupation to approach Mendoce.

"Señor cavalier," he said, subjecting him to a searching gaze, the gaze that ordinarily determines the more or less gracious manner with which innkeepers receive travelers, "I greatly regret that all my provisions have been reserved by the noble stranger whose rich carriage you have seen at my door, but if you can content yourself with an excellent omelet, an *olla podrida* and the best wine that can be drunk in La Mancha . . ."

"I'll be content with what you give me," Mendoce replied, distractedly. Sitting down on a wooden bench placed beside a table to the left of the fireplace, he did not appear to perceive that he was made to wait for an hour.

When he had finished his modest meal, he ordered the child to summon his valet.

"Your valet?" the hotelier replied "Scarcely had he arrived than he left again with his mule and your horse to prepare lodgings in Calatrava, although you would have been as comfortable with your servant Gregorio Gonelès."

"Gone! Gone with my horse!" cried Peres, as if he had woken up with a start. "I'm the dupe of a rogue! Find me a horse right away . . . a mule, it doesn't matter . . . so I can catch up with the scoundrel." And, searching his belt in order to take out his purse, he realized that the perfidious Pedro had found a means of stealing it from him.

It would be difficult to describe Mendoce's consternation, and the ignoble expression of insolence that was suddenly painted on Gregorio's face. He was dealing with a young man who seemed timid and inexperienced, and, thinking to obtain an advantage from the adventure he cried in a shrill voice: "Don't think I'll be content with all those grimaces! You've conspired with that so-called valet to rob me, but by Saint Gregory my patron, you won't get away with it. You won't leave here without having paid me in full. Here's something that will serve as a pledge." At the same time he grabbed the cloak that Mendoce had set down beside him while he was eating.

"What will become of me now?" murmured the unfortunate young man. "How can I get back to Toledo with no money and no horse? And to complete the humiliation, I have to suffer the insolent suspicions of this wretch! A fatal journey! Inezille, Inezille, into what abysm of misfortune and suffering has my deplorable love for you cast me?"

And, falling back on the table, he covered his face with both hands, to hide the tears that he was shedding.

"What's the meaning of all this noise?" asked a newcomer who had just emerged from the next room. "Is that the way that an impertinent fellow of your sort ought to talk to this young stranger, and abuse the embarrassment in which a rogue has put him?" He turned to Mendoce, and added: "Señor cavalier, I offer you my purse; and although I do not have the honor of knowing you, I hope not to receive the affront of a refusal. Would you hesitate to make me the same offer if I found myself in the same predicament? No, undoubtedly. Well, accede to my plea, then, I beg you."

Mendoce parted his hands, and cast his eyes over the unknown man who was speaking. He was a small man, aged about sixty, who was no more than four feet tall; and nature had attached his bald head in a fashion so bizarre that it seemed to take the place of his breast. His fiery gaze, his symmetrical and agreeable features, announced intelligence and an ardent imagination, but his smile had something strange about it; it resembled simultaneously that which one allows to escape on receiving an insult of which one is scornful, and the kind of convulsive contraction that agitates the lips of a gambler when he sees heaps of gold, objects of his covetousness, pass into the hands of his adversary.

It was legible in Mendoce's visage how much it cost him to have recourse to the purse of a stranger; the latter easily divined his agitation, and with the exquisite tact that is a certain sign of a good education and great familiarity with society, he continued in these terms:

"I reside, Señor Cavalier, in a castillo near Calatrava; come and spend a few days there with me, while the Alcalde carries out research to discover the rogue who has robbed you. In the meantime, you can, if young judge it appropriate, send one of my men to Toledo, who will bring you back the money necessary to return there."

Mendoce shook the hand of the generous stranger, and, as someone had come to announce that Count Alvares della Ribeira's coach was ready, the two new friends took their places therein beside one another.

Gregorio, hat in hand, followed the brilliant carriage and its numerous cortege with his eyes for some time; then, when he could no longer see it, he turned his gaze with satisfaction to the numerous group that such a rare spectacle outside the little inn had attracted to his door.

Chapter II
A few observations made by Don Alvares.
He arrives at his Castillo della Ribeira.
What happened there, and his conversation with Mendoce.

While the carriage advanced rapidly toward Don Alvares' castillo, that señor, who strove in vain to extract Mendoce from the profound reverie into which he incessantly lapsed, soon wearied of looking out of the window at a bare and deserted landscape; he sank back into the carriage with a discontented expression, yawned, tried to go to sleep, hummed a *seguidilla*, and, in sum, employed all the means that travelers employ to escape the idleness and ennui to which they are condemned. His directed gaze finally arrested on the silent stranger who was traveling with him; he set about examining him with an attention all the more minute because Ribeira was still at least three leagues away, and that examination offered him an occupation that was perhaps puerile, but which his boredom did not permit him to disdain.

A blue velvet doublet embroidered with silver designed Mendoce's frame, which could only be reproached for being a trifle too slender; following current fashion, his hair descended to his shoulders in elegant waves, and a light moustache also covered his upper lip. When his large dark eyes, full of expression, were not raised toward the sky, he attached them with a sigh to a ring that he was wearing on his left hand, from which Señor Alvares concluded that Pedro's theft was doubtless not the greatest subject of his traveling companion's distress.

Perhaps, dear reader, you have sometimes experienced the malaise and timidity that one cannot help feeling in the presence of a person who imposes upon us by his age, his reputation or his rank: a blush rises to the visage; the mind refuses to form thoughts and the mouth to articulate them; one suffers, one is tortured. Such was Mendoce's situation when, on arrival at the castillo, perceiving his distraction, he thought that it must have disposed Don Alvares against him, and caused that señor to think him impolite. Exaggerating his faults, he wanted to repair them; he strove to lend a more attentive ear to his host's discourse, and even to provoke his questions, but bitter memories returned in spite of himself to take possession of his imagination, and when it was necessary to reply, he had not heard a single word that Don Alvares had addressed to him. It was, therefore, with a sort of joy that he heard the señor ask him for permission to retire, alleging the fatigues of the journey.

Left in the apartment that had been prepared for him, Mendoce gave free rein to his sobs and abandoned himself to the violence of his dolor. From a nearby room, Don Alvares heard him uttering groans and pacing precipitately. Fearing that he might be led to some act of despair, the old man came to see him and sat down beside him.

"Señor Mendoce," he said, "I don't know what can be afflicting you to this degree, but at your age, one feels things very keenly, and perhaps your troubles are not as great, and not as real as you think. I'm old, I have some credit, and if my experience and my advice can . . . "

"Señor," replied Mendoce, "my misfortunes are without remedy. If you deign to listen to me, I'll tell you the story of them; I can only thank you for your generosity by giving you that mark of the confidence that you inspire in me. In any case, I sense that I shall experience a dolorous pleasure in pouring out my troubles into the bosom of the respectable and generous friend that fate has enabled me to find today in you. In sum, it's the sole consolation that is still permitted to the unfortunate Mendoce."

Chapter III
Mendoce's story: how he encountered Don Garcias and his daughter;
what service he rendered them; the cause of his despair.
The hunchback's strange system of philosophy.

"I am the only son of a merchant of Toledo. Raised by a tender mother who cherished me, surrounded me with attention and care from the cradle, I never knew the torments with which the benefits of education are bought by children. My father, a learned and enlightened man, wanted to direct my studies himself; he was able to make them a veritable pleasure for me, and the little knowledge I have acquired has not cost me a single tear. From the age of eighteen I was associated with my father's commercial enterprises, and thanks to his active generosity, they have never had anything arid or repulsive about them for me.

"I was therefore leading a pleasant, placid, uniform and, in consequence, happy life when one evening, at the corner of an out-of-the-way street, I perceived an old man and a young woman who were being abused by two scoundrels. I threw myself upon the wretches, sword in hand; one of them fell to my thrusts, and the other took flight in a cowardly manner.

"'Brave cavalier,' the old man said to me, 'I'm a stranger brought to Toledo by important business. My name is Don Garcias de Puebla; and the King, in recompense or my long service, has deigned to confide the commandment of Merida to me. The lodgings I occupy are only a few steps away, and as you might be troubled because of the man you killed in lending us such generous assistance, I urge you to accompany us there.'

"Impelled by a violent desire to see the young lady who had taken Don Garcias' arm again, I accepted the offer that he had made me; but Señor, how can I describe my admiration and my disturbance when that lady, lifting her veil, offered to my delighted gaze a dazzling beauty? No, nothing can compare to the charms of Inezille! The grace of an enchantress, the sweetness of her physiognomy . . ."

Mendoce, following the custom usual to lovers such cases, was about to paint a portrait of his mistress . . . but, casting a glance at the hunchback, he saw him trying to hide a smile—and, as I have already said, the hunchback's smile had something strange about it, which disconcerted Mendoce; after a momentary interruption, which he pretended to employ with a cough, he continued his story.

"On my father's return, I didn't conceal anything of what had happened to me, and I had no difficulty in making him promise to favor the violent passion that Inezille inspired in me. In sum, señor, Don Garcias had permitted me to visit him sometimes during the remainder of his sojourn in Toledo. I had obtained from Inezille a confession that filled me with joy, and my father was about to go on my behalf to ask Don Garcias for his daughter's hand, when that officer was suddenly obliged to quit Toledo to return to his government.

"I did not take long to follow him to Merida, but—would you believe it, señor?—neither the memory of the service he had received from me, nor the violence of my love, nor Inezille's tears, could make him consent to our union.

"'Inezille is necessary to my old days,' he replied. 'I cannot do without her cares.'

"'Señor,' I cried, 'I'm rich; come and live with me; come and live in Toledo with your daughter . . .'

"'Renounce the honorable post that the King has confided to me?' replied the cruel old man. 'And to put myself at the mercy of a son-in-law! No, Mendoce, never. Abandon your impossible project.'

"The next day, I wanted to try once more to bend his will; the ingrate refused to see me, and I was returning to Toledo, deploring my fatal love and the revolting egotism of Don Garcias, when you extracted me so graciously from the unfortunate situation into which a rogue of a valet had cast me."

"Señor Mendoce," said Count della Ribeira, "I am not like the majority of old men, who are unable to feel compassion for the troubles of youth because those troubles are no longer of their age; whether the subject is real or not, they are no less vivid. You are unfortunate, young man, that's true, but time will lessen—I would even add, if I did not fear being accused by you of blasphemy, that it will quickly cure your dolor.

"However, do not let that dolor render you unjust; you accuse Don Garcias of egotism; are you any less egotistical than him, you who want an old man, at the expense of his wellbeing, to deprive himself of a cherished daughter? Why? To give her to a stranger whose seductions have inspired in that daughter a passion of which he disapproves? Have you not abused the rights of hospitality? Have you not deceived the confidence that he showed you? But do not let that reproach of egotism afflict you; it is a sentiment that nature has placed in the hearts of all men; they only act for themselves, for themselves alone; if they do good, it is because divine wisdom has given their conscience remorse, and the interior and sublime joy that they receive from a good dead. Examine attentively the most hideous vices, and the most heroic virtues; they take their source from egotism."

The desire to show himself grateful, or at least polite, toward Don Alvares, had not been able to extract Mendoce from his sad reverie; and yet, as soon as he heard expressed a manner of seeing that was not his own, he no longer thought of anything but combating it, so natural is the spirit of contradiction to human beings.

"But señor," he exclaimed, "such a paradox isn't even specious! How can you attribute to egotism amour and amity, affections that render possible the most dolorous sacrifices; benevolence, which refuses the necessary and risks its life to help the unfortunate; glory, to which repose, wealth, happiness and life is immolated?"

"Amour!" said Alvares, becoming heated. "Amour! Is anything as egotistical as that frenzy? Does it not demand of the beloved object the renunciation of all other affections? Does one not experience an involuntary frisson of rage and terror when someone else allows his gaze to fall upon the woman one loves? Amity! It's the need to fill the void that pursues us everywhere, to free us from the secret ennui, the work of nature, that forces us to seek the society of humans, without which we live grim and insolated. If

263

we're benevolent, it's to savor the enjoyment attached to the benefit. Finally, strip glory of its dazzling radiance, and what do you have left? Vanity."

"What a revolting theory!" said Mendoce. "It desiccates and withers the soul, and it degrades human dignity. Oh, my heart refuses to submit to it; it's too odious to be true."

"That's typical of mortals!" Don Alvares continued. "Remove the scales from their eyes, and they complain because the bright light has wounded their delicate sight, because they don't find the imaginary charm with which it pleased them, in their blindness, to dress all objects." Taking him to a window, he added, in a melancholy tone: "Señor Mendoce, your illusions won't take long to dissipate, and the world will offer itself to your gaze like that moonlit landscape; in spring, the foliage hides those sad potholes and those chains of rocks; the melodious tones of the nightingale charm the attentive ear, and the shepherds come to dance in the ferns, to the sound of guitars, singing naïve *seguidillas*; now, winter has arrived, the fields are deserted; no more birds, no more songs and joyful fandangos; and the black and leafless branches allow the eye to plunge into those horrible precipices or pause fearfully on those deformed and sterile masses.

"Young and without experience, you refuse to believe the sad verities that I've just revealed to you; but I have traveled the road of life almost in its entirety, and it is the result of sixty years of reflections and sufferings that I've just made known to you. I can also confide my story to you, and after having heard it, you'll say with me that the motive of all human actions is a vile egotism."

After pronouncing those words, Don Alvares left

Mendoce, without giving him time to respond; the latter was not sorry, however, for, after all, one does not like to irritate a rich señor who is giving you lodging, admitting you to his table, generously lending you his purse, and who is the commander of the cavaliers of Calatrava. As my savant friend Dr. Geronimo Valerio says, with reason, such a person cannot be entirely wrong.

Chapter IV
In which one sees new characters who do not play a great role but
whose acquaintance it is important to make.
The hunchback tells Mendoce his story:
his childhood; his amours; how he became a misanthrope.
Mendoce returns to Toledo.

The slumber of lovers, especially unhappy lovers, is not usually peaceful and of long duration; nevertheless, it was broad daylight when Mendoce woke up. For a long time he passed through his memory the sad events that had succeeded one another for him in recent days, but in the end, extracting himself from those painful reflections, he went to look for Alvares, whom he found conversing with two richly-clad cavaliers, and whose attentions to the Count seemed servile and despicable, so prodigal were they.

"My guest, this is Don Fernando de Lunès and Don Gabriel del Ribosa, my distant relatives . . . and my sole heirs."

Those words of the hunchback were accompanied by his strange smile, the expression of which seemed even more bitter to Mendoce. The young Toledan was also astonished to see, during lunch, Don Alvares taking pleasure in wounding his relatives' self-esteem, and lacking for them the regard that was lavished upon him. Furthermore, they scarcely perceived it, or at least pretended not to perceive it, and redoubled their protestations and accolades when they took their leave of their relative.

While they drew away, the latter attached his piercing and malicious gaze to them, and remained plunged in a profound reverie for a few moments. Then, suddenly turning to Mendoce, as if he were annoyed that he had been seen in that reverie, he said: "I promised you yesterday to tell you my adventures; I'll keep my promise. You'll find some consolation in the story, for humans are so egotistical that they feel their misfortunes less keenly on seeing someone more unfortunate than them.

"Doña Bianca, my mother, belonged to a poor but noble family of Calatrava. Smitten with her beauty, a Spanish grandee, Don Antonio della Ribeira, married her in secret, and promised to recognize his marriage as soon as he succeeded in appeasing the anger of his father, who was irritated by the misalliance. You see in me the fruit of their union.

"The deformity that I bore at birth, which was caused by Dona Bianca's precautions in concealing her pregnancy, inspired so much aversion in my father that he always refused to see me and render public a marriage that had given him a hunchback for an heir. That unjust conduct caused my mother a chagrin to which she succumbed a few months after my birth.

"Don Ribeira soon contracted a new marriage, and on his orders I was put in a convent, under the supposed name of Pedrillo. While the son of his second wife received a brilliant education analogous to the rank of which he judged me unworthy, I languished in the most shameful abandonment. An old monk took pity on me, cared or my frail and valetudinarian infancy, taught me the little Latin that he knew, and engaged me, when I reached my sixteenth year, to enter into holy orders.

"I was about to follow his advice when I was told that I was the son of a Spanish grandee and that my father, the noble Count della Ribeira, had summoned me. I left, weeping for the good monk, my benefactor. Alas, he was the only person who had loved me sincerely during the sixteen years that I had lived.

"All of Count della Ribeira's other children were dead; there only remained, to inherit his titles and his immense fortune, the poor hunchback abandoned in infancy, and as it was important to the Count that those advantages did not pass into foreign hands, the same pride that had made him refuse me even the name of my ancestors was the unique cause of my recall.

"A year after my emergence from the convent, my father died in my arms, but while I wept by his side, he could not vanquish the repulsion inspired in him by the deformity of the person he had never called his son.

"So there I was, at eighteen, the possessor of an immense fortune and absolute master of my actions. Isolated since birth, I felt keenly the sweet need to love, so I did not take long to link myself in close amity with Don Juan Salzedo, a young cavalier, an orphan like me, but whose feeble patrimony did not respond to his noble birth. We were inseparable, and our friendship soon became celebrated in Madrid and the court, for I had quit Calatrava to go and live in the Spanish capital.

"I was abandoning myself with intoxication to the charms of that pleasant union when a new sentiment caused my heart to palpitate. Placed, at a bullfight, near a young woman of a rare beauty . . ."

Smiling, the Count added: "Señor cavalier, I was only twenty years old, and I'm long cured of my love, so I shall not paint you the portrait of Doña Margarita, nor tell you the story of the means I employed to please her, and the obstacles that my love had to overcome; let it suffice for you to know that I believed myself to be loved.

"Preparations were made for our marriage. One night, on returning to Madrid after a journey of short duration, in my tender impatience, I wanted at least to see Margarita's residence. What was my astonishment to find her door ajar! I advance, I listen; bursts of laughter strike my ear. 'My dear Juan,' said an only-too-familiar voice, 'you imitate delightfully that amusing eccentric who, in his stupid vanity, imagines that one can love a monster for himself. Poverty imposes upon me the painful obligation of marrying him, but your love . . .'

"I did not give her time to finish; I hurled myself upon them, sword in hand, and I was about to strike the perfidious individuals, who were fleeing . . . when a mirror placed before me suddenly offered me the image of my sad deformity . . .

"That sudden sight disabused me in an instant of all my illusions; I understood that amour and amity cannot exist for a paltry being, a reject of nature, and I went home, radically cured of my amour and appreciating friends at their true value.

"Perhaps another would have deplored the loss of his illusions, but I, on the contrary, applauded myself. I was scornful of human beings; I did not take the trouble to hide that scorn from them, which my observations justified from day to day. I even found pleasure in diminishing what they call beautiful, great and virtuous, in unveiling the egotism that alone makes them act; in brief, I forced people to see themselves as they are.

"Nevertheless, I have never hesitated to be useful to them when I can—but in acting thus, I only seek the enjoyment that one savors, the superiority one obtains in taking vengeance for a benefit."

Don Alvares would doubtless have continued his invectives against humankind for some time, when he was interrupted by the arrival of the Alcalde; the latter came to tell Mendoce that Pedro had been arrested in Calatrava by the Santa Hermandad, in the home of honest receivers, and that he would inevitably be condemned to the galleys.

The young man thought that he was about to re-enter into possession of his valise and his horse, but as they were pieces of evidence, the law did not judge it appropriate to release them, and he never heard mention of them again—except that he saw one day in Toledo a tall, thin man whom he was told was a judge in Calatrava, and who was mounted very comfortably on one of the pieces of evidence.

Two days later, the valet that Mendoce had sent to Toledo brought him the money necessary to complete his journey. In spite of the insistences of Don Alvares, who wanted him to stay with him for a few more days, the young Toledan left immediately, not without expressing once again his gratitude to Señor della Ribeira or without leaving his domestics marks of his generosity.

Chapter V
What visit Mendoce received. He returns to the Château della Ribeira.

The motive for his voyage. His traveling companions.

He is finally able to marry Inezille. Conclusion.

Time is ordinarily an infallible remedy for amour; however, although two years had gone by since the events we have related in the previous chapters, Mendoce's affection for Inezille had lost none of its violence, and tears bathed his face every time one of the old duennas whom gold renders sensible to the pains of lovers brought him a letter from the daughter of Don Garcias.

One day, he saw a carriage bearing the arms of Don Alvares stop outside his house. Believing that the Count, of whom he had not had news since his departure from Merida, had come to spend a few days in Toledo in the home of the man he had so graciously obliged, he ran to the door, getting ready to receive him as best he could. To his surprise, however, it was not Señor della Ribeira; he only saw descending from the carriage the two relatives, Don Fernando and Don Gabriel, clad in black and affecting a hypocritical dolor. They told him that their dear and worthy cousin Don Alvares was dead, that he had appointed Mendoce as the executor of his testament, and that they begged him to accompany them to Ribeira in order to make the dispositions of the deceased known to them.

Astonished by that mark of confidence, Mendoce offered sincere regrets to the memory of the Count and, in haste to fulfill his last will, he departed with the two señors, who, during the journey, could not conceal their joy well enough for it not to be continually betrayed. Sometimes they discussed plans for embellishments they projected to the castillo; sometimes they talked to one another about the pleasures they would savor in Madrid with their cousin's great wealth. At the expenditure they made in his establishment and the generous manner in which they paid him, the estimable hotelier Gregorio Gonelès said, cracking his knuckles: "By Saint Gregory, my patron, these people are surely heirs, and I only ask the holy Virgin to send me such guests once a week!"

Having arrived at Ribeira, Mendoce and his traveling companions were received by the Alcalde and the notary Metellino; Don Fernando and Don Gabriel did not leave any repose to the two men of law and the Toledan until they had been taken to the room where the testament was to be opened. In the presence of the Alcalde and numerous witnesses, the notary observed that the deceased's seal was still entire and tact; after which he broke it, and read the following in a loud and intelligible voice:

"I, Alvares Antonio, Count della Ribeira, Señor of Tormosa, commander, etc., appreciating at its true value the noble character of my worthy relatives Don Fernando de Lunès and Don Gabriel Ribosa, declare that the evidences of affection that they have lavished upon me and the numerous gifts with which they have overwhelmed me . . ."

At this point, the two cousins wiped away a tear and inclined modestly. Metellino, whom that mark of sensibility had interrupted, resumed his reading in these terms:

". . . And the numerous gifts with which they have overwhelmed me have not dazzled me, and that, having no right to my succession, those two hidalgos shall not have a maravedis.

"I institute as my universal legatee Don Luis Garcias de Puebla, commandant of the town and fort of Merida, under the express condition that he will abandon his government to go and live in Toledo, and that he will give his only daughter in marriage to Mendoce Peres, my testamentary executor."

It is for the reader to imagine the rage of the two relatives, who went out cursing the hunchback, and the transports of joy to which Mendoce allowed to burst forth. Not daring to believe what he had just heard, he took the testament from the notary's hand in order to assure himself of the reality of his good fortune . . .

Suddenly, a blush of shame covered his face; he had read these words written in the hand of Count della Ribeira:

Mendoce, are you convinced now that all men are egotists, that you are an egotist yourself? I know the human heart well enough to know that all your thoughts, at this moment, are for your marriage, and that you have not thought, I will not say of regretting the hunchback—one does not regret those from whom one inherits—but only of blessing his memory.

Theriaki[1]

Better one grain of opium than twelve gourds full of rice.
(Oriental proverb.)

Happiness? It's drunkenness that takes away reason.
(Anonymous.)

"ALAS, my feeble and convulsive hands can scarcely raise this cup to my lips; the shaking is making its contents spill. Oh, I would bless the angel of death if he would extend his redoubtable blade over my mouth! Life weighs upon me so heavily! There is no true believer more miserable than me; my contracted muscles are inclining my heavy head toward my left shoulder; a cup seems a burden in my trembling hands; my stiff legs are buckling beneath my paltry body and the slightest light closes my eyes, too weak to support it.

"I would like to be in a shroud on which the pious hands of a dervish has inscribed verses from the Koran; I would like the servants of Mohammed to prostrate themselves

---

1 This term, referring to opium, was exceedingly esoteric in 1831 and has fallen into disuse since, but Honoré de Balzac was fond of it and used it in several stories, including one reference to a cadaverous face with "a theriaki smile."

on seeing my abode illuminated by funeral lamps; yes, I would like them to repeat, while striking their breasts: 'The Aga Massoud is no more! There is no God but God and Mohammed is his prophet.'

"What is there left for me to do on the earth?

"In vain the most delicious dishes are set forth before me; they only excite my disgust.

"What use is it to me to have slaves in my seraglio from Georgia with white shoulders, Kaffirs with passionate movements and coppery complexions, Africans with large eyes and black breasts? Their smiles leave me cold; their voluptuous dances weary me; it is necessary for me to lower the triple bans of my turban over my ears when they marry their voices and play the lute or the Persian flute; the softest sounds shake my debilitated brain and are too noisy for it.

"Yes I would like to be in a shroud on which the pious hands of a dervish has inscribed verses from the Koran; I would like the servants of Mohammed to prostrate themselves on seeing my abode illuminated by funeral lamps!"

Such were the thoughts of the Aga Massoud.

Lying sadly on a vast sofa, pale and motionless, his eyes half-closed, one might have mistaken him for a corpse if one had not heard the rattle of his slow respiration.

Soon, the effects of the opium that he had drunk began to manifest themselves: a more rapid breath elevated his bosom; all his limbs quivered with a convulsive frisson; his swollen face became red; a wild expression caused his eyes, previously dull and bleak, to scintillate.

At the same time, a coolness, an indescribable wellbeing circulated in his veins and rendered an artificial existence to that demi-cadaver; a magical influence caused reflections of dazzling light to gleam in his eyes from all the surrounding objects.

Suave visions rose up, passing back and forth, rotating before his charmed gaze; there was the vertigo if an intoxication, not like that produced by the fermented beverages of Europe, but a divine intoxication, an inexpressible, sublime ecstasy.

"Oh," he murmured, in a halting voice, "Oh, what sensations of happiness are inundating all my senses! They are too delightful for the strength of a mortal: it's necessary that I succumb to them!

"A soft languor is half-closing my eyes; my warm and supple limbs allow themselves to relax into the sweetest abandonment. Make the celestial melody sounding around me stop . . . take away those houris who are fluttering and smiling at me and lifting up garlands of flowers entwined around their semi-naked breasts . . . leave me alone, beautiful phantoms, oh, leave me alone! Do you want to make me die of voluptuousness?

"I need to get rid of these fantastic images . . . it's necessary to flee . . .

"A magic power is dragging me away and making me glide lightly over meadows enameled with flowers, shores sparkling with light, without me having the fatigue of having to lift my feet, without my will directing my body: a delightful sensation in which the inertia of repose is mingled with the wellbeing of movement . . .

"I'm no longer gliding now; a vague and languorous swaying is cradling me voluptuously, and mysterious beings are lifting me slowly into the clouds.

"They're angels who are supporting me in their interlaced arms, they're the angels of the divine Allah! I can glimpse their smiling heads over my shoulder; their warm breath exhales over my forehead, and the blond curls of their beautiful hair gently brushes my lips.

"Will I never be able to stop, being borne away for ever and ever by the unknown impulsion that it drawing me? No, divine messengers of the prophet, not even to visit those innumerable palaces sparkling with emeralds and carbuncles, which flee before my gaze, not even for those houris whose modulated voices are calling to me!

"No, no, don't stop! One is rocked so softly in your arms, one palpitates with such sweet ecstasy, on breathing the air with which this region is embalmed. The air of mortals makes me die. Keep flying! Let's fly without stopping, like the rapid arrow of the angel of wrath! Let's fly and fly, further . . . let the celestial wind that is blowing over my face never cease to blow . . ."

And Massoud's voice, fading away and becoming inarticulate, no longer murmured any but rare and inconsequential words; and his eyes closed; and he went to sleep: a profound sleep excited by fantastic and voluptuous dreams.

The next day, when he woke up, Massoud was pale and suffering; his extenuated voice could hardly make itself heard by his slaves. He summoned them so that they could give him another dose of opium.

Nocturnal Terror

I am one of those who are most sensible of the power
of the imagination: everyone is jostled by it,
but some are overthrown by it.
(Montaigne, ch. 11.)[1]

"Ha ha! You make me laugh uproariously!
Boasting about your reason and your courage!
It only requires the most ridiculous accident to
put the latter in default and ruin the former forever."
(Anonymous.)

OH, what a delightful day Lord Edgard was about to
spend! To depart at daybreak for the ruins of the priory of Saint Ruth, to depart with the naïve Miss Arabella,
and the witty and piquant Duchess MacMoran! And to
have the mild and indulgent Milady Tirnson's carriage for
a conveyance, and for a guide the jovial and knowledgeable
Dr. Raleigh!

Let's go then! Forward ho! Farewell to old Edinburgh!
There isn't a cloud in the sky; the refreshing wind is making

---

1 In fact, these are the opening words of chapter 20 of volume I of
Michael de Montaigne's *Essais*.

the foliage of the oaks tremble gently. Let's go! Onwards, onwards!

And there was, to begin with, a merry mélange of frivolous remarks, tender words, ingenious pleasantries; I would have defied the most careworn brow not to have cleared; I would have defied the most phlegmatic of men not to have felt the electric gaiety that sprang forth from every direction in sparks.

But a cloud has formed at the extremity of the horizon; it is extending like a lugubrious veil; instead of the light of a little while ago, of the radiant day that ornamented nature with a soft and living glare, everything becomes dull and inanimate; one can no longer breathe freely, one no longer experiences an indescribable wellbeing; and I don't know what sadness comes to squeeze the heart and freeze the imagination. Still, if one were to shiver at the sudden glare of lightning, which flashes, dies and is reborn, with the majestic din of thunder . . .

But no; it's a slow, gray, monotonous rain that clutches the limbs with an icy inconvenience.

They do not have their picnic on the grass; the semi-ruined arcades of the monastery do not resound to their joyful bursts of laughter; shut up in a poor cottage where an old woman is dying hoarsely on a wretched bed, they spend two long hours of rain, disappointment and sadness, without saying a word.

Finally, the horses are rested; they can leave, and quit that black dwelling where the fetid air makes it so difficult to breathe, where they have been embarrassed and inhibited beside the bed of a dying woman. A few gifts are left to a tall, pale and thin young woman, the only creature weeping by the invalid's beside. She murmurs, by way of thanks: "This will serve, my ladies, to bury my mother."

To complete the misfortune, the roads have become bad; the horses' feet slip, the wheels sink into profound ruts. Night will have fallen by the time the berlin reaches Edinburgh.

Night? No, it will be tomorrow, for now it's the axle that has broken; the carriage is lying on its side in a ditch . . .

Thank God no one is injured! A great fright for the ladies; for everyone, a rainy night spent under the stars: those are the only inconveniences of the accident that has just occurred. It's necessary, however, to seek shelter. In which direction? They are five miles from any habitation, and how are they to reach one, with frail footwear, along muddy roads, in rain like this?

Luckily, a short distance away, there is an old ruined manor house, whose owners, if there are any, have not been in residence there in living memory; today, the only living beings to be found there are an old Scots woman and her daughter; they have come to set up home in the ruins, rather like swallows taking possession of the corner of a window to build their nests.

After holding a discussion, they decided unanimously to go seek a refuge in the old manor while one of the domestics would keep watch on the carriage and the other would go on horseback in search of laborers.

The hospitality was not as poor as might have been feared; the good woman in the manor received the strangers as best she could; dealing, as she could easily see, with people of high status, who would reward her zeal generously, she displayed the utmost reverence, and put her abode and the manor at the disposal of her guests.

To begin with, the ladies exchanged their sodden clothes for the Sunday garments of the old woman's daughter, Betty. The travelers' cheerfulness was briefly reanimated: that was when they saw the two young ladies dressed in scarlet skirts, whose Scottish cut allowed the sight of their legs clad in blue stockings and shoes with big buckles; for headgear they had muslin bonnets, which fell over their shoulders and were certainly not unfavorable to their charming features.

The entire evening was spent around a large fireplace where a peat fire was burning. Insensibly, the conversation became sad and lugubrious, and they began to tell terrifying ghost stories.

It was the old doctor who, seeing his audience marvelously disposed to feel the somber impressions of that kind of story, amused himself greatly in following the progress of the vague and insurmountable terror that gradually took possession of the ladies during the narrations, and even attained the gentleman, Edgard.

It must be said that the irritations of the journey, the memories of the cottage and Saint Ruth, the howling wind, the deceptive light of the fire and the walls charged with Gothic sculptures could not have seconded the doctor any better; never had he had such a satisfactory audience.

The hoarseness of his voice, and Lady Tornson's eyes, which were beginning to close, indicated that if he wanted to keep such a great success intact, it was time to bring it to an end, so, taking out his watch, he announced that midnight had chimed some time ago.

The ladies then took possession of the only lamp that their hostess had in the house, and the doctor and Sir

Edgard went their separate ways to lie down on pallets of straw set down in the only two rooms in the manor into which the rain did not penetrate through the dilapidated roof.

Hazard had placed Edgard in the remotest part of the building; his tender imagination, inclined to excitement, had experienced the effect of the doctor's tales keenly. Then again, after having groped his way through a long, narrow corridor, he was alone, far away from everyone else, in the large deserted hall of a ruined building; he could not, therefore, prevent himself feeling a kind of mysterious dread.

While recognizing the absurdity of such a sensation, he was nonetheless subject to its effects; wrapped up in his cloak and lying in a corner, in the midst of a profound obscurity, he felt his heart beating forcefully. The only glimmer of light he perceived was that which the moon sometimes projected through the large clouds, which the wind was driving rapidly; the only noises that reached his ears were the hooting of an owl and the roaring of the wind.

He was nevertheless dozing off when the badly-closed door flew open with a bang. He woke up with a start: the moon half-lit the place where he was . . .

Great God! A white phantom was standing over him!

He tried to cry out, but his voice failed; he tried to fell, but a powerful, inexorable hand held on to his garments . . .

He fell unconscious.

The next morning, at daybreak, the domestics brought the berlin to the old manor house, restored as best they could to a condition in which it could reach Edinburgh.

At that good news, everyone assembled—but Edgard was missing.

"He's asleep, the idler. Come on, we need to go and wake him up."

They found him pale and motionless, with the pocket of his jacket caught on the foot of an old stone statue. His hair had turned white.

They had a great deal of difficulty bringing him round. As for his reason, he was never able to recover it.

A PARTIAL LIST OF SNUGGLY BOOKS

CPSIA information can be obtained
at www.ICGtesting.com
Printed in the USA
FSOW01n1054190218
44762FS